One Last Heist

Lyndon Hardy

Volume 7 of Magic by the Numbers

Bartizan Press
Los Angeles

Print ISBN: 978-1-7330950-9-9

Library of Congress Control Number: 2023912206

Version 2

Other books by Lyndon Hardy

Master of the Five Magics, 2nd edition

Secret of the Sixth Magic, 2nd edition

Riddle of the Seven Realms, 2nd edition

The Archimage's Fourth Daughter

Magic Times Three

Double Magic

Visit Lyndon Hardy's website at: http://www.alodar.com/blog

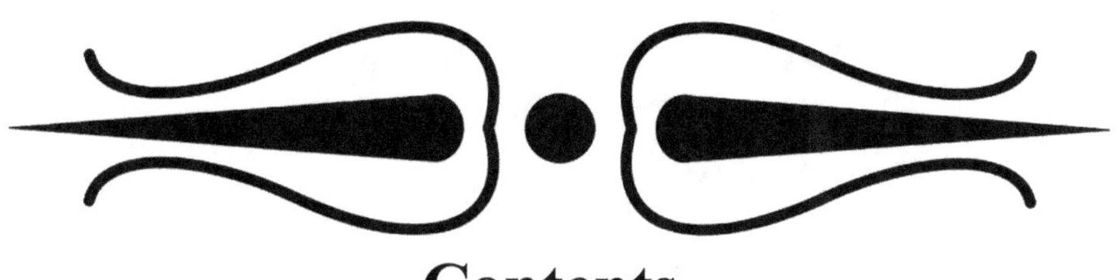

Contents

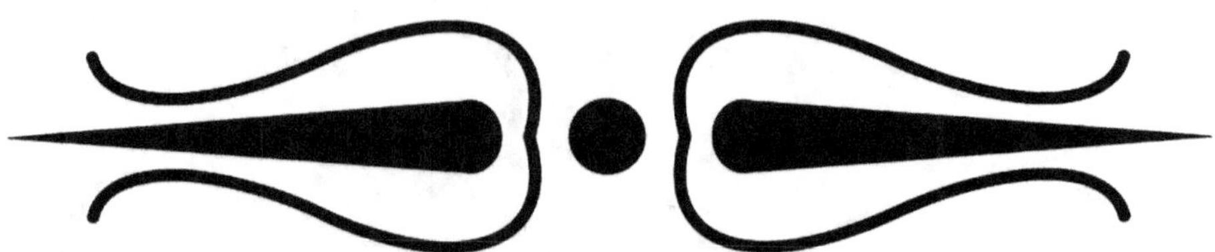

Part One *Aspiration*

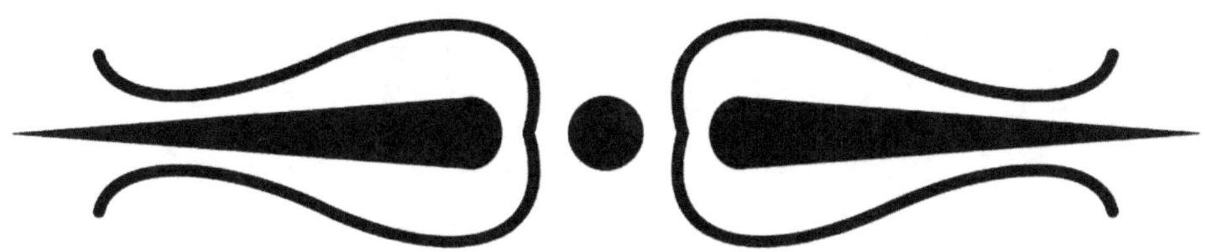

Part Two *Struggle*

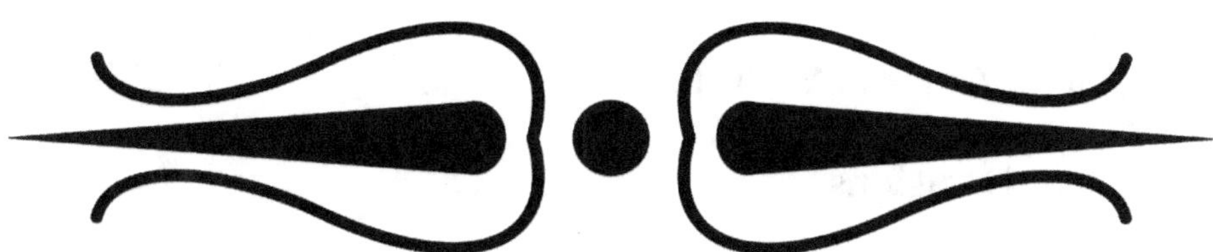

Part Three *Resolution*

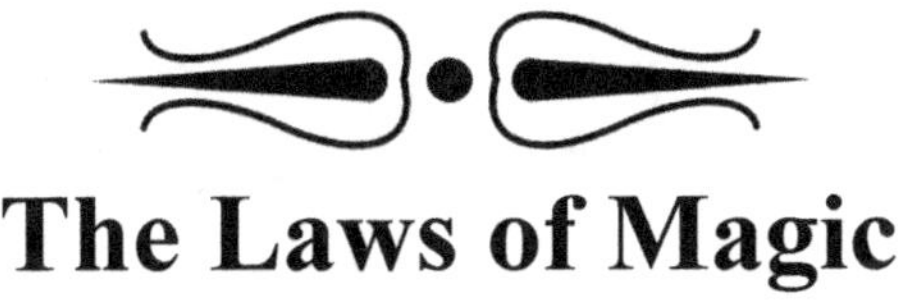

The Laws of Magic

Thaumaturgy

The Principle of Sympathy — like produces like

The Principle of Contagion — once together, always together

Alchemy

∇

The Doctrine of Signatures — the attributes without mirror the powers within

Magic

○

The Maxim of Persistence — perfection is eternal

Sorcery

◉

The Rule of Three — thrice spoken, once fulfilled

Wizardry

The Law of Ubiquity — flame permeates all

The Law of Dichotomy — dominance or submission

DEMONTOOTH TOWER
PROCOLON
BARDINA
THE IRON FIST
FUMUS MOUNTAINS
AMBROSIA
YTTERBY
CARMELA
ARCADIA
OXBRIDGE
SOUTHERN KINGDOMS
N

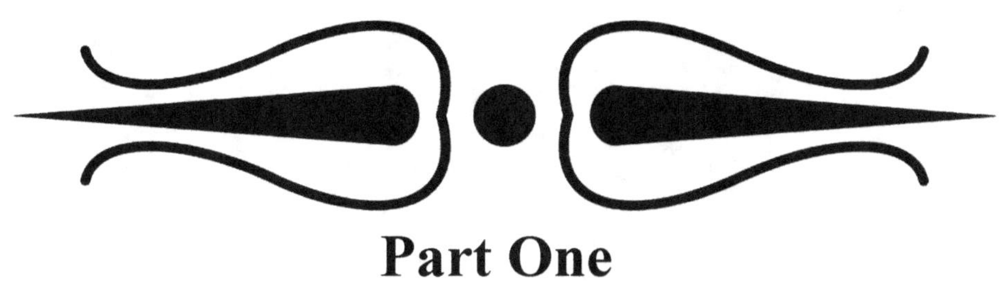

Part One

Aspiration

Three Times a Charm

IT WAS high noon. Diana felt the sweat trickling down her back. The thick black robe, adorned with a scatter of sorcery icons hung heavy on her slight shoulders. Air inside the tiny beige tent was hot and humid, barely enough room for herself, the lordling facing her, and the two small stools on which they sat. Outside, the dusty path leading away from Ambrosia's biggest slum was empty of travelers. There was no danger of being overheard.

Involuntarily, she covered the obvious patch on her robe near her waist, then realized the noble was far enough under that he would not notice. It was more important to concentrate. Keep the pattern of the charm flowing smoothly. Three repetitions, each one more difficult than the last, and the lordling would be under her thrall. 'Thrice spoken, once fulfilled' — the basic law of sorcery.

Diana grimaced and almost shuddered. What the law didn't reveal was that each of the three recitations became more difficult to accomplish than the last. No one knew why that was so. It just was.

As she continued, her tongue became increasingly numb and more reluctant to obey her thoughts. And the tiniest falter would break the flow of the charm. She pushed aside the thought that it might fail to complete. But already she was feeling the beginning of a stabbing headache, nausea starting to bubble in her stomach.

Diana completed the second recitation and distracted herself from how difficult the third time was going to be. It was the usual type of request — not just one simple question, but a bunch of them. How would he fare at the state dinner in the queen's castle tonight? Especially after the dining was done. Would someone new be there? What would she look like? How lucky would he get?

And as Diana always did, she faked peering into the future. There was too much risk in doing that for real — enchanting herself instead of the lordling. Using up too much of her lifetime supply of whatever was the essence of every sorcerer's craft.

Instead, she took pleasure creating her *own* image in the lordling's mind to be the prediction of whom he would meet. Auburn hair, cropped almost as short as that of a man. A long face with a jaw jutting too strongly to be judged a great beauty. Her eyes were her defining asset. Large and beckoning. Deep blue with flecks of gold. Of course, they were. After all, she was a sorceress.

Why did she include this bit of fakery along with the rest? Diana did not know for sure. Perhaps, it was because her own life was so depressing. Each and every day, as far back as she could remember, absolutely the same — sitting in her little tent to earn a few coins for her uncle. The one meal of the day and then to bed because there was not enough money for a splurge on candles.

Diana finished speaking the charm for the third and final time. Then, more rapidly, she planted her image into the lordling's mind. All that remained was the final suggestion — the one her uncle Izzy insisted she use.

"It squashes complaints after the sale," he had explained. "No demands for refunds. Failure was the client's own fault."

IT WAS totally bogus of course, but Diana did as her uncle had directed. She brought the lordling out of the spell. "There is one thing to be aware of," she explained when she judged his mind was again clear. "Predicting the future is fragile. The littlest of things can deflect the greatest of events."

"What little thing?" the young lord asked. He was tall and well-muscled. A week's growth of beard. In real life, what the ladies of the queen's court might imagine as they read their boddice-ripper fantasies. But there was something more as well. Defiance in deep-set eyes. Someone who wanted to plot his own course in life rather than blindly follow the norms of the court.

"Above all else," Diana replied. "Before the evening is over, refrain from saying or even thinking the word 'griffin.'"

"Why?"

"If you do, the prophecy may not come true."

"Griffin? I have not thought of such a creature in … months."

"Nevertheless, starting this evening, you would do so at great peril for your desired outcome."

The lordling shrugged. "I can handle that." He looked Diana up and down as if she were a slave being auctioned off. "I liked the prophecy you put into my head. You do a good job. How much?"

"Whatever you think knowing about the possibilities tonight is worth." Diana knew that stating the fee this way usually resulted in a bigger payment. Even a few coppers more would make a big difference.

With a theatrical gesture, the lordling tossed a brandel in the air for Diana to catch as he exited the tent. "Never let it be said that Lionel, scion of Talusan, was a stranger to largess."

Her eyes widened. A brandel! A solid gold brandel. More than she could garner in a fortnight of toil. She would not even have to make change — although for an entire brandel, it was much more than she had any means to do so anyway.

Wishes she had long learned to suppress bubbled up within her. How wonderful life must be for someone like the lordling. On an impulse, tossing off a coin of gold as if it were a speck of dust. Striding out to get dressed for a ball in the queen's palace. A life she would never come close to having.

Diana shook her head to vanquish the thoughts. As always, they served no purpose other than to make her desire even more what she did not have. With a sigh, she hastened to collapse the stools and strike the tent. She should rush back and tell her uncle the good news right away.

But then she stopped and considered. Money seemed to seep through Uncle Izzy's fingers like water. He certainly would use a brandel to buy into some new get rich quick scheme.

No, instead she would go to the street of the money changers. Exchange the brandel for smaller coins. Spend a few of them on herself. Pass on to her uncle what was left. He still would be pleased — and never know the difference.

Diana walked eastward on the northern bank of the wide river that split Ambrosia into two parts and drained into the great ocean. She left the hovels and walked past the homes and shops for those who worked at keeping the city running. Carpenters, thaumaturges, roofers, alchemists, smiths, market-keepers, fishermen. And the sorcerers and wizards past their prime, slipping into dotage.

Across the bridges, the buildings on the southern bank were noticeably finer. The farther one climbed the steep hill dominating the landscape, the more luxurious the dwellings became. Street lamps full of buzzing imps made the travel easier. Only the rich could afford to pay wizards to keep them full. At the pinnacle, Diana could see the curtain walls of Queen Vendora's castle.

Most of the buildings higher up the hill were personal

residences; some also fulfilled other purposes. Merchants to the rich displayed alluring signs announcing their services to everyone who journeyed by. They wanted to reside near their customers.

At last, she spotted one of the signs she was looking for, a large scale with a stack of coins in each pan. The exchange accomplished, she then sought out a dress shop farther up the hill. At first, she was hesitant about entering. Two women exited with frowns when they saw her in her shabby robe. The clerk inside raised his eyebrows and twitched his nose as she approached.

"Ah, we sell only fine gowns here. The discount store is two blocks closer to the river."

Diana reached into one of her pockets and pulled out the sack of coins. It jingled when she clanked it down on the table. "There are ninety-eight silvers in here. Keep a civil tongue, and some of them might become yours."

The expression on the clerk's face immediately changed into one of welcome. "Ah, certainly, my lady. What is it you desire? Perhaps a new frock for the summer. Shorter lengths are the rage this time of year."

Diana's heart fluttered. She felt a warm glow course through her and savored the feeling. Attention. Respect. Pampering. Things she had missed for her entire life.

She chose quickly. Not one dress but two. A small accent bag. She did not know if she was expected to haggle and did not care. With a flourish, she added a last silver to the total. "For yourself," she said to the clerk. "You have been most helpful."

"Thank you, my lady. And to be fair, here are six coppers in change."

Diana tucked her purchases into one of the large pockets of her robe. She knew she could hide them away in her own blanket easily enough when she returned to Uncle Izzy's hovel. He would be excited enough to receive six coppers from her rather than the usual one or two.

But the good feeling that had accompanied her spending was fading away. She wanted to maintain it as long as possible. Rather than immediately returning home, she would go to — the street of the butchers and buy a roast! Yes, a *fresh* piece of meat. The four of them wouldn't have to pick off the maggots from whatever remained in their larder. Uncle Izzy would just have to accept what she had done.

Diana sighed. Uncle Izzy. She had to admit her feelings about him were conflicted. He stuck fast to his tale that his original name was something like that, but somehow everyone began calling him Izzy as a nickname. As she had grown up under his wing, she surmised it was because he always began pursuing a new scheme before the old one even had a chance to fail.

Despite that, somehow, she did manage to grow up. Her parents were both mortally wounded in the horrible business with the snowdevil when she was only three. Uncle Izzy told her he had sworn to her father as he died that, no matter what, she would be looked after.

Yes, despite everything else, her uncle *had* looked after her. Diana caressed the remaining coppers in her palm. But recently, he got a far-away look in his eye when they chatted, and that bothered her. What was he thinking?

Even so, she concluded, she would not abandon him — well, maybe only disobey once in a while. With a light step, she shouldered the tent apparatuses and hurried towards the street of the butchers.

She did not notice the neophyte magician hurrying the other way, obviously late for some important appointment.

2

The Neophyte's Hurdle

NICHOLAS, THE neophyte magician, ran his free hand down the sides of his pale blue robe, but it did little to help dry his palm. Even though it was a cool afternoon, he felt drenched with sweat. A trickle snaked down from his unruly black hair onto his broad forehead. His plump face was full, his eyes a deep blue. Having the nickname of 'babyface' did not help, nor did his less than average height. Even in the society of the scholarly, appearance was important.

In front of him sat three masters on high backed stools, their faces stern. They were crammed together inside an abandoned apothecary on Honeysuckle Street, now repurposed as their new magician's palace. The layout left much to be desired, there had been no other choice. The price had been all the guild could afford.

The first question had been the traditional soft toss, something to ease the mind of the candidate wishing to advance to be an initiate. Nicholas knew each subsequent challenge would be harder than the one before. Eventually, every candidate failed. It was part of tradition. The goal was to answer enough to advance to the next level.

Nicholas's thoughts froze. This might be his only chance to pull himself into respectability. What was at stake for him was his entire future. He was not adept with his hands. No craftsman would accept him as an apprentice. He would become a piggy. That is what happened to his two older brothers. A ring through the nose. Movement constricted by a confining rope. Pulled hither with no ability to resist. Forced to grovel for coins tossed into the gutter by the gang of boys who controlled them. No, Nicholas was convinced. Employing his mind was the only way to prevent such a fate.

"Come now, neophyte Nicholas," the master with the long bushy beard sitting in the center asked. "If one cannot be proficient with the simplest of mathematics, what hope is there for understanding the intricacies of magic rituals?" He shrugged. "And when I say simplest, I do not mean we are discussing the 'Mathematics of Commerce' course you took when you first came to our guild. That was merely to ascertain if you could listen to lectures and parrot them back.

"It is geometry that is fundamental to many of our rituals. This first question is about that. Use the unquenchable marker in your hand on the slate. Prove that the sum of the number of degrees in the three angles of a triangle, regardless of its shape, is equal to one-half the number of degrees in a circle."

Nicholas turned his attention to the board behind him. It was smooth and clean, as new looking as when it was first created hundreds of years ago. "Well," he said, "the number of degrees in a circle is 256, so the number in a triangle should be 128."

"Yes, yes. That is obvious," the bald master sitting on the left said. "Get on with it. Prove the sum is 128, no matter what shape. Use the drawing slate and marker if you must."

Nicholas drew a wiggly line with the unquenchable marker and then pressed the small button on the side of the slate to remove it.

"Just testing," he said over his shoulder.

"Both the slate and the marker are magic, neophyte," the bald master snapped. "Of course, they are still working. Everything magic survived the explosion. And will continue to do so for eons after this exam is over, no matter how long you continue stalling."

"Now, now, Hector," the master in the center said softly. "Remember your own candidacy exam. Give the young man some slack."

"I have an idea for an experiment to flesh out this afternoon, and if it makes sense, a visit with the queen." Hector smoothed down the folds on the front of his deep blue robe. "Some very important ones, as you well know. No matter what changes we make to the interior walls and partitions, this place still reeks of alchemy, not a palace of magic. Our rituals must be modified in order to compensate."

"Calculations," the master on the right snorted. His left eye twitched when he spoke. "You have no mind for mathematics. What did you do, add two to three and state the sum was five?"

"What good is your, what do you call it, celestial mechanics, Randolph, if you can't use a screwdriver without hurting yourself?"

"If we followed the path I originally suggested, we would not need to have any dependence on our surroundings," Randolph said.

"Enough bickering," the master in the middle spread his arms wide. "And you as well, Hector. Give the neophyte a hint if you are so impatient."

"Very well, Archmaster Antron," Hector growled. "Neophyte, draw the triangle first and then a second line through the top-most vertex parallel to the base. The second line is a key to making the problem easy."

"Thank you, Master," Nicholas managed to say with a quiver in his voice. Now, with the help, the need to solve the problem quickly became even more crucial. He felt his chest constrict. It was becoming difficult to breathe.

He turned to the slate, followed the instructions, and

stepped back to look at what he had done.

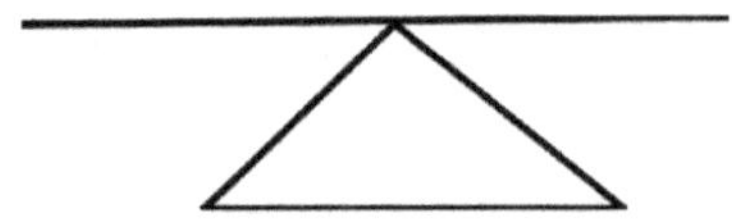

He tried to draw a deep breath, but could not. No inspiration surfaced. He had aced simple geometry, was first in his class, but now, in the heat of battle, nothing came to mind.

He had always been like this, he sighed. As quick-witted as any of the masters, he was sure of that. But to stand in front of them with his entire future at stake was too hard to bear. Yes, magic was grounded on rituals. Everything in the craft was built upon them. But the hoary performance he was part of now, one repeated over and over again starting centuries before was not real magic. It was merely an initiation because the masters had gone through the process themselves when they were neophytes.

"We are wasting our time here," Hector said. "Those of us who survived the disaster were lucky. But we may as well not have if we have no wherewithal to pay for our daily bread. The neophyte is useful doing what he does now. Death by starvation is as final as one by explosion."

"And we will need every mind we have focused on understanding what was Gavarak's miscalculation," Randolph said as he stroked his well-trimmed goatee. "He was on to something new, something none of us had dreamed of before. If we can get an understanding of what it is, how it works, our status among the other guilds will be assured. Neophytes and initiates will abandon them and flock to us. Our place in the lore of our craft will be cemented there forever."

"Gavarak claimed the copper spheres he had fabricated were sufficient safeguards." Hector shook his head. "Nothing could get out of one once the clasps were sealed. Obviously, he miscalculated somehow." He stopped for a moment and glanced back at Nicholas.

"Idiot, don't you see it now?" Hector pointed at the slate. "The proof why the sum of the three angles in a triangle, any triangle, always add up to 128 degrees?"

"Ah, I know that, by definition, there are 256 degrees in a circle — " Nicholas began.

"And if we bisect the circle with a line, the number of degrees on one side is?" Randolph offered. He looked at Hector and then Antron as if asking for approval for what he had said.

"128, of course," Nicholas replied. He felt the acid-burn in his stomach get worse. His mind was blank. He had only barely managed to divide 256 by two.

"We must keep up with our rituals," Antron said. "All of them, even those not meant for creating magical objects. Otherwise, what will we become? No more than mere alchemists pandering to the poorest street beggars."

"Time is our most precious asset," Hector said. "And there are two things we must focus on now. First, we must think of new means of generating income. The meager reserves we have will not last forever." Hector studied Randolph and Antron, waiting for both of them to nod.

"Second," he continued after the brief pause, "we must proceed down Gavarak's path of exploration. The payoff could be large. There can be glory and adoration by our peers from what we may learn." The master looked directly at Randolph and raised his voice. "Only this time, there will be more safeguards, better careful, well-thought-out experimentation."

"Gavarak's hypothesis has a grave error." Randolph shook his head. "He was enamored with the myth from ancient times. If I can deduce from his notes where he made his mistake, then my repu — I mean the reputation of our guild will be much enhanced.”

“Explore what escaped from Gavarak’s sphere and reduced our palace to a pile of rubble, many bodies, and only a few unscathed?” Hector asked. “Yes, the exact ritual must not be repeated. But I am close to understanding the modifications we must make, a much more controlled experiment. Once I am sure of those — ”

“Masters, masters,” Antron said. “I remind you that we are in the midst of a candidacy exam. The neophyte is the one who has the floor to speak.”

Hector turned his attention back to Nicholas. “Well?”

Nicholas was still dumbstruck.

After what felt like a fortnight, Randolph said. “Look at the line you drew above the triangle, neophyte. How many angles are there next to one another?”

“Three. One inside the triangle, and another one on each side,” Nicholas answered tentatively.

“Yes, half of the number of degrees in a circle. And so, their sum must be?”

“Ah, 128 degrees — obviously.”

“I can’t believe I am doing this,” Hector fumed. He pointed at the top of the triangle that touched the horizontal line. “And the middle of those three angles is also within the triangle, right?”

“Right, I see that.” With each passing second, Nicholas felt his advancement to become an initiate slipping away. He had to finish the proof on his own now before —

“So, is there anything else you can say about the other two angles in the triangle, the ones at the base?” Randolph prompted.

Nicholas felt a glimmer of hope. Randolph wanted him to get past this. The first problem was merely a means to calm the neophyte down so he could think his best. He knew that. So, take the time to …

"Vertical angles!" Nicholas shouted suddenly. Of course. It was obvious. "For this diagram, each of the other two angles in the triangle is what is called a vertical angle, one that pairs with one on the underside of the line." He rushed on. "Vertical angles have the same number of degrees. So, if the sum of the values of the angles on one side of a line is 128 degrees, then so also must be the sum of those in the triangle. It is so simple that even a child can understand it."

"Exactly!" Hector said. "Even a child." He shook his head. "Unfortunately, this is not a candidacy examination for childhood. I vote 'No.'"

"Hector, he was rattled," Randolph said. "Give him a chance to recover."

"By the rules of our guild, the decision must be unanimous. Therefore, the neophyte fails."

"He does get a second chance," Randolph countered.

"Yes, a second chance in one month. And if he performs the same as he did today, then he is booted to the street. Our guild is not awash in cash like some others. Not anymore. You know that. One less mouth to feed would benefit us, those who are sufficiently skilled."

Nicholas walked away from the drawing slate. On top of the results of his examination, he also found himself troubled. How could Randolph and Hector continue to dabble with what had happened? They both continued to think about something that promised death and destruction. Would there be another explosion in a crowded city merely because of vanities yearning to be inflated?

His shoulders slumped. No sense in dwelling on the macabre. He had enough in his cup. Now, he was down to his very last chance. His one goal in life was to be a master magician. If he were, he could even mingle with the highest of society, the nobles and the queen. But, rather than concerning themselves with ritual, at this very moment, they probably were preparing to enjoy a royal dance.

3

A Bird in a Gilded Cage

THE NUMBER of candles in the wall sconces lining the walls was inadequate. Lionel, the scion of one of Procolon's most powerful lords, widened his eyes. It was dusk. The so-called ball was about to begin. Vendora, the Queen, insisted on the name even though the purpose was quite different. The lack of light was on purpose, of course. He understood that. Shadows cast by the flickering hid uncomeliness. So many of the marriages were arranged. Mere appearances couldn't be allowed to interfere with more important plans. Nevertheless, he wondered if the sorceress's prophecy from this morning would come true for him.

Lionel walked slowly towards the young woman awaiting his approach. Even in the dimness, he saw her limbs tremble. She was short and thin. Fourteen at the most. Old enough to wed, but with an adult mind only beginning to form.

"The young ones are best," Lionel's father had said. "You can shape them to what you want. And after you have sired a son or two so that our lineage continues, a more mature appetite can be satisfied discretely."

Lionel sighed. So much ritual cast in iron, as binding as a magician's cage. He glanced about. A dozen or so couples were converging onto the dancefloor. A small ensemble seated on the platform at the far wall tuned instruments for the first gavotte. No thrones were present. Evidently, the queen would not be putting in an appearance.

As he grew close to the young woman, Lionel hesitated. He suddenly felt fuzzy-headed. He could barely make out her features. Blinking a few times did not help. For a moment, his balance faltered, and he flailed his arms to regain it.

Finally, he was at her side, and whatever had stolen into his mind for an instant was gone. Now, the woman's features were sharp and clear. Well, at least her face seemed interesting enough. With dark hair, cut very short. A brunette? No, more auburn than that. And a face that was more mature. Definitely older than fourteen. A blossoming woman rather than a child. Had he seen her before?

The sorceress had foretold the evening would turn out well for him, and now that he had seen his partner for the first time, he felt a tickle of arousal as well. This evening might not be wasted after all.

Just so long as he did not think of griffin — Damn, he thought. Damn, damn, damn. The word 'griffin' had not occurred to him the entire day after the meeting with the sorceress — not until this very moment.

Lionel scowled at himself. As he had been warned, he had broken the charm. The enticing prophecy was not going to be fulfilled. He was seeing again the young girl he had first noticed when he entered the room. Her face was full, a gibbous moon. Long black hair combed into two long tresses poked over her shoulders and down both sides of her gown. They were strewed with little flowers and tiny works of art.

She looked terrified. Poor thing. She was much too young to have to play this mating ritual. How many centuries has this been the custom? Was there any decency left in the peerage?

He decided that he would try to get her at ease as best he could. "My name is Lionel," he said. "And you must be Rachel, right?"

The girl nodded.

"Let's dance." He smiled. "Don't worry. I won't bite."

Rachel stifled a quick shudder and held out a trembling hand.

"That's better," Lionel said. "While we dance, tell me a bit about yourself."

As the music swelled, Rachel warmed. With Lionel's coaxing, she began talking more and more. At the end of the piece, she sighed with relief.

"Do you, do you find me attractive?" she asked in a tiny voice.

Lionel smiled as wide as he could. "Ah, of course," he said. "You are a — a flower beginning to bud."

"Then it is settled, just like that?"

"Wait a moment. Not so fast. You know the saying, right? 'Don't pick the first pup you see in a litter.'"

"But my cousins said — "

"Yes, yes. I understand. But time is not so much of essence as it is led to be. One must sample many fruits before selecting a favorite."

"But my grandaunts said — "

"Look, I will speak to the queen's secretary before the next ball. I have two younger brothers, much closer to your age. The next paring will be more to your liking."

"So, I am so ugly that you don't want me as a bride despite how that boosts your status. I have failed." She bolted for one of the many doorways that ringed the ballroom.

As she left, a portly man, making as much haste as he could, rushed up to Lionel.

"What did you do this time?" Lord Tetris wagged a thick finger in Lionel's face. "We have been over this I can't remember how many times. An alliance of Talusan with the house of Alamain would be a great advantage to us. The fiefholder is old. His girth is wider than mine. Only daughters and no sons. If you play the game as you should, we could end up with your heir becoming lord of not one fief but two."

"I know all that, father," Lionel sighed. "You have drummed it into me more times than I can remember. But can't you see? Alamain's oldest is, what, fourteen? Still a child, not a woman."

"I have it on the authority of Alamain's alchemist that she is old enough to bear children. That is all that is necessary."

Tetris grabbed Lionel's arm and started propelling him away from the center of the ballroom. Lionel did not resist, and soon they were seated at one of the small tables scattered around the periphery.

"Another of our rules, Father," Lionel sighed. "Another of our blindly followed rules. You have made it clear."

"And the benefit is?" Tetris asked.

"A lack of chaos. Reduced bickering and strife." Lionel replied by rote. "Yes, yes, I know. Wars and skirmishes do still occur but they are less than they otherwise would be. Every lord swears fealty to the one who is his superior in exchange for land of his own. Forwards some of his collected taxes to the one he in turn has sworn to. So long as everyone follows the rules, we all will be safer. At peace longer.

"But, in the longer view of things, everything we do will not matter. We will have no tales of glory entered into the sagas." Lionel sighed again. "Safer, but merely birds trapped in gilded cages."

"I have just the thing to get you thinking right," Tetris said. "A position has opened up on one of the city patrols. I have nominated you to the queen to be its new leader, and she has accepted. It is part of your coming-of-age tradition. You start tomorrow."

"Tomorrow!" Lionel said, then pondered a moment. "Well, at least it trades one monotony for another."

"Monotony? What are you talking about? Like these

dances, it is all part of the same game. In the evening, you court the females. In the day, you build alliances with the young men, the scions of the other lords. Learn who would come to your aid and protect your back and who would not.”

“Yes, yes, I understand the reason, but it is boredom, nonetheless. You probably don’t remember how carefully you have instructed me to play the card games. I must allow slow-witted Eugene to win occasionally at the Gambling House or else he will insist on playing Old Spinster instead.”

“So then, you agree! Out of the target sight part of the day would be a good change. Not worry about an assassin’s knife thrust whenever you enter a new passageway alone.

“You could see how fortunate your life is, Lionel. Mingle with the lower classes. Find out first-hand how lucky you are to be born into the peerage — despite the few shortcomings.”

“I want nothing of the fiefdom and the jockeying for position that goes with it. In fact, if I find no suitable mate, I am thinking of journeying south and joining the artist’s colony in Carmela.”

“Nonsense! Don’t be sarcastic. What would you eat? It no longer would be choosing between roast duckling and fried tuna flank.”

“I don’t know. Somehow, the colony persists. Successful artists get paid for what they produce. I guess they may share. And if I have to, I will abdicate. Let one of my two younger brothers assume my role as heir.”

“Which twin? You know as well as I that there is no undisputable evidence of who emerged from the womb first. There would be chaos, and one of our ambitious neighbors would decide it was a good time to invade. In fact, as far as we know, there is a target on both our backs even as we speak.”

“You are not listening to me, Father, not answering the most basic question of all.”

“What is that?”

Lionel waved his arm around the ballroom. "For me, for the rest of the nobles, why do we embrace all this? What part of our lives are truly our own? Might it not be better to be low-born and choose what it is that we do? At this moment, surely none of them are contemplating with whom to have the next dance or looking around each doorway to see if assassins are lurking on the other side. Even the sorceress I encountered this morning is better off than I."

This Time Will Be Different

DIANA PATTED her stomach and smiled. Every bite of the roast tasted as good as she had imagined. The makeshift tent she sat in was small, one of many scattered about on what was called the Beggar's Field. As the sun set, she wiggled to get more comfortable while sitting over the lumpiness of the stools and other paraphernalia she used for her enchantments stashed under her sleeping blanket.

It was a close fit being nestled against Uncle Izzy on one side and Claymore on the other while they ate, but she knew that was where she had to be. Intrepid, at least that is what he called himself, eyed her with a slight smile from the other side of the small table. Between every bite, he looked at her, teasing her with his eyes. But fortunately, not yet anyway, he had not tried anything further.

The two warriors had been part of their little group as long as she could remember. Not skilled enough to be part of a more prominent gang, nor smart enough to survive on their own, they put up with Izzy's schemes because they had little other choice.

Claymore was a giant of a man, stout arms and legs each as large as a bursting bag of flax. He would look formidable if only he could change his easygoing smile into something else.

Intrepid was tall, taller than Diana. He prided himself on

his swagger, leather vest and leggings squeaking with menace when he walked. But that visage was reserved for women and children, not another warrior who could do him real harm.

Izzy was short and beginning to stoop. His deeply sunken eyes darted from place to place, always seeking the next opportunity, the one that finally would put them on the road of ease he insisted he deserved.

"I wish you had handed over all your proceeds as you usually do, Diana," Izzy said as he wiped his hand on the tatters of what was once a vest. "I'm really on to something this time. All I need is a large enough bribe for the dimwit I plied with a few drinks in my evening of ah … information gathering."

Intrepid snorted. He smoothed his long black hair into place on his neck. His eyes closed to mere slits. The effect was meant to be one of menace, Diana had deduced long ago, but it came across more as someone roused from a deep sleep. She knew what was coming next, another challenge to her uncle.

"Old man, you said something like this before. Remember? When we almost lost even this shelter. Why will this time be any better?"

"And why do I even put up with you?" Izzy shot back. "If you don't think I should lead, say so."

"So."

No one spoke for a moment. Finally, Claymore cracked the knuckles of one giant hand in his other. With some effort, he arched his back and stretched. His face tightened into his best attempt at a snarl, like a tamed circus bear a mere instant from breaking free. "You have never left, have you? Confess, why do you hang around?"

"You will not get anything as a reward for protecting Diana, pudding-brain." Intrepid shook his head. "You are such an idiot."

"Boys, boys," Izzy said. "Our talents complement one

another, right? I think we all agree we are better as a team. Much better than acting as individuals." He paused for a moment. "Now, pay attention. What I have learned is quite intriguing. Well, intriguing if you know what to listen for."

Intrepid sighed and stretched out to rest on his side. A single arm propped up his head. "What is it this time then? A lady's ring? An heir who parades around the city unguarded?"

Before Izzy could reply, the door flap suddenly flung aside. "Saddar!" Izzy exclaimed. "You are a bit late tonight. We have already finished our dinner meal. I had hoped we could delay payment until tomorrow. You see, today is a … a holiday for us."

Saddar's face was a riverbed of lines. He squinted when he looked at them. Izzy was old, but the intruder was older. "You worked the street today, didn't you?" Saddar challenged. "No one gave you any trouble. You were protected to go about your business. No interference from outsiders in your territory. There is no time off for a, whatya call it, a holiday."

"Diana did not bring home a single coin," Izzy protested. "Neither Intrepid nor Claymore saw any purses worth snatching. It happens that way sometimes. You know what they say, 'either you starve to death or get liquid gold down your throat.'"

Saddar grabbed the old man's tunic. "See these two goons standing behind me outside. They have to eat every day, too. They don't take holidays. I have expenses every day."

"I guess we should have invited you," Diana said. She rubbed her stomach and stifled a small burp. "There probably would have been enough for that."

"You don't get it, do you?" Saddar pointed over his shoulder. "Ambrosia is a big city. Two guys like these can only protect a part of it. There are others like me doing the same elsewhere."

"So?" Intrepid said.

"So, somebody has to keep things in order. Handle squabbles at the boundaries between the territories. That sort of thing."

"So?"

"So, a percentage of my take goes up a chain of collectors to the guy at the top. You see, Izzy, if you are short, then I am short. I have to make it up somehow — no, you, Izzy, have to make it up."

Saddar leered at Diana. "You know, Izzy, your, what, niece, is rounding out nicely. You could get out of this bottom-of-the-barrel stuff and sit back and enjoy some of the profits. For a small fee, I can get you connected."

Diana tensed. She looked at Izzy and saw the far-away look fill his face. After a moment of silence, Saddar shrugged. "Maybe not this time, but soon." He turned to leave. "Tomorrow, double the usual and an extra copper thrown in for my trouble. Think it over, Izzy. You are getting too old for this."

EVERYONE WAS silent until they were sure Saddar had gone. "Nothing as commonplace as what you surmise, Intrepid," Izzy continued as if the interruption had not happened. "Nothing so mundane. The fellow I am talking about is newly hired to stand evening guard at the apothecary that had been abandoned on Honeysuckle Street. Well, he is no longer there now, since he has stopped being paid."

"An apothecary," Intrepid snorted. "What are we going to do? Rob a few of the more popular potions and hawk them on the street ourselves? That would last three days, maybe four, and then a royal patrol would swoop us up. The cut of our take we would have to give Saddar for his so-called protection would be too much. He has a daily minimum as you well know."

"This is not about street drugs." Izzy shook his head. "Something bigger than even Saddar would want to get involved with. It is not about alchemy at all. A new set of alchemists are not moving into the apothecary." He paused for effect. "Instead, it now is a guild of magicians. And the — "

Intrepid bolted upright. An involuntary gasp exploded from Claymore. Diana's mouth dropped open. Over all the years they had been together, she had become quite jaded about her uncle's crazy schemes, one after the next. But magicians. That was something entirely different.

"Magicians," Claymore scratched the stubble on his massive jaw. "They stay isolated in guilds — like the one in the south that blew up a little while ago. A very secretive lot. Perform complex rituals that sometimes take centuries to complete. 'Perfection is eternal' — the basic law of magic, it is said. Make objects that command a queen's ransom to purchase. Why would any of them want to set up in a shop in the oldest part of the city?"

"Precisely, Claymore," Izzy said. "Something very peculiar is going down right here in central Ambrosia. And where there are magicians involved, there is gold, lots of gold. If we can figure it out first, we could retire from the game. Play our cards right, and this could be our last heist."

"Another of your dreams, Izzy" Intrepid shook his head. "We know absolutely nothing about magicians."

Diana forced the every-night bickering out of her thoughts. She looked around at her simple and cramped surroundings. Wondered about how it would be if things were different, if she lived in a dwelling with solid walls rather than cloth, one centered on the pomp of exotic rituals and filled with results of true magic. What would it be like to be a magician rather than a sorcerer?

(5)

Image and Reality

THE NEXT morning, after his exam failure, Nicholas stewed in his thoughts. He was alone, outside the makeshift vault in the center of the abandoned apothecary's shop. Located behind the stronghold were the chambers of the masters. They seldom left them, spending almost all their time there eating, sleeping, and thinking.

Near the draped front windows was the stage with the drawing slate and the facing chairs. Yesterday evening, he had failed his initiate examination there. He knew he should begin studying again right away, but the task of remembering everything for instant recall felt too formidable. He could not make himself start cracking the books.

A knock on the front door broke Nicholas out of his mental churning. He went to answer, and, peering through a peephole, saw another young man wearing a robe standing there. Instead of a pale blue like Nicholas's own, the color was white and covered with triangles, the garb of a novice alchemist. Nicholas scowled. Triangles. After what happened yesterday, he felt as if the cosmos was now mocking him.

"What do you want?" he managed to ask.

"You're one of the magicians, right?" the man called out.

"A magician? You mean a master magician?"

"No, no, any — what do you call yourselves — neophytes will do. Someone who has the authority to buy and sell. My name is Urias. I wonder if you are in the market for some alchemical equipment. I, ah, represent several apothecaries on the street and have some items that might interest you."

"Like what?"

"Like potions that guarantee sleep, memory enhancers, factory machinery that drill, sand or bore."

"Not interested," Nicholas said.

"No problem," Urias waved the words away, turned to leave, and then paused. "But before I go, I do wonder. Do you, by chance, have any left-over glassware here. The outfit that left probably took everything of value, but one never knows. Doesn't hurt to check. You get some cash, and my alchemist gets equipment for a good price."

Nicholas scowled. Anybody could steal a novice's robe and assert he was being trained by a master. He hesitated.

"My money is good," Urias said as he jingled coins in his hand. "Brandels of solid gold."

The thought sprung into Nicholas's head. An opportunity to help the guild's finances! He brightened a bit. "Come in," he said as he cautiously opened the front door. "Yes, there is some gear we have no need for. Like everything else that might be worth something, it has been moved into our vault."

"You are going to let me look into your vault! Really?"

"No, of course not. Wait here. I will fetch what I am talking about."

"Yes, yes. I understand. It's common lore about magician vaults," Urias rattled on. "Built by magic so that they were impenetrable if the entrance was properly closed. Had to be. Ransoms for kings inside, right? Objects hundreds of years in the making. All the partially completed projects safely stored inside awaiting their next ritual step in which they were involved."

Nicholas did not answer. Anyone who knew anything about magic enclosures would not be fooled by what he saw if let to peek inside. Yes, the latch to the one access door could only be released by the possessor of the proper magic ring. But the door and walls themselves were merely thick, not magic. Drilling through one would be only a small matter for a dedicated marauder.

It was all that could have been done. A real magician's vault took at least a century to complete all the necessary rituals. Obviously, Antron, Randolph, and Hector did not want to devote that much of their personal time to the task. Three masters and one neophyte. They were the only ones left of what once had been a powerful guild. All the others were killed by what Gavarak had unleashed.

"Any more, what do you call yourselves, neophytes, around?" Urias asked.

"Once there was," Nicholas said. The next words came hard. "Felicia and others."

"Felicia! A woman? Let me guess. You were a twosome."

Nicholas said nothing immediately. The shock of what had happened from the explosion had long since settled into a dull but persistent numbness. Only now could he think of the initiate, Felica, without surrendering to tears.

She would have wanted him to struggle onward, be awarded the robe of sea-blue that indicated an initiate. Originally, they had planned to become masters together. Then find another guild who would welcome two new additions to their rosters.

"Yes, we were a couple," Nicholas managed to say quietly.

He took a ring out of his pocket and slipped it on his finger. The gentle tingle reminded him that it was indeed magical. He touched the vault door with it, and the lock clicked.

Nicholas pulled the door open a crack and slithered in. Inside, things looked a little better than they had yesterday. The shelves on the left still sagged with weighty tomes of lore, but at least now there was some order to them. He had puzzled why some like The Game of Ferret and Geese for beginners, Famous Battles of History, and When to Raise the Price, were even relevant to the craft of magic. But so that he would not dwell on what might have been, he had spent most of the time before his failed examination putting the books into order.

Urias stood on tiptoe and peeked over Nicholas's shoulder to glimpse of what lay beyond. "How were you able to construct a vault so fas — this is not quite as impressive as I thought."

Nicholas scowled at the dismissal and slammed the door shut after himself. It had been part of the tragedy that their original vault was open when the blast occurred. Most everything not magic had been destroyed. Only a few things were salvaged.

Next to the shelves, short, thin panes of unadorned magical glass propped against the wall. They were the first of many steps in the production of magic mirrors. Farther along the floor sat the remaining flask of resin that had survived the blast along with two of fixer. They were next to worthless now since alchemists had started hawking a glue of their own — one produced in a fraction of the time and with much less effort.

On a small table were several trays of magic rings, thousands of them, each little orb as plain as the next. Near the vault wall on the other side stood two short stacks of Gavarak's nestled hemispheres of copper. Each one bristled with stout stoppers from a slew of portals. Place a half globe from one stack atop one from the other, give it a short twist and an impenetrable sphere was created.

Nicholas shook his head. No, that was not quite right, he corrected himself. The assembled spheres were strong, yes, but not completely impenetrable. Not truly magic, and that had been Gavarak's mistake.

A stool was tucked under a table to the right of the hemispheres. Upon it was an open cashbox with most of its partitions empty. Nicholas's cot lay on the floor next to the table. On the far wall was a crude box of abandoned alchemical equipment. He scooped it up, slithered back outside, and the door shut again with a satisfying click.

Urias ran to the collection of flasks, condensers, and beakers, eyeing them critically. "Three brandels for the lot," he said, plonking the coins onto a nearby table. "That is my first and final offer."

"Agreed. Three brandels," Nicholas said quickly. "Take the stuff away. There is no need for any of it here." In his head, he recalculated how much longer the addition would help keep their guild afloat. He was good at arithmetic. Of course, he had to be to even begin to think about becoming a magician.

"How many of those finger rings come with the purchase?" Urias asked suddenly as he pulled a wrapping parchment from a pocket in his robe. "I got a glimpse of them in the box near the door. They are magic too, right?"

Nicholas pondered for a moment. The existence of magic rings was not a deep mystery. No harm in saying a few words about them. "Yes, they are, but do not possess any true power yet. They are what we call *blanks*."

"Ah, that is clever. Yes, give me a few. I bet they can be used in another apothecary's shop."

"They are magic," Nicholas said. "Not to be frittered away for a mundane purpose. One of our rituals has made them indestructible, but no additional attributes have been bestowed on them yet. Now they are similar to what one could see in any jewelry shop window."

Urias frowned. "If all they are is merely being indestructible, what good do they serve?"

"None yet, but eventually, after many more rituals, they could have a power worth fortunes."

"Interesting." Urias paused for a moment, then smiled at Nicholas. "So how many of these rings are part of the deal?" he asked.

Nicholas did not immediately respond.

"Your decision," Urias said. "A lost opportunity." He shrugged and began unwrapping the flask he had just handled and put it back into the box from which it had come.

Nicholas scowled. Urias's boldness irritated him. It was a standard sales technique called the *last nibble*. He recognized what it was. For an instant, he had looked at the three golden coins and imagined how many provisions he could buy with them. Then he let the temptation pass. It was a manipulation, nothing more, he reasoned. He was not going to be pressured this way. A master alchemist had no use for two blank magic rings.

Urias slowed his unwrapping and then finally stopped. "So, it looks like the title neophyte doesn't really mean anything, then. They give you a robe so you can feel good about yourself while you dust and mop. But in reality, you are a servant, not allowed to make even the simplest decisions."

Nicholas grit his teeth. "I am not a mere servant. Much more than that, I am the one who has to take care of everything, no matter what the shade of my robe. I have to manage the purchase of all the meats, vegetables, breads, and wines. Supervise the day-workers who cook, wash the underwear, and change the beds.

"Make sure ink and blank vellums are always in supply even at all hours of the night. Fetch and return volumes of what was left of our library to their proper shelves. Maintain the perfect environment so that the masters can think their heavy thoughts."

"Still sounds like a servant to me. Do they pay you anything besides room and board?"

Nicholas felt he had endured enough. He shook his head, walked back to the front door, and motioned Urias to follow.

The visitor paused, reluctant to leave. "If I could only talk to one of your masters, they would see the merits of what I have to offer."

"What merits?" Hector suddenly emerged from his chamber. "What is the racket here? How could alchemy have any relevance to magic?"

"I have seen the primitive nature of your, ah … vault," Urias said. "I have conceived a machine that will make digging into the ground much easier. Putting your vault into a basement has got to be better than what you have here."

"A machine?" Hector scratched his chin. "What do you mean?"

"Well, the details are, of course, private," Urias answered.

"Then I will speak to your master," Hector said. "At which apothecary on the street is he located?"

"Well, the concept is my own invention and — "

"Of course," Hector laughed. "Every underling of the crafts assumes that he can bring something new to the practice." He looked at Nicholas. "Well, perhaps not every single one. Begone with your ideas, novice. If a master is not interested, then whatever you are espousing has no merit. I have better things to do. Next time, Nicholas, keep the noise down."

Hector vanished back into his chamber. Urias shrugged. "Oh well, always worth the try." He finished preparing the glassware for transit. When he was done, he flung the brandels on the floor and left.

Nicholas's burden upon himself immediately returned. Neophyte or floor sweeper — what difference did it make to Hector and the others anyway? Urias had been correct. The masters did not care about him as a person at all. He was no more than a servant. They were merely going through the motions before eventually taking his robe away.

He should walk out the door right now and let the masters

discover they were on their own. Find something else to do. But then …

But then that would sever his last connection with Felica. Without being involved with magic in some way, his memories of her would fade all the faster. Above everything else, he did not want that.

He surveyed the vault one final time and made a decision. Maintaining the guise of a viable guild could not continue much longer. The masters denied the existence of the dire circumstance. They hid the truth beneath their deep thoughts about rituals.

Figuring out what Gavarak had stumbled upon might prove to be profitable someday. But even a sorcerer could not determine how long that might take. A steady flow of income had to be generated and soon.

Nicholas frowned. He probably should check with Antron first, but he was not sure of the answer he would get. No, there was no way to avoid it. Three unexpected brandels helped, but some of their magic trove, meager though it might be, would have to be sold.

The most valuable asset they had were the glass panes, of course. But no other guild would pay much for unbreakable glass with not a single additional capability impressed into them.

The rings then, Nicholas concluded. Their guild had what must be several thousand of them. They were all blanks, but what was important was that they invoked that slight suggestive tingle when one was slipped on a finger. They were more than mere fabrications freshly cooled from a smithy's furnace, but indestructible loops of true magic. No one would deny that they indeed seemed to wield some power. Certainly, a few could be spared to keep the bills for food and upkeep paid.

Nicholas rubbed his cheek. They might need some convincing embellishment to convince a customer. A bit of a pretty stone bound to a ring by a strand of wire and a convincing patter to go with it. Cheaply enough obtained from one of the 'new age' crystal shops that seemed to be the rage recently. Yes, he could do this. First, acquire some small crystals, attach them to a few of the rings, and finally to a market before sundown …

He stopped. Wait a moment. Was this unethical? True magicians did not do such things. Was it even legal? Weren't there lordling-led patrols constantly inspecting the markets to ensure nothing improper was offered for sale?

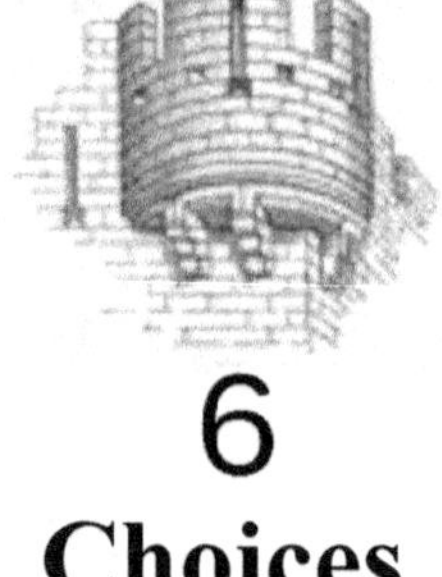

6
Choices

LIONEL SIGHED. 'Make a show of being helpful.' The words of Vendora, queen of all Procolon, flashed in his mind. Her legendary beauty that had aroused so much tumult in her youth had long since faded. Now, she resorted to craft to keep her rule secure. Her commands were part of her largess for the populace — the duty of the eldest son of every lord attending court to spend time on the city patrol. One of the bars of the gilded cage. Another obstacle to overcome if one were to be truly free. Free to do whatever one wanted — to create astounding art — write a great saga, become known as a renowned sculptor ...

Lionel shook his head. He was fooling himself again. It was not so simple as merely being free to choose the life he wanted. The problem was, what would that be? He remembered having canvases stacked to face the wall in his room at his father's stronghold. None good enough to show to someone not seeking favor. Next to them was the tangled pile of vellums, the attempt at a saga, the shorter works intended to amuse. In the corner, the hammers and chisels covered with dust ...

The sun reached its zenith and began its descent. Walking around in armor through the heat of the day was tiring, no matter how formidable he might look. The two pikemen who strode behind him kept pace without protesting at all. But then, why would they? They were being paid, and their vests were made of leather, not heavy steel.

Well, at least he did not first have to spend time on training. As a scion of a wealthy lord, he had endured that ever since he could ride a horse without falling off. The pikemen accepted his commands without protest. They did whatever he said. After all, he was a lord, not a commoner. And since it was his first day, the routine was at least interesting. He was seeing parts of the city into which he had never visited before.

Lionel glanced briefly at a trio emerging from the tavern just ahead in one of the poorer parts of Ambrosia. Two men were struggling to hold erect a third between them. 'Make a show of being helpful.' The words of the queen were again in his thoughts. Be clearly in the present, do noble duty, and keep the peace.

"Is there a problem here?" Lionel asked as he approached the struggling trio.

"No, my lord," Intrepid said. "No trouble at all. My, ah… uncle here did not guess accurately how much he could hold. Claymore and I are assisting him home."

"How far away does he live?" Lionel asked.

"Not far. Not far at all. Among the indigents to the east."

Lionel made a snap decision. Maybe at least a little value might come from today's duty. A good story that his father could brag about to the queen. Save himself from another parental lecture. "Pikemen, render assistance," he decided. "Help this citizen get to his home." He glanced from Intrepid to Claymore. "You two can go about your business. The patrol will take it from here."

"You don't know where we live," Claymore protested.

"I am not an addled idiot," Izzy slurred. "I know exactly where my abode is."

Intrepid grabbed Claymore's arm. "Come on," he whispered. "We are owed another round just to pay for listening to the babble we heard back there. Magic spheres, explosions. Something straight out of the sagas. It's gotta be. The stuff of fantasy."

Claymore started to reply, then shrugged as Lionel's pikemen relieved the pair of having to keep Izzy vertical. He licked his lips. "Yeah, I guess so. Let's go."

For a moment, Lionel watched the two men walk into the distance. There was something suspicious about them, but he could not fathom exactly what it was. He glanced at his pikemen with their hands full holding the drunk erect. Focus on seeing him safely home, he decided. Enough of an accomplishment for his first day in service to the queen.

It had always been something on the agenda, he mused, from as far back as he could remember. A duty, a task he must perform with no say in the matter. He stood at attention next to his father when a higher ranking noble deigned to visit their manor. Hours upon hours learning how to fence, wield a whirling mace, and cock a crossbow that never would be used.

What the titles of duke, marquis, and earl implied — know instantly the status of a stranger to which you were being introduced because of what he wore on his sleeve. Understand the implications of the subtle moves at court. He was born into the peerage. He had had no choice. But he was not like his father at all. His father welcomed these rituals, the lack of any necessity to think. Just finish one and move on to the next.

And rebelling, slipping away and learning, say, one of the five crafts was no better. Thaumaturge, alchemist, magician, sorcerer, wizard. They all required the crushing weight of what had to be remembered. Exactly like the military; one had to work up through the ranks. Lionel shook his head. He doubted even the archimage, Alodar, could have had any joy.

The grinding poverty of common laborers, smiths, carpenters, and masons, also did not appeal. Slaving from dawn to dusk to earn enough to feed a family that depended on you totally for their very lives must eventually sap one's every essence.

What then? What was it that he was best suited for? He didn't know. Carving little caricatures in soft wood was his current fancy. Get enough skill into his fingers so that working with stone would be next. But really, he had difficulty in even giving them away. Did he have any true talent or was he fooling himself? Well, maybe he was.

"Begging your pardon, sir," one of his troops said. "Which way are we to go?"

"Let the drunkard show the way," Lionel said as he looked eastward. "I suspect it is among the tents a half league straight ahead.

Surcharges

DIANA WAS alone in the tent as the sun became serious about its decline. She busied herself tidying up the few possessions their group had accumulated in their tent. First, she covered the canvas, post and stools from her daily work along with her purchases the day before, all well out of sight in her bedding. Then she arranged the 'furnishings' — her mother's fancy comb, Intrepid's spare dagger, and Claymore's little dexterity puzzle — the challenge to get the two small steel balls simultaneously in holes at opposite ends of their enclosure.

Diana smiled. The day had gone well for her. More patrons than usual wanted to sample the thrill of an enchantment, mild though it might be. All by herself, she had made enough for her group's payment to Saddar when he came — not for only one day, but enough for both. She had been able to return much earlier than usual.

No one else was present. That was a good sign, she told herself. If everyone had tried harder, they might be able to breathe easier for several days more.

"It must have been a good take," a voice interrupted Diana's thought. "Left you here alone while the three of them are out spending the excess."

"Saddar!" Diana exclaimed. Her brow furrowed. She did not like the way he was looking at her. His hunched stature, dirty shirt with ragged sleeves, never washed, pock-marked face, and eyes dripping rheum were the same as always, but this time there was something even more sinister there.

"Ten coppers for yesterday, and ten more for today," Diana quickly reached into the communal purse and poured out the coins.

Saddar shook his head. "The total is twenty-four, not twenty."

"Why? Even with the late payment, it was to be twenty-one."

"Interest, my dear, one copper for the delay and three more for the annoyance."

"Twenty-one coppers. That is all that I will give you."

Saddar glanced over his shoulder to his two henchmen standing outside the door flap. "Listen Up and Pay Attention," he called out. "Go and take a pee somewhere."

He turned his eyes back on Diana and shook his head. "'That is what I will give you' is not a correct statement, my dear. There is something else you can give me instead."

Diana knew instantly what this was about. The minds of female customers of her craft had explained much. She looked Saddar in the eye and started the first recital of a chant.

"Oh no you don't, lassie," Saddar put an arm across his eyes. "I understand more about your craft than you realize. Now, come to me. It will be so much more enjoyable for you if you do."

Diana looked about for Intrepid's spare dagger, but Saddar blocked her way. Perhaps the words alone would be enough, she thought desperately. Maybe the eye contact was merely lore, passed down from one sorcerer to another. Something to keep the subject's attention from wandering. After all, 'Thrice spoken, once fulfilled' was the basic rule.

She shook her head to get rid of the thought. No time for

that, not now. Saddar reached out for her. Without thinking more, Diana bit down on his arm, then coughed to spit out the taste. Saddar roared in pain, clutching the injury with his other hand. "I'm bleeding," he cried in disbelief.

Diana saw her chance. She scrambled up and out through the tent flap. She had to run away as far and fast as she could, but to where? Saddar's two goons stood impassively in front of her as they always did. They had not gone anywhere after all. Both their faces were expressionless and bored. They probably had witnessed Saddar's behavior many times before.

"Stand aside!" Diana commanded, and to her surprise, the two men pulled apart from one another. She looked into the distance and gasped in shock. There was Uncle Izzy being propped up by two guardsmen, and more importantly, a lordling she recognized. What was his name? What did he say the day before as he departed? Yes, Lionel — that was it. She looked quickly right and left.

Diana framed her cheeks with her hands. Each time the same subject was enchanted, the task became easier and easier. Shorter and shorter charms could be used to bring one back into thrall.

She took off running towards Lionel, yelling the first pass of the charm as loudly as she could. She heard Saddar stumbling after, but now she felt she had a chance.

LIONEL BLINKED. A tall young woman was running towards him, shouting out something he could not quite make out. He blinked again. There was something familiar about her …

"Yes, the woman I was to have met at the queen's ball," he said out loud. "I recognize her face."

"Diana!" Izzy shouted as she drew closer. "What is it? What's the problem?"

"Him!" Diana turned and pointed. "Saddar … he … he

attacked me!"

Lionel's attention sharpened. "Fear not — my, my lady," he said. This was a role he had been trained to perform. He drew his sword and pointed it at Saddar as the thug panted to join the group. "Stand, varlet. You are under arrest."

"For what, my lord?" Saddar halted his pursuit and smiled. "There is no issue for you to concern yourself with here. This vixen was fleeing because she could not pay me what is my due. I was merely trying to collect."

"Is this the man who attacked you?" Lionel asked Diana.

Diana hesitated. The cad certainly had intended to. She had no doubt about that. But … but he had not even touched her yet.

"What is the punishment for such a thing," she asked. Maybe a few days in a cell would do Saddar some good.

"Usually months in Vendora's dungeon, my lady." Lionel shrugged. "And if there is persistence after that, castration. I know for a fact that, as a woman herself, the queen is quite stern about this kind of thing."

Diana frowned. If she were perfectly truthful and said that no attack had actually occurred, that she had been merely threatened, Saddar would go free. And he certainly would not forget this. It was quite likely he had been caught for this before. Demanding the payment of a few additional coppers would be the least of what he would want. On the other hand, probably every woman in Ambrosia would applaud if he were removed from society — one less menace to be wary of.

"My lady?" Lionel asked.

Diana took a deep breath. "I said that he attacked me," she uttered slowly in a small voice. "One such as he deserves to be punished."

"Very well, then," Lionel said. His words rolled off his lips as he had been trained for many years. "Pikemen, release the citizen you are escorting and take this one into custody instead." He smiled at Diana. "And if you ever again are in need of my services, my lady," he paused for expected effect. "I am yours to command."

"Thank —"

"I will get you for this, you guttersnipe." Hate boiled out of Saddar's eyes. "You will rue this day for the rest of your life. I swear that you will."

"Enough blabbering, knave," Lionel said. "The lady is well done of you. Pikemen, attend to your duty, and we will be off. Even the queen herself will be pleased by what we have done today."

Diana watched as Saddar bolted, but the pikemen were quicker. One shoved the handle of his weapon between the legs of the rogue, and he tumbled to the ground. His hands were quickly bound behind him, and the pair hoisted him to his feet. In an instant, without another word, the quartet marched off. Diana did not feel good about what she had done, but maybe, just maybe, she rationalized, it was for the best.

"Diana, dear sweet niece, can you give me a little support," Izzy asked. "I still cannot quite make it all the way home by myself."

Diana sighed. She motioned to Izzy that he could lean on her. With an arm around his waist, she steered him towards their tent. As they approached, she sighed again. There was another problem to deal with. Saddar's two henchmen still stood in front of the entrance flap. Surely, they would let her take care of Izzy first.

A New Possibility

IT WAS nearing dusk. After Diana had got Izzy comfortable, she climbed back out of the hovel and faced the two henchmen still standing there. They were tall, near the same height and clothed in leather, with sheathed swords at their sides. Their most striking features were their faces — brows furled like plowed fields, eyes squinting with menace, lips taut and straight, unyielding.

Intrepid and Claymore were not there. Izzy was not in any shape to handle this. She had to act on her own. But she found herself distracted, unable to think through what she should do. The lordling, Lionel, had addressed her as 'My lady.' The words warmed her to her core.

"Look, I — I guess I'm sorry about what happened to your boss." She grimaced. That was not totally right. Saddar was bad. No, worse than that, he was evil. But, even so, he probably did not deserve the fate she had thrust upon him. "I don't think he is coming back today." She attempted a slight smile. "It is me that you will have to deal with. Sorry for the complication."

"Complication?" The henchman on the left shrugged. He looked at the other, who answered. "It's simple. The clients pay for the service, and we make sure nothing interferes with what they do. It is a bargain, Saddar would always say. No one who paid for his services has ever been bothered."

"Yes, well, you see, there is a small payment problem. All I have to give you today is twenty-one coppers, not twenty-four."

"We don't keep track of the numbers," the one on the right said. "That's your job, not ours."

"*My* job?"

"Yeah, that's the way it works," the one on the left said. "In our line of business, a boss keeps doing what he does until someone better at it comes along. Then the first one is history. And whoever did in the old boss starts running the service."

"You got rid of Saddar, correct?" the one on the right continued. "That's clear enough. No doubt about it." He pointed at his comrade. "Listen Up and I saw what happened. So, now you take over what he was doing."

"I am listening," Diana said. "But you are not. I am asking that you take the twenty-one coppers, and agree we are done for today."

"No, not for you to listen. Saddar has called the two of us Listen Up and Pay Attention so long that I have almost forgotten what my mother named me. I'm 'Pay Attention,' and he's 'Listen Up.'"

Diana held out her hand holding the coppers. "Do you want these or not?"

"Not me," Listen Up and Pay Attention said simultaneously. "We merely want to follow the rules, stand around looking menacing, and keep our noses clean."

"You are the one who got rid of Saddar," Pay Attention continued. "That means you are the boss now. The three of us make the rounds daily, just like before. The only difference is that now you are the one who collects the fees. At the end of the day, you give the higher-ups their share, then ours, and keep the rest for yourself. Like I have already said, it's simple, really."

"I don't want to get involved." Diana shook her head. "Take the payment for Izzy's hovel and go to your next stop."

"Can't do that," Listen Up said. "We know the route but not how much each client is to pay."

"I don't know that either," Diana protested.

"Play it by ear. Do whatever Saddar must have done. The only important thing is to turn in a percentage of our daily take. So long that is greater than a minimum, everybody is happy."

"I refuse," Diana shook her head. She wanted no part of this and would rather think about what had happened with Lionel. She had enchanted him of course, so his attention to her meant little. But … being treated like a lady rather than a tent tramp had an irresistible lure to it.

"Then, you're a goner," Pay Attention said. "We will squeal who you are right away. No sense to endure any of the torture ourselves trying to cover anything up."

"It's easy," Listen Up said. "You go to the next tent while we stand outside and look menacing, like always. Then, collect the payment, and we move on to the next. By sundown, we should be finished with everybody."

Diana sighed. Stay focused, she managed to command herself. She looked down at her tattered sorceress's robe. The smell probably was not from that but from how infrequently she bathed. She remembered how the butcher store clerk had treated her until she showed that she had money. If only she had a few more coins for soap, she might be treated differently.

"Diana," Izzy called out from the hovel. "I seem to have had another small accident. Be a dear like you always are, and get the mess cleaned up."

Diana's resistance crumbled. Izzy's words were the last stroke. Her thoughts took flight. Suppose she did what the henchmen asked but only for a few days. Learn enough in that time so she could foist them off on the higherups, whoever they might be. Distribute the payoffs required and maybe have a little left over for herself to buy soap and even something called 'makeup,' whatever that was. Rather than spend the entire daylight hours performing light enchantments, she would stop that early in the afternoon and let these two thugs guide her through the slum while there was still light. Appear at dinner time as before. Hold back a few of the coins. Give herself a chance to live out the fantasy of being treated like a lady, if only for a short while each day.

And things might begin looking up, she told herself. Maybe, Izzy would abandon the idea of dealing with magicians. The strange things rumored about what they did were nothing to get involved with. Finally, there was the lordling, Lionel. Who knew when their paths might cross again?

"Let's go," she said with weak conviction. "I will do it. The city guard with its lordling commander probably will not reappear here today."

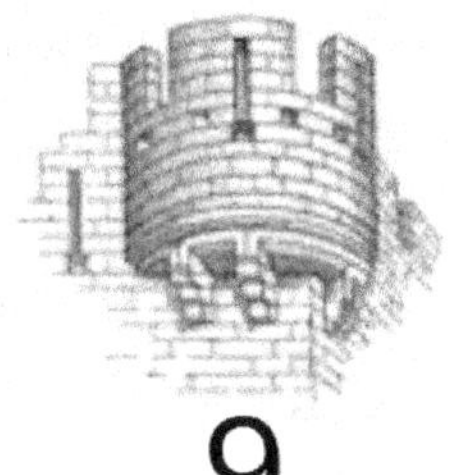

9

The Queen's Treasury

LIONEL FLEXED his shoulders as the attendant unbuckled his chain mail, and it chattered to the armory floor. It was not yet time to light torches, but he was already tired. Tomorrow, he would try to stay out longer. He stretched to release the tension in his shoulders. Why did the sagas never mention the effort it took to wear battle gear all day?

For patrolling city streets where the greatest threat might be a drunken ruffian, the leather of his pikemen would have been enough. He shook his head. Dawn to dusk in the service of the queen, and then no chance to do something that he had chosen to do himself.

"I have informed the queen of the rescue you performed today." Lionel's father burst into the armory changing room. "She was much impressed. Especially the part about coming to the aid of a lady. It is a shame you did not think to ask her name."

Lionel frowned and then shook his head. "It is now a blur, Father. I told you that. Whatever happened somehow is a fading memory."

"Nevertheless, I do have much influence with Vendora. She listens to me, and now is aware of your name. Old Bovine cannot last much longer. Your name might be at the top of the list when he goes. A younger man who could be useful rather than a sinecure holder as the new Captain of the City Guard."

"Captain of the City Guard!" Lionel exclaimed. "When would I have time to do that?"

"The captain sits at the desk near where you are standing. He does not go out on patrol. Instead, he makes the assignments for those who do."

"That somehow still fills up the entire day?"

"Well, yes, not totally, but it certainly enhances your chances to become lord of two fiefs when Atrium passes without a male heir and you are the husband of his only daughter."

Lionel sighed. "This is such a wonderful plan, Father. All that has to happen is for not one but two men to pass and then — "

"Not so loud, my son. There is someone else here who asked me to intercede for him. He would like to speak with you. I will talk again with you after the ball."

"Who?"

"A magician. One who is newly arrived in Ambrosia."

"What does he want?"

"A simple request. He wants to see the queen's treasury."

"The treasury! Of course not!"

"You must garner allies and supporters wherever you can, my son. The skills of a magician might be useful. Look, what can it matter? One little peek. He seems curious; that is all."

Lionel sighed. Someday, he would find the strength to resist his father's wishes, but right now he was too tired. "Very well, I will walk him to the door in the keep that leads below, but show him no more than that. And you must accompany us. The guard stationed there will recognize you, but I am still too new to this."

"Of course, my son. Whatever it takes to move us a step closer to our family's destiny."

Lionel sighed again, plastered a smile on his face, and opened the armory door to meet the new arrival. "So that it is finished and done," he muttered.

"Excuse me for intruding, scion Lionel," Hector said as he entered. He ran his hand over his bald pate. "My guild has only recently … relocated here. On the street, I have heard that you are acquainted with the ways of the court and, well, are also easy to approach."

Lionel did not immediately reply. Instead, he examined Hector's robe, hesitant to start a conversation. "Why would a master magician have any interest in the ways of the court?"

"Wherever magic is involved, any master would be curious. Isn't the craft used by Vendora's household the same way as she employs the other four?"

"Well, yes, magic has its uses — although the price is dear."

"I assure you, we of the guilds charge only enough to recover our expenses. Profit is not a motive. Do you know that some of our objects take centuries to perfect, the efforts of scores of neophytes, initiates, and masters?"

"I have heard this explanation many times before. That does nothing to lessen how much one must pay. Look, I have to change the rest of my garb for a social event of the queen. Most minions are not allowed in the armory to help, and it takes a surprising amount of time to get it right. Tell me directly. What is it you want of me?"

"Ah, a man after my own heart," Hector said. "Direct and to the point. What I desire is a tour of the royal treasury."

"Why?"

"Well, one never knows. Vendora keeps the peace by maintaining many men-at-arms such as yourself. You all must be housed and fed. But, if perchance the wherewithal to pay for such services were to vanish, then there would be no one to staff the army, no one to keep the peace. Our society would dissolve into chaos.

"We magicians much prefer order to chaos. Order over extended periods. The possibility of robbery of royal treasure upsets us greatly."

"Yes, there is much gold in the queen's vault," Lionel said. "I, myself haven't seen it, but as you can suppose, it is well guarded." How to get rid of this man gracefully, he thought.

"And well-guarded is defined as …"

Lionel glanced at a nearby table. On it lay two small glass bulbs connected by an even smaller passageway between them. A little imp imprisoned in one of the bulbs pushed a grain of sand from one container to the other. It looked like there was still plenty of time, and the prospect of immediately exchanging heavy coils of steel for fluffed collars stiffened with starch was not appealing.

For a moment, he studied Hector. This magician was not going away. His father also was still standing there, wringing his hands in his usual anxious way. "All right," Lionel said. "I will show you where the entrance to the queen's vault is, but that is all. You will see that it will turn out to be a wasted trip."

"I presume you have heard of eternal calendars of course," Hector said. "I can also supply you with an eternal clock for a reasonable price. It's magic of course. Will never lose a single heartbeat of time." He waved at the table. "It gets rid of this demon-infested approximation."

"Enough words," Lionel said. He looked at his father and sighed. "Follow me."

IT TOOK less than a minute for the trio to walk from the armory to the central keep, the highest and most massive building in a bailey bustling with activity. They had to dodge not only horse droppings but skirt the mud beneath the adjacent water tower that was always out of repair. Countless royal servants scurried past in all directions to keep the daily ritual of the castle running.

Lionel pointed to the sentinel manning the entrance to the keep. The magician labored to keep up with him while raising the hems of his robe as high as he could. "They are with me," Lionel's father said to the guard as they entered.

Stairs leading upwards circled around the wall and disappeared into the ceiling. On the other side of the room stood a shut, rough-hewn door reinforced with thick crossmembers spanning it from side to side and supported by thick angle irons.

Hector looked about. "I see no treasure here," he said.

"Of course not," Lionel answered. "Exactly right. Now, if you will excuse —"

"I think a little more information will make the master's trip worthwhile," Lionel's father interrupted. "And clearly, it will do no harm." He pointed. "That is merely the first door — the first one of five. See the beam anchored in the iron braces on either side of the jamb? The chains with links thicker than a wrestler's wrist locking it in place. Even if somehow one of the curtain walls was pierced by invaders, it would take hours to pry open the lock."

"The first of five?" Hector asked.

"Yes, the one here is only the beginning. There are four more doors in a downward passageway, each one secured the same as you see. Even if the entire castle falls, it would take days to get past all five to reach the treasures stored below."

"Approached perhaps then from the river?" Hector asked. "I have heard tales of other less well-guarded passageways in the castle besides those in the keep."

"There are many more chambers of Vendora's castle than those within this one tower. Kitchens, the ballroom, the private royal abodes —"

"Wouldn't it be a bother to go through five doors in order to give a minor lordling a small boon?"

"Going into the vault rarely happens. The queen uses scrip instead."

"Scrip?"

"Yes, scrip." Lionel's father reached into a small vest pocket and extracted two small rectangles of vellum. "Note what it is said on each one."

Hector examined one of the small scraps. "'Exchangeable for one brandel of ninety-nine percent pure gold from the queen's treasury on demand.'" The magician was quiet for a moment. "I think I understand," he said at last.

Lionel nodded. "Yes, a new fad among the nobility. They use them instead of having a minion carrying a purse of gold wherever they go. Each vellum is a substitute representation of an actual coin residing in the vault. Probably not widely employed by anywhere else yet, but as you surely must know, the nobility thinks it is beneath themselves to merely barter instead."

Hector again was silent for a few moments, then asked, "How do you keep track?"

"Keep track of what?"

"How do you know that for each and every scrip, there is a coin of gold residing in the vault?"

"There are ledger books in the small bailey building used by the accountants. You know, those who have the talent for computing sums in their heads without using their fingers or moving their lips. They must be the ones who keep track of such things."

Hector did not speak for several moments. His brow furrowed. "Interesting," he said at last. "Thank you very much, scion Lionel. You have given me much food for thought."

Lionel watched his father and the magician depart. He felt

uncomfortable. This Hector did not learn much, but every little bit of knowledge chipped away at the castle's defenses. This magician was up to something, but he could not figure out what. He shook his head. Masters, initiates, neophytes. None of them could be trusted.

57

(10)

A Day at Work

THE SUN drew nearer to the horizon. Nicholas spread a blanket on bare ground in the market and arranged his display case containing the rings to which he had added simple chips of stone. There was not much space. He barely had enough room in which to sit. The area was not as spacious and fashionable as those across the river and frequented by the wealthy.

He looked both ways down the winding pathway. Stalls were scattered like jacks tossed from the hand of a child. Fresh fruit stands stood next to seated palm-readers. Carved wall sconces hung on a portable frame behind an oldster hunched down on a low stool. Although it was not yet near dusk, some torches were already being lit atop tall posts along the pathway to attract attention. The noise was irritating. Each hawker tried to outshout the one standing next to him.

Nicholas sat and folded his legs under himself into what he hoped would be a comfortable position. He studied the crowd, trying to decide if he should sit quietly and let the rings sell themselves or compete with the cacophony around him. Perhaps watch for a while, he decided.

Two men strolled down the path and stopped in front of him, bickering among themselves, one tall and slender, the other short and stout. The slender one looked down at Nicholas. "A neophyte, eh?" he said as he touched the pommel of his sword. "We need this space. Move somewhere else."

"I was here first," Nicholas protested. "Those are the rules."

The slender man reached down and grabbed Nicholas's arm. He pulled him to standing. "I said that we need this space. Get lost. Keep your mouth shut, and you won't get hurt, understand?"

Nicholas felt himself involuntarily nod. He had no weapon. He was no match for either of these two men. It was too late in the day to call for help from the city guard. Everyone knew that they had taken off early. And even if some were near, they could not arrive in time against the crush of the crowd.

He glowered and picked up his blanket by its corners, catching his display of rings inside. He shuffled across the path and squeezed between two other vendors squatting on the other side. Both had their heads down on their chests, apparently asleep. They had covered their wares with thin pieces of cloth.

Nicholas hunkered down, trying not to attract any more attention to himself. He saw the stouter of the two bullies rub his stomach as if trying to recall the pleasure of the meal the night before.

"That one, Claymore," the slender man pointed, speaking so loudly that even Nicholas could hear the conversation. "See? He just bought something and keeps his stash in a rear pocket. You keep him distracted while I work the incantation."

"How come I have to take all the risks, Intrepid?" Claymore asked.

Intrepid sighed. "We go over this every time. If you don't slip the words of power inconspicuously enough into the chatter, then even a dullard like you could pick them out as being different and important."

"I can spout nonsense jabber as easily as you," Claymore scowled.

"Indeed. That part you are very good at."

"So then, why not — "

Nicholas watched Intrepid thrust his hand into a pocket and withdraw two small pieces of wood carved and decorated to look like grasshoppers. "Because you don't have these," the brigand said. "Both created out of the same oakwood at the same time. Coiled springs snipped out of adjacent pieces of wire. Bent into shape on the same spindle."

"I know all that. You have explained it to me enough times. One recites a nonsense incantation that disguises the words of power and then, what one pincer does, the other follows. Basic thaumaturgy."

Intrepid said no more and scampered to mount a stool grabbed from an adjacent stall. The owner started to protest, but the brigand stared him down just as he had Nicholas. The neophyte looked up and could see the thug, now standing higher than the crowd, move one of the carved grasshoppers slowly through the air until it was about the height of his waist. The other did the same in unison, but lower and belt high to anyone walking the market path.

Nicholas pondered. Should he stand up and call attention to what was about to happen? He started to rise and shout a warning, but then what? The thugs both had swords. He certainly would be skewered.

"The mark is getting closer," Intrepid said. "Do your thing."

Claymore waited for the man Intrepid had spotted come his way, weaving in and out among the others on the path. When they were beginning to pass one another, Nicholas saw the heavyset thug lean in with his shoulder and staggered the mark backwards a step.

"Hey, watch where you're going, you big oaf," the target said.

"If you know what is good for you, you will stay out of my way," Claymore shot back.

The mark scowled and withdrew copper knuckles from one of his pockets.

"Good," Claymore said.

"Good? Did you just say 'Good?'" The man waved his armored hand in front of Claymore's nose. "Are you hungry? See these? Want a taste of a metal sandwich?"

Claymore took a small step backwards and put up his hands, fingers spread. At the same time, Nicholas saw one of the grasshoppers alight on the mark's hip.

The mark drew back his arm and aimed a punch at Claymore's nose. The giant blocked the onrush with one hand and clamped his other around the man's wrist. The mark's eyes widened. He tried to pry Claymore's fingers away but could not.

The flow of the crowd quickly stopped and surrounded the engagement. Nicholas had a hard time continuing to keep track of everything that was happening. Claymore was tall enough to keep his eye on Intrepid, but no one else was paying his partner any attention. Who would more than glance at an adult, obviously addled, playing with a small toy?

Nicholas saw Intrepid maneuver the grasshopper he was holding. The brigand dipped it slowly, somehow managed to snap its wooden jaws together and then quickly made it rise again. In an instant, it was joined by the lower one now dangling a money pouch in its grasp.

No one else noticed. All eyes remained on the struggling two men. Soon, Intrepid signaled he had successfully retrieved the purse and tucked it away. The incantation had been a success. The words of power that linked the two pincers together had been disguised in gibberish. Intrepid had been able to pick the target's pocket with one of the grasshoppers by manipulating its twin some distance away.

Claymore snapped two of the mark's fingers, then let him back away, mouth open wide with surprise and pain. Nicholas understood now. By using the spell, the duo was able to rob their victim totally unaware of what was happening.

Nicholas shook his head, ashamed of himself. The thiefs had bullied him into silence. He did not do a thing. No shout of alarm. No cry for help. Nothing. He was a coward. A failure with his body as well as his brain.

But before he could get the conclusion out of his head, a loud bang sounded that hurt his ears, and not long after, it was followed by a blast of sand-blown wind. Then there were cries of pain. It was clear to Nicholas and everyone around him that this was not a close lightning strike — no flash. There had been an explosion, a strong one.

"The alchemists. They are at it again!" someone nearby shouted.

"They should brew their potent formulas farther out of town, not only on this side of the river."

"Help me! I can't get out from under my table."

"My arm! I don't feel it anymore."

For Nicholas, everything sounded chillingly familiar. He recognized it as the awful memory flooded back. His heart started racing. The swirling dust made him cough. Could it be? Was it alchemical folly or ... another of Garavak's spheres, one bursting asunder in a crowded market.

A Toe Dipped into the Water

DIANA HESITATED at the entrance to the tent adjacent to her own. Next to her, Listen Up carried an unlit torch, ready to light the way if needed. While she dithered, a loud, rolling clap of thunder sounded from the west, louder than anything she had ever heard before. But there had been no warning flash. Was this a sign she should not be doing this?

She looked at the two henchmen. They seemed unperturbed. For them, nothing significant had changed. She steeled herself and decided to proceed.

Diana was only on barely speaking terms with the older woman inside the tent and could not tell her six brats apart. She looked back at the henchmen for a final confirmation, and they both nodded that this was the right place.

The sorceress stiffened herself and pulled aside the door flap. "Anybody home?" she asked. "It is that time of day."

"I recognize you — " the woman said. "Stop it, Ianson! You know better than to jostle Gilbertson while I am nursing him." She turned her attention back to Diana. "You picked a bad time to visit. Saddar is due any moment now. Did you hear that thunderclap? For a moment, I thought he had added some drama to his appearances."

"About that …" Diana said.

"No matter, no matter, come in and find a place to sit. We probably will benefit by comparing notes anyway. Should have done it a long time ago. How much does the pissbucket charge you guys, anyway?"

"I imagine what Saddar demands is based on how much he can get one to pay," Diana scanned the squalor not so very different from her own. Her chest began to tighten. Should she really be doing this?

"Right, right," the woman replied. "That is what I keep telling him. I don't have three able-bodied men … well, two anyway, bringing home some coins every day."

"How much does Saddar charge you? What is his 'protection' fee?"

"Over and over, I try to explain to him that my income fluctuates. Some nights, there is a line of men outside. You probably have noticed that, right? On others, not a single customer."

She stopped and moved Gilbertson from one side to the other. "But Saddar won't have anything to do with, say, a single transaction once a month. Says that paying each and every day keeps me on my toes. On my toes! That's a good one, get it? I get paid for being on my back, not my toes."

Diana grimaced. Her situation with Uncle Izzy was not the worst one she could be in — at least not yet. She increased her resolve. "You said we should compare notes. How much a day from you then?"

"Three a day. Three coppers every frigging day."

"Three!" Diana blurted. "Saddar charges my uncle ten."

"Well, that makes sense. Like I say, you have three workers to earn what is demanded. You're lucky he doesn't charge for four." The woman's eyes narrowed. She looked at Diana critically. "Although it won't be long before he decides to raise the daily take to twelve."

Diana pondered. The implication was obvious. She had dismissed it from her thoughts over and over again. But, except for herself, were Izzy's plans for her common knowledge throughout the tents? "What happens if, ah, business gets slow?"

"Well, you know, lassie. Sometimes I pay with goods rather than coin."

Diana steadied her thoughts. She didn't know how many stops had to be made and how much time was available. It was better not to even think about the dire situations she would encounter were going to be. How guilty she was going to feel. Instead, she should move forward as best she could. "Well, Saddar can't make it today. I am, I am collecting in his place."

The woman peeked through the tent flap at the two familiar henchmen standing there as always. "Hmmm, Saddar might be a little smarter than I give him credit for. It probably will be much less of a hassle if a woman gets what he demands from female, 'customers' like myself. Adamson, get three coppers from the lootbag on the peg. Mustn't have the apprentice late on her first day out."

THIS WAS not so bad, Diana told herself as she followed the henchmen weaving their way through the squalor. In fact, it had been amazingly easy. The woman with the brats had not questioned that a payment was due, nor that the job of collecting had been delegated to someone new. The ones that followed were pretty much the same. There were no arguments other than a repeated daily recital about how steep was the fee.

But, on the other hand, every tent contained a depressing sameness: occupied by the defeated, the outcasts, and even those who had to resort to nefarious activities so they get food and have shelter from the rain.

The last stop was far apart from where Diana's own tent was pitched. She had never been this way before. But, as she followed the henchmen, she noticed that the tents were even more crudely made than hers. The canvasses covering the sapling frames bore many patches; some had rips that were only partially sewn closed. Others hung with gaping holes open to the elements. A few had no covering at all, merely the arch of poles that defined what ground was reserved by someone for sleeping.

Diana ducked into the tent indicated by Listen Up and Pay Attention. Like the first stop, it was occupied by a single woman, this one not much older than Diana herself. But, unlike Saddar's other clients, worry and strain filled the inhabitant's face. Obviously, she did not accept her lot at all.

"One of them should have worked," the woman mumbled. "The attributes without mirror the powers within — the basic law of alchemy."

"I am here to collect the daily payment," Diana said without hesitation. Listen Up had cautioned her to spend time with a payer only if there were trouble with producing the coins.

"You don't understand," the woman said. "The formulas I usually try have a high chance of success." She shrugged. "Sure, once in a while, a batch will not completely finish, but after enough tries there will be success."

"I know little of your craft," Diana said. "Only that the more powerful the desired result, the less likely it will be produced."

"Yes, yes, that is what I have just said. Did you not hear me? I used to own one of the most highly regarded apothecaries on Honeysuckle Street. My potions were the best. Results guaranteed or else a money-back guarantee.

"But I hit a dry spell. Had to borrow to pay for more ingredients. Their formulas failed, too. So, I was forced to try and create elixirs that were even more potent, ones for which I could charge enough for to pay off my debts.

"The spiral continued unabated. More failures. More

borrowing. More surrender of my assets until I was evicted. Forced to move here and create the simplest salves: itch cream, wish vapors, hallucinators — ”

“And now, you do not even have three coppers,” Diana interrupted. She felt pity for the woman’s plight. She seemed buried in a deep depression. Despite the dark days she had to experience under her uncle’s care, Diana could remember none like this. “When was the last time you ate?” she asked.

The woman shook her head slowly but said nothing. Diana realized that this scene could just as well have played out in her own tent on any given day.

“I, I feel for you. I really do. But …”

Diana stopped. But what? she thought. She touched the pouch at her side. It felt good to finger the coins through the hide. She glanced back over her shoulder at the two henchmen. They held the same stoic frowns they always did. She considered for a moment and then told herself that this could be over soon enough anyway. What happens in the days following could be somebody else’s problem. For now, who was to know? What difference did it make?

“For this time only, I’ll —I’ll forgo payment today and give you enough to get by on for a little while.”

“Oh, thank you, thank you,” the woman gushed. “Wait until I tell the others. They won’t believe this.”

Diana felt her heart suddenly start to pound. Having what she had done become common knowledge would not work at all. Everyone would demand the same treatment. Worse, word much more likely would find its way up the ladder. “There is one stipulation,” she said quickly. “Not a word to anyone else. This will be our little secret.”

Diana left the tent quickly. The hint of dread over what she had just done did not go away. She, herself, had become numb to what her life was about. But for others, the pain was not as well hidden. Should she go back and give something to the woman with the six children and all the others as well?

No, they would be too many. The henchmen had said she had
to hand in a minimum.

"That's it," Pay Attention said, breaking her out of the
spin of her thoughts. "The last payment collected. Now we go
and settle up, and then we are done for the day."

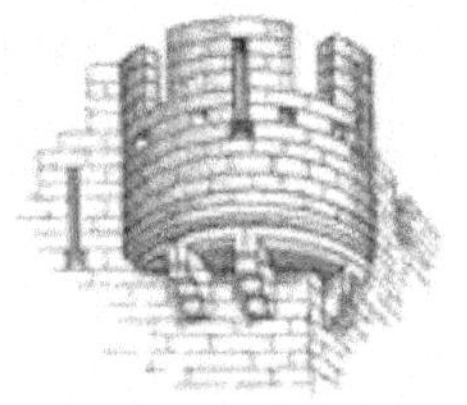

12
A Mere Suggestion

THE SUN had set an hour ago. Lionel paced with his father outside Queen Vendora's small audience chamber. The command had come quite suddenly. Another hour had gone by waiting outside.

"I hope this summons is not about the mysterious loud noise," Lionel's father, Tetris, said. "Not if you have no explanation for it. Vendora is quite sensitive to what the rabble is thinking."

"I have no idea, Father," Lionel said. "Possibly, the brew of an alchemist did not go right."

"Your every thinking moment must be spent on solving riddles such as these." Tetris lowered his voice to a whisper. "As the queen ages and her beauty fades, her popularity continues to wane. Her consort wallows in the distractions of the court. His barbaric fierceness is long in the past. The kingdom of Procolon has always been ruled by the strongest. Who knows what will happen if these 'unexplained omens' continue."

"You may enter," a servant said as the door swung open. "The queen will see you now."

The father and son complied, and Lionel could not help but blink. The queen was seated as always, but Hector, the magician was also there.

"This master has told me that he spoke with you earlier today," Vendora stated, not wasting time explaining Hector's presence. She glowered at Lionel, and her voice was stern. "I want to hear exactly what you have told anyone about the accounting ledgers for the scrip."

Lionel frowned. Vendora said nothing about the loud noise. Wasn't she at least curious? He knew enough to keep quiet until the queen had finished, but he did not like the way this conversation was starting. There had been rumors enough already throughout Ambrosia about Vendora living above even the means of a monarch — having more scrip than there were corresponding disks of gold for them. As the queen had aged, her spending had increased in lavishness. Parades, festivals, and more than two royal dances a week rather than one a season. Perhaps it was better to speak up after all.

"Master Hector asked where the accounting ledgers that link gold brandels to corresponding—"

"I know what the ledgers are for," Vendora snapped. "What did you tell him about them.

Who else knows? Leave out not a single word."

"I said that the royal accountants were in charge of the ledgers," Lionel answered. "And they were maintained in another structure in the bailey other than the keep."

"As I also have informed you," Hector said smoothly. "The lad here did not do anything wrong."

Vendora took a moment to compose what she would say next. "You have pointed out to me, Master, that there are rumors stating someone has obtained access to the ledgers. Added entries for coins that do not exist and hence illegitimate scrip would be generated.

"But all the accountants are under the spell of a sorcerer. Everyone knows that. None of them can falsify an entry. No sham pieces of scrip could ever be generated. Every slip would correspond to coins of gold."

"Only a suggestion, my queen," Hector smiled. "A mere suggestion … and I have proposed a remedy as well."

"What then?"

"Merely that the ledgers also be protected. I can provide your majesty with special binding guards for each volume, ones that prevent opening without the exercise of a proper ritual. One that only those loyal to you can know. So long as the access is restricted, there can be no more than possibly some additional idle talk among the riffraff."

Vendora was silent for a moment. Her brow furled. "Why would anyone want a book that they could not open?" she asked.

"Who can fathom the inner workings of the mind of a thief?" Hector shrugged. "Maybe the volumes could be held for ransom. Without them, how does anyone know for sure that all are correct?"

Lionel was not sure Hector's proposal had any merit. Couldn't everyone just agree that the gold was safe and the exchange of scrip proceed as it normally did? In fact, didn't a similar event happen years ago in a kingdom across the great ocean?

Vendora frowned at him. "That is all, captain," she said.

Lionel bowed and left. The queen's audience chamber, he thought. Not such a grand thing after all. Not nearly as elaborately decorated as the royal ballroom. The royal ballroom … His thoughts skittered. Why had he never seen the lady who had intrigued him at any of the balls?

Diana at the Counting House

IT WAS completely dark outside. Torches provided the only light. Diana would be late back to her tent. What would Izzy and the others think? She looked up at the rafters. A dusting of termite droppings slowly settled from the roof. The shanty certainly was better constructed than any of the tents, but not by much. She glanced over her shoulder. Listen Up and Pay Attention were standing off to the side some distance away. With nods in unison, they propelled her forward in the queue.

Diana was the last in line. She was apprehensive about what was going to happen when she reached the very front. Four or five other short queues were on her right, each terminated in front of a long table with visored men behind it. To the left, three leathered-clad guards slumped in boredom.

"Next," a man older than Izzy called out to her. He did not bother to look up.

"Ah, west-central," Diana said as the henchmen had instructed her to do.

"West-central," the counterman intoned in a bored voice. Almost instantly, a sprite appeared out of nowhere, settled onto a scrolling frame, and began cranking a rolled parchment from one reel to the other.

A sprite! An actual sprite with gossamer wings and rough scales everywhere. Diana would have been delighted by the sighting if the circumstances had been any different. Larger than an imp and much rarer as well. There was little reason for such creatures to hang out in the tents, with no wizards there to command them to do so. And for now, she had to focus on not making a mistake that would give away her charade.

Diana watched the pages slowly move from right to left in the frame. She felt fortunate that, before the accident, her mother had taught her the fundamentals of reading and writing. Large letter headings were on the top of each page cranking by. The one in the queue before her must have been from a territory with a name starting with 'Aardvark' or something because it took a while for 'West-central' to appear.

"Empty your take onto the scale," the counterman droned. "Come on. Hurry up. The day is almost done. I don't get anything more by staying late."

"Scale?" Diana asked. She looked from left to right along the table but saw no device with two pans balanced on a fulcrum and a set of weights arrayed nearby. Instead, there was a cup resting on a single pan held by another sprite above his head, a fearsome looking thing, muscular and frowning fiercely.

The counterman looked up. "It won't bite. Completely dominated as would be a full-sized djinn. Dominated — a basic law of wizardry.

Empty your pouch into the cup," the counterman continued. "Otherwise, its weight will be included in our take." He shook his head. "What's the syndicate coming to? When I started, everyone was taught his job and did it without error."

Diana acted as she was instructed. She was nervous. More importantly, she did not want to make a mistake that called attention to herself. Trying to act as natural as she could, she feigned disinterest in what the sprite was doing. The little demon sagged under the weight for a moment, then said in a high squeaky voice totally out of place with its demeanor, "It weighs eight hundred and twenty-four coppers."

The first sprite dashed down to the scroll and entered the date and amount. Then another the same size scooped out a portion of the coins and flew off with them to somewhere in the rafters. The counterman glanced at the new entry.

"A little off today, isn't it? Well, it happens." He glanced back up at Diana. "But don't make it a habit. Too low an output more than once could mean it is time for a replacement. Understand?"

Diana nodded, not trusting herself to speak. In a few moments more, it would be over. She poured the coppers remaining in the cup into her pouch and walked back to the henchmen — with a little quicker step than she had first intended.

"The last thing to do is give us our share," Listen Up said as she rejoined the two henchmen.

"How much?" Diana asked.

"You don't know, do you?" Pay Attention smiled. "We could tell you anything."

"No, I don't know. I don't even know how much is left in the pouch now."

"So, what do we do?"

Diana thought for a moment, then said, "Let's go somewhere quiet and divide what we have left into three equal piles."

"*Three* piles!" Listen Up and Pay Attention said in unison. "One for you and one for us. Who gets the third?"

Diana could not help a smile. The henchmen had made a wrong assumption from what she had said. She expected a protest and more bartering, but the pair merely nodded. They assumed their share was one for them to divide in half. Saddar must have set up things with them that way.

But that did not feel right. Without saying more, she

handed one share to Listen Up and the other to Pay Attention.

"Missy, we will follow you anywhere," the pair replied in unison.

Diana finished the allocation and smiled in satisfaction. In her entire life, as far back as she could remember, she had never been close to a fountainhead of wealth. Hundreds of coppers each and every day! For many of the higher-ups on the hill towards Vendora's castle, a handful of coins was close to nothing, but to herself, she felt as rich as the queen. She recalled the intoxication that accompanied spending the lordling's brandel. Now, for the first time ever, she could continually act like one. She dismissed the henchmen, all the while savoring what she was going to do next. Yes, she would be late back at the tent, but how late probably made no difference. Yes, then, a visit to the marketplace again.

Hope

FROM OVERHEARING snatches of conversation in the marketplace, Diana had learned that the explosive noise had originated there. Several people had been killed. But an hour or so later, the damage had been cleared away and business continued as usual, as if nothing out of the ordinary had happened. Such was life north of the river.

Diana felt a little giddy. She carefully protected the newer, fancier frock draped over one arm while holding the bar of soap in her other hand. Spending so much all at once felt almost as good as self-enchantment — self-enchantment without the risk of misspeaking the words. Even better than with her first splurge with the lordling's brandel. And she still had many of her coppers left to spend on something else before they all were gone — possibly the rental of a small vault in a storage shop across the river. She did not want to hide anything actually of value in her bedding.

What she was doing was basically shameful. Diana understood that. But the frock and odor of the freshly made soap made it hard to condemn herself for what she had done. She looked around eagerly as she strolled the crooked isles. The sun had long set, but nearby torches were sufficient. A low table on her left caught her attention. A light-blue robed neophyte magician sat behind it. A sign above him read. "Rings of true magic on sale here. Twenty coppers each."

Diana looked down on a tray lined with finger-rings of steel. Each was adorned with a small dull stone.

"These are not really magic, are they?" she asked.

"They in fact are," Nicholas said. "Try one on, and you will find out."

Diana looked at the young man. She could see he was distraught. With sagging shoulders, his eyes darted away from looking directly at her. Her training as a sorceress made that quite clear. "I am called Diana," she said. "What is your name?"

"Nicholas, Nicholas the neophyte."

Diana shifted her focus to the rings. She selected the one with the smallest stone attached and slipped it on her finger. Her eyes widened. She gasped as the sensation coursed into her hand. It was not an unpleasant prickling at all. No something far better than that. Something seductive, soothing, repeated caresses from a warm rising tide, a promise of good things that would come. She had never felt anything like it in her life.

"Yes, true magic," Nicholas said. "There is no way to fake that feeling."

"So, what power does the ring possess then?" Diana asked.

"Well, none." Nicholas shrugged. "Other than the fact that they are indestructible, these rings have no additional power at all. They are the first step in a series of rituals. More capabilities are added by subsequent steps after they have been created, and sometimes these additional efforts take eons to complete."

Diana pondered for a moment about how the end of her day had gone. "I see that your tray is full. It looks like none have been sold. Maybe you should hawk that they can at least do something."

"Like what?"

"I don't know." Diana shrugged, then smiled. "Perhaps tout them as substitutes, placeholders. If you had the task of tossing a magic ring into a volcano, using one of these might be a better choice than losing another that had the power actually to do something."

"Wouldn't work. All magic rings are indestructible."

"Well then, perhaps associate them with something intangible." She thought again of the hovel-dwellers she had met during the day, each one meekly handing over a portion of the results of their hard work without real protest. A trap from which they had concluded there was no escape. No, what they needed more than even protection was …

"Hope," she said aloud. The concept had burst into her mind. "These magic rings could be touted as providing *hope*. If one were worn, hope would always be present, always tingling the hand of the wearer, always reminding that there was hope even when things looked the darkest."

"But that is a deception," Nicholas shook his head. "Nothing good will happen for the wearer because they are wearing a ring. At best, a false hope, no more."

Diana shook her head as well, but more forcefully. "That is faulty logic. All hopes are based on wishes. None on certainty. Something good may happen to a ring bearer, or perhaps not. The outcome does not matter. What is important is that so long as a ring tingles, it is a constant reminder that maybe, just maybe, everything will end well no matter what."

Nicholas thought for a moment. Then he smiled. "That is a good way to look at it," he said at last. "Thank you. When I return tomorrow, I will have the signs altered."

"Well, there would still be a problem. Those most in need of hope will be the least able to spend twenty coppers for one. I know for a fact that your price is too dear."

Nicholas shook his head again. "If they are not expensive enough, then no one would want them either."

"Have a sale," Diana said. If my Uncle Izzy had taught

me anything, it is the lure of a bargain.”

“What do you mean?”

“I don’t know. Maybe, for example, offer one ring for, say, five coppers and three rings for a total of ten. Buy two at the stated price and get one for free.”

“Magical objects are not like gourds to be bundled together when they start to rot. No one would be tempted by such a thing. I am a neophyte magician, not a street hawker. Can’t you tell from the color of my robe?”

Diana felt a tinge of irritation. She had only been trying to help. Help someone like … like the failed alchemist in the slum. Yes, there was still enough in her purse. “I will give you ten coppers right now for three of the rings.”

“Sold,” Nicholas said. “Show me your money.”

“Hold my soap for a moment,” Diana said as she handed the bar to Nicholas. “I have the coins in my purse right here. I am — well as you can tell, despite my appearance — by the frock I am carrying you can see that, after all, I am … I am a lady.”

“The saying is that ‘merely a frock does not make a lady’,” Nicholas said.

“And a pale blue robe doesn’t make one a master magician either,” Diana snapped back. Maybe it was her fatigue after a stressful day. Maybe it was having her fantasy interrupted, but she did not care for this neophyte’s words.

But what her thoughts had stumbled upon still shown like a beacon in her mind. Hope. Hope was a balm everyone in the slum could use, regardless of their situation. She took a deep breath and decided. The lingering guilt she still felt about what she was doing melted away.

Yes, she would revisit all the hovels and collect their payments again tomorrow. And to a couple of them in particular, she would also give a magic ring — a magic ring of hope. And after that, in the days that followed, she would continue. More rings for those who needed them. Excitement bubbled in her as it never had before.

I have made up my mind, she told herself. I will continue the collection of protection money tomorrow.

(**15**)

Possible Suspects

NICHOLAS WATCHED Diana leave. Somehow, he felt a little better. A glimmer of renewed purpose blossomed, a reason for being. One that did not involve strutting around and beating one's chest. Or making a fool of himself in the front of master magicians. And this woman was responsible for that.

He cocked his head to the side and pondered. Diana. Diana. Her name echoed in his thoughts. She projected a soft and pleasant image; someone he would enjoy getting to know better. And there was something else about her. Her quickness of mind; how she had quashed his misgivings about himself. Yes, he was shorter than she; that was nothing new to him. But perhaps, just perhaps, she might not care.

The ethical dilemma he had felt before was gone. Selling the blank magic rings was a worthwhile thing to do. No need for the gaudy semiprecious stone additions. Truly, if one believed in their hearts what they were getting, then he was performing a great service — selling magical rings of hope.

But the good feeling lasted only for a moment. Yes, his dilemma was gone. The marketplace had long since forgotten about the explosion. Like a hive of industrious bees, business hummed as usual. But, unlike everyone else, he had a new question to worry about — *who* was responsible for the blast?

All Ambrosia's alchemists claimed they were not trying

to brew risky formulations in the city — and probably they were not. It was standard practice that hazardous formula brewing took place far into the country side.

So, … he drew another conclusion: it had to be one of the masters of his guild. Yes, but which one?

Antron was unlikely. He had no motive. His only goal was to have the guild survive. He was the stoutest of the three in favor of tradition. Continue going forward one step at a time. Insisting upon the initiate exam taking place even though it made little sense until a solid inflow of income was secured first.

Randolph was the vainest of the three. The street talk was that he was a fourth son overlooked by a family that had three famous warriors to brag about. He proceeded one tiny step after another. He would study Garavak's notes over and over until he understood them well. Find the flaw in the ritual that let things get out of control. Then deduce what should be changed in the detailed steps so that he could broadcast his intellectual triumph to whomever was in earshot.

Hector was the greediest of the three. Raised in poverty, he lusted for sufficient wealth so that he could mingle with nobility as an equal. He had the 'Damn the catapult bombardment' personality. Sally forth into the enemy king's pavilion no matter what the cost. So of the three, he would be the most likely to assemble another of Garavak's spheres. Screw the two halves together, instrument the thing eight ways to Wednesday, and then …

But perhaps it was none of the three masters. Was there sufficient reason for any of them to do this? There was no cause to have innocent people die.

Nicholas faltered. But why was he, himself, mulling all this over again? It was none of his business. He had to admit he was merely finding another excuse not to focus on his candidacy exam.

And if it were one of the masters, then whoever caused

the explosion likely would learn from what transpired. The next part of the experiment, if indeed that was what was going on, would not have any fatalities. No concern of his; he did not have knowledge of the tools yet to do anything about it anyway. He was not yet a master himself.

LIONEL PUT down his pen and looked at the blank vellum. There was nothing he could report to Vendora about the mysterious explosion. And she seemed to dismiss it as if such things occurred on a regular basis. He arose from the cot he had brought into the armory and began to pace. Two hours had passed since the audience with the queen. Time wasted that he should spend in preening for the ball.

But there was something that did bother him. Perhaps that would be worth informing Vendora about. The magician, Hector, wanting to see the vault obviously was an excuse so he could pitch magical gadgets he was selling.

He visualized the small latches, as Hector had called them, glued somehow to the covers of the accounting books. The magician had proposed such things to Vendora, but the plan did not feel properly focused. Why a separate latch for each volume? Who would care? Was the magician merely trying to make his sale as large as possible?

No, if the security of the accounting books was important, then merely preventing them from opening was not the only thing to guard against. They could just as well be stolen and held for ransom. And if the accountant building somehow were attacked, semaphores on its ceiling could signal what was happening. No need for any magic at all.

And by whatever means an attempted robbery occurred, there should be an alarm mechanism. One that should come to the City Guard not the queen's personal one. He and his comrades were responsible for repulsing such an attack, not showcase minions. The latter were all rum-sotted ne'er-do-wells, lessor sons of unimportant outland nobles.

On the other hand, there had not been an attack on the royal treasury for over three hundred years. No matter what they were, Hector's schemes could not be of any consequence. Lionel sighed. He looked again at the unmarked vellum on the desk mocking him.

It was all very well to grouse about being encaged and not free to do what he wanted. But how true was that, really? He did enjoy the respect shown to him by the men who accompanied him on patrol. He looked forward to the challenges brought by each new day, sometimes hoping there would be a situation that required decisive action.

Yes, the guard duties did consume the part of the day illuminated by the sun. And most evenings were required to stay in the queen's good graces, but …

Before Lionel could ponder more, an aide rushed into the armory. "Come at once," he said. "Bovine, the Captain of the City Guard, has keeled over and died."

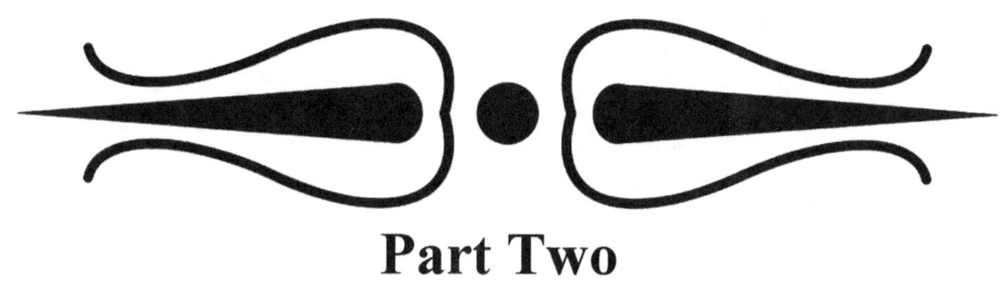

Part Two

Struggle

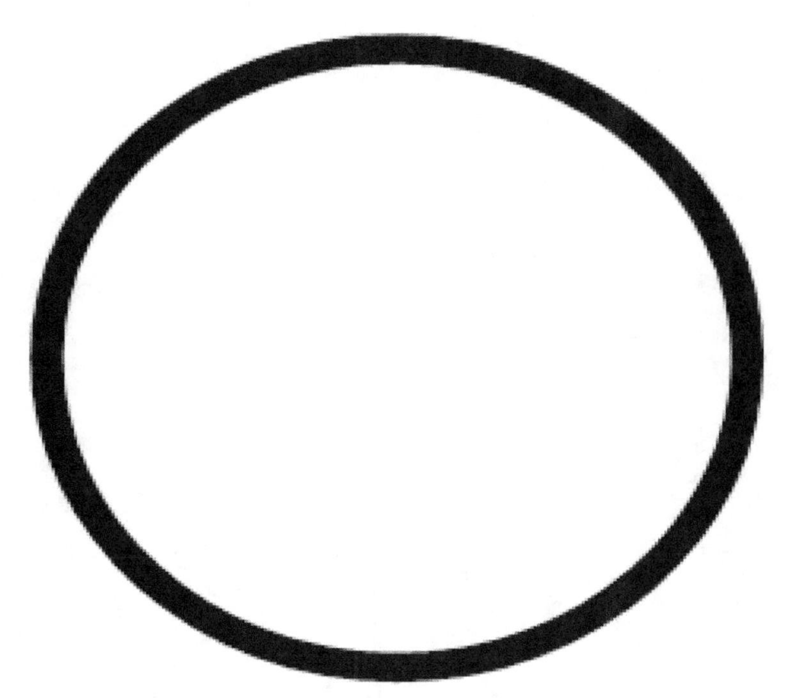

A Reward for Good Work

DIANA WAITED nervously in the check-in queue. A month had passed. And over it, each day she had been forgoing any collection from several hovel-dwellers in her territory — usually somebody new but not always. The difference she made up most of the time with what she had left over after buying rings the previous day. Other times, when there were too many who should not have to pay, she shrugged and turned in less. She had stopped shopping for any more frivolous things for herself. The novelty of doing that had worn off completely. Her mattress in Izzy's tent could not become any lumpier. The expectations of her uncle, Listen Up, and Pay Attention remained the same.

Most important of all was the increased effort to rationalize to herself what she was doing. If not her, she told herself over and over again, there would always be someone like Saddar making the rounds. She was acting as a shield against that, but nevertheless, her charade could end any day now. She felt as if she were on a scaffold with the noose tight around her neck and waiting for the trap beneath her feet to be sprung open.

"Wait a minute," the counter said as she handed back Diana's collection sack. "Bossman wants to see you."

Diana tried to hold her expression neutral. She hoped her suddenly racing heart beneath her tattered robe did not show.

She wished she could be wearing one of her fancy frocks instead. "What about?" she managed to say.

"Look, you do your job, and I do mine," the counter said. "It doesn't pay for either of us to ask too many questions. Just cross the street and knock on the door immediately in front of you. Answer the challenge with 'Sweetcakes', and you will be let in."

Diana gave her henchmen their shares and pocketed the rest. The visit with Nicholas would have to come later. It was somewhat surprising when she thought about it, but chatting with the neophyte had become part of her daily ritual at the end of each day.

She steeled herself. No one higher up was the wiser, she reasoned again and again. So, today would be only a little different, nothing to be apprehensive about. She exited the shanty and crossed the street. The building she faced was constructed of brick rather than salvaged timber. The façade was recently painted. Hesitantly, she clanked the knocker.

A slit opened in the center of the door. "Yeah. Whatya want? Who are you?"

"Ah, Sweetcakes," Diana said.

There was a long pause. Diana could feel eyes crawling all over her. She shuddered.

"Yeah, that's right," the voice said as the door clicked open. "Come in. Bossman is expecting you."

Diana did as she was told and found herself in a long dark corridor dimly lit by wall sconces containing glowimps. A sudden hum heralded the approach of a sprite barely managing to keep airborne as he lugged some sort of apparatus. It was a box with a lens in the front. Before Diana could speak, the sprite rubbed his wings together and a sudden flash left an afterimage in her blinking eyes.

"It'll go away in a few moments," the sprite said. "This is for the Bossman to help remember you by. Follow me."

The small demon, laboring to keep aloft, lugged the instrument and zigzagged uncertainly down a corridor. Diana obeyed and followed. She breathed deeply, but her heart rate did not slow. It was so dark and foreboding. What had she gotten herself into?

She followed the sprite through a doorway and watched it hover for an instant over a vacant chair in the gloom. As her eyes adjusted, she saw that the chair was in front of a large desk, and behind it sat an obese man with a face from which two jowls hung like wet blankets on a clothesline.

"Sit down, Sweetcakes," Bossman said. "It is not often one of the gentler sex is as successful in a craft as you are. I think it is time for a change."

"I, I am having a little dry spell," Diana said. "The, ah, clients in the slum are giving all that they can."

"Yes, yes, that is always the case. The trick is to extract as much as possible without the desperation boiling over. You must have a discerning eye."

"Well, I — "

"No need to explain," Bossman said. "Some have the talent. Some do not. For me, what is key is the number of complaints I get. Too many, and my enforcers have to get involved. That in turn arouses the attention of the queen. Bad for business. Increased patrols. Round-up of suspects. Harassments. That sort of thing."

"Why am I here?" Diana managed to ask.

"Why, your promotion, my dear. Your promotion. I don't know how you do it. The details are unimportant to me. But with you at the head of all the protection collections throughout Ambrosia, I think you can teach the other agents, how to behave. Decrease the number of visits my enforcers have to make. There have been none at all from your territory after you took over from what's his name — "

"Saddar."

"Yes, Saddar. That's right. Someday, when I have more time, you will tell me your secret."

"There may be a little misunderstanding here —" Diana began.

"It's simple really. You keep track that all the collectors are turning in above their minimums. One of the imps takes care of everyone's numbers for you. Your share from each collector is automatically deposited in our bank. Another imp manages that."

"But —"

"The thing to keep track of is the number of complaints for each collector. When customers are squeezed too much, they complain. Call the screwup in for a conference with you. Teach him what it is that you do so successfully. Point out the consequences of the bad behavior if it continues. Help keep everything running smoothly, and we all profit, right?"

"I think there has been some mis —"

"Later, my dear, later. Your work speaks for itself. For now, you are just in time for our regular staff meeting. I will introduce you to the others. Come. Follow me."

Diana hesitated. But only for a moment. In charge of all the protection racket in the entire city! That was nonsense. It had to be. She merely was a simple…

"I want to keep the route I have now in addition," she blurted. She could not let someone like another Saddar take over. And with what additional she would get from supervising the others, she could probably dispense collecting from anyone in the slum.

Bossman nodded. "It will take a while to train someone to take your place," he said. "That of course will be your task as well." He rose, waddled towards a doorway behind him in the dimness and pulled it open. Diana did not know what to do. She took a deep breath and followed.

Inside, there was a bigger room that was better lit, but

only barely. Diana saw a long table for ten with both sides filled with men whom she immediately did not like. All seemed to be trying to stare each other down. Bossman sat at the head of the table and motioned Diana to the last remaining chair on his right. The last on his left was empty.

"Druman had an accident," Bossman said as Diana sat down. He paused for a moment. "Yes, this is a woman, a young one at that. But how she looks does not matter. Pay attention to what she says and does. It might rub off on you." He motioned around the room, pointing out each man as he did so. "Blackmail, Gambling, Narcotics, Arson, Embezzlement, Kidnapping, Burglary, Pimping, and Enforcement, meet the new Protection."

There was immediate silence. No one spoke. After a moment, Bossman filled the void. "We are not some pipsqueak operations like those down south. We use magic in our work. Wizardry for blackmail, magic for gambling, alchemy for narcotics, thaumaturgy for arson, sorcery for embezzle — "

"A woman?" Pimping interrupted. "Boss, I understand that you are progressive. I admire that. But a *woman*?"

"You are here because of results, all of you," Bossman said. "So is Protection. She has proven she knows how to dampen the waves. For her, I have decided. It is final. Let's move on. As usual, look at my little reminder first, and then we will get on with the reports."

"This is a waste of time," Arson said. "We get it. We all do. No need for the little show each and every meeting."

"I think it does not hurt," Bossman said.

Almost on cue, a sprite near the ceiling began to glow brightly in front of a reflector. It illuminated a back corner of the room. All turned to see four armored men standing there. They were behemoths. Muscles barely confined in their armor. Scowls that made one shudder. To Diana, they looked able to slash apart the likes of Listen Up and Pay Attention almost as afterthoughts.

"A reminder about my enforcers," Bossman said. "All of you know what you should do, what you must provide each and every cycle of the moon."

No one else spoke.

"Any comments?" Bossman asked after a few more moments of silence. The spotlight quenched. "Good. Reports then. Blackmail, you're up first."

Blackmail stood and squinted at a vellum scrap. He snapped his fingers, and a smaller glowimp immediately hovered over his head. "For the last month, only one client required any need for enforcement. Total take for the cycle is three thousand, two hundred brandels."

"Quit your bragging," Robbery said. "You guys have it easy. You send spy imps into the fief holdings, even into Vendora's castle itself. Mixed in with the mosquitos always buzzing around. Some of them get flattened, but so what. The ones that do not return with the dirt, no problem. Not a bit of risk for yourselves. On the other hand, we have to confront targets who are prepared to defend what is theirs."

"*We* have risks as well," Blackmail said. "Sometimes, the payoffs are ambushes."

Diana could barely pay attention to the argument. Her jaw had dropped. Blackmail had garnered over three thousand brandels in a single month! By comparison, protection was merely a wart on the back of the hog of crime. She guessed that all the Bossman controlled all the illegal activities, no matter how small they were. Peace was kept over all the dealings. Not so different than the lords of Procolon reporting to a single head of state, the queen. And now she was a part of it. How had this happened? What was she going to do?

2

For A Few Good Men

LIONEL SIGHED. He signed the last document on his desk and slumped into the highback chair. The setting sun cast its final beams through the narrow window of the small chamber in the queen's armory — the office of the Captain of the City Guard.

The door opened and Lionel's father entered. He waved his arm across the chamber. "See, this is not so bad, is it?"

"Father, it was a mistake to have taken on the job after old Bovine suddenly died," Lionel said.

"No, no, the timing was perfect," his father replied. "The number of complaints from the tents has decreased remarkably. I made sure Queen Vendora was made aware. Told her your good work was responsible."

Lionel shook his head. "I'm not convinced that parading around the slum has anything to do with reducing the unrest." To himself, he thought that the only thing remarkable about the area was the woman. The tall one with the short auburn hair. The lady who had asked for his assistance. The one he never saw again. Somehow, the one he could not shake out of his mind.

A whole month had gone by, and despite every day directing his replacement along the same route he had taken before, there was no report of any sign of her in the squalor. All he could do was fantasize about another daring rescue like the ones recorded in the sagas.

He rose and stretched, sighing that his day was far from over. "Another ball tonight, father. Another pairing with Rachel and before that, selection of the new recruits for the guards. My day starts with the sun and does not end until the wee hours of the night."

"Look at these tasks as an opportunity rather than a chore, my son. You already know that bonding Rachel in marriage is important. And that who sits on the throne is not chiseled in stone. Having a cadre of soldiers at your command might prove important. Who knows what the future will bring?"

"Yes, Father," Lionel sighed. "I understand." He was a grown man, one who should be able to make up his mind. But his mother had died giving birth to his twin brothers. There had been no one else to guide him for over two decades — no one without an agenda of their own. For reasons he did not fully understand, his father's wishes were almost impossible to resist. He reached into one of the desk drawers and withdrew the scroll with Bovine's final notes — 'New recruit selections.' At least that would be a distraction before two hours of trying to make interesting conversation with a teenager who still slept with a doll.

FLICKERING TORCHLIGHT ringed the bailey of Vendora's castle. In the center stood a line of ragged men. All were roughly clothed and unshaven, hopeful of receiving three meals a day and a roof over their heads that did not leak.

"Not a very good selection this time," the man standing next to Lionel said. Age had etched the wrinkles around his eyes. With an expression of a cat who had cornered a mouse, he looked the young scion up and down. "I am Wandred. Wandred the Wily," he said. "The head of the queen's Royal Guard. And you must be Bovine's replacement, right?"

"Yes, Lionel is my name. We probably should get together more often and exchange what we know."

"Like what?"

"Well, for instance, I happened to go into the keep earlier today. Saw a strange little disk stuck against the door leading to the treasury. Do you know anything about that?"

Wandred laughed. "You know the queen. Once she gets her wagon on a rutted road, she will ride it to the very end."

"What do you mean?"

"That magician, what's his name, Hector, continues to have her ear. He is a hustler who would make a legitimate salesman proud. In addition to plastering latches on each of hundreds of accounting books, he also has managed to sell her what he calls 'alarm patches' for the treasury doors. Every time one opens, a bell rings in my chamber.

"And loudly, too. At first, I jumped out of my chair every time the one on the ground floor started ringing, but now it is only a nuisance. I am prepared for the four more that follow shortly after. Do you know how few times a day an accountant visits the treasury vault?"

Wandred shook his head. "For years, I don't know how many times I told myself I would get a small pension to live on, and therefore the job was worth it."

He sighed for a moment, then shook his head. "Never mind that now. Today brings back fond memories. Many a time I have contested with Bovine over selections like this. He was a shrewd opponent. I will miss him much."

"Opponent?" Lionel asked.

Wandred laughed. "Of course. No one to instruct you. So much the better for me."

"Opponent?" Lionel repeated.

"See the scribe over to the left," Wandred pointed. "The one with the sheet of vellum on the stand. There is a line down the center with the names of 'Queen's Royal' atop the column on the left and 'City' on the right. Below that are our starting values — one thousand points for each."

"I still do not understand."

"The recruits stand before us, one by one. We make a single bid on them and like for an auction, the higher one wins."

"Bid on them with what? I thought the queen paid for maintaining the Royal Guards and the City Guard both."

"Yes, yes. But you see, you have only the one thousand points to use altogether. Spend it all on the first recruit and you would have none to use for the rest."

Lionel unrolled Bovine's scroll and understood. Besides each possible recruit's name was inscribed a number, obviously the amount to bid.

"First up — Melidon," a barker called out.

Lionel had more questions about how to proceed, but it was clear from Wandred's manner that this was a competition. He was not going to receive even a hint on how to play the game well. He shrugged and looked at the man who stepped forward from the line. The applicant was short but his quadriceps bulged. His face held a brutish scowl. Lionel consulted the scroll and found the number 200 written next to it. One fifth of all the points. Evidently, Bovine had thought him to be a strong addition to the guard.

Shrugging, Lionel wrote 200 on a bid token and handed it to the scribe. Wandred did the same. The scribe looked at both slips and announced, "Melidon to Wandred for 210."

For the next two recruits, the results were the same. Wandred outbid Lionel by ten points for each of the first three. Lionel grimaced. Obviously, Wandred had arranged a peek at what Bovine had prepared. He started to protest, but then clamped his jaw shut. Instead, for the fourth selection, he ignored Bovine's scroll and bid 220. Two could play this game.

"Cranspat to Wandred for 235," the scribe announced after glancing at the two bids. Lionel's scowl deepened. Wandred laughed.

"It takes a while to size up the offerings correctly," he said. "If you manage to hang on to the City Guard captaincy long enough, you might get a little better."

Lionel did not answer but glared at Wandred instead. Was he giving something away? A glimpse at his bid? A signal from the scribe? He did not like being the one on the losing end.

The next man that came forward could barely stand. His voice was slurred and filled with hiccoughs. He must have come straight from a tavern. Lionel bid zero. Wandred did the same. The applicant was dismissed.

"I want none of the rest," Wandred then said. He laughed. "Pick from what is left as you will."

Lionel surveyed the seven remaining. Some were tall, but thin as reeds, others shorter and rotund. One common feature, however, was the desperation on their faces. Serving as a guard meant having shelter and food each day. And, by the laws, he did not like being made to look the fool.

"I will take them all," he blurted. "None of them might be great warriors, but all seemed to possess a desire to succeed."

Wandred laughed again. "You have much to learn," he said. "Whatever tunics you have in stock will have to be retailored. These men are all too small."

"So, that is what will be done," Lionel said.

Wandred shook his head. "By magic, you are indeed unprepared for this. It is a shame that Bovine did not give you any tutoring. You probably don't even know about the budget shortfall from last year. All the money spent but not enough results to show for it. Altering the tunics will be an additional expense for you this year. I don't really like to disrespect those who have passed, but Perhaps Bovine's own pocket was a little too deep."

Lionel started to sigh, but stifled it at the last minute. It sounded like he had inherited a mess that could lead to a personal scandal. He had to straighten things out as soon as he could. Before being Captain of the City Guard turned out to be quicksand that would pull him under.

The sigh escaped anyway. Set things right as soon as he could, but first attend another ball.

Helping A Friend

DIANA BUMPED into the door jamb as she exited. She reviewed what her final instructions had been. First, continue with her own route until she had secured a replacement. Second, scan the list prepared daily by the office imps to review the take of each protection collector from the day before. Then, if necessary, inform the counters so they could pass on the word that she needed to speak with one of the collectors. Finally, request an enforcer or two to be present for the conversation as needed.

It felt like more than she could handle. What had she gotten herself into? Now in charge of all the protection racket collections for the entire city of Ambrosia! Unbelievable. She should go back immediately and tell the bossman there had been a mistake.

Diana shook her head. No, no, that wouldn't work. After learning so much about the criminal organization in the city, she would not stay alive for a heartbeat if she explained the big error. She needed some time to figure out what to do. And that meant, at least temporarily, playing the role. Making the collections daily was not all that bad. At least she was managing to return most of what she collected with magic rings that gave some hope. And she was taking fewer coins from the people who needed them each day.

And the other responsibility, rebuking collectors from

other parts of the city, might not become an issue until she could figure something out. Yes, that was it. She stiffened herself. Continue her daily routine. Hope that no other collector's techniques aroused the attention of the queen and nobles. Pretend nothing at all has changed.

Diana still felt uncomfortable. What she was doing was just plain evil. Despite the rationales, she struggled to justify her actions. Grabbing hold of the fact that she was giving others hope was a salve, but in the end, she should not be collecting money from anyone against their will. She needed something else, a deed that stood on its own merits, not twisted by circumstances that gave it a soiled grey.

It was now a habit for her to enter the market and jostle with the late afternoon crowd after her collection task was over. It did provide at least a little pleasure, a little relief. An image flashed into her mind, and she smiled. Nicholas was always near the same place every day. He had no permanent stall, merely a blanket on the ground, a makeshift sign flapping above, and his trays of magic rings. It seemed as if his supply was inexhaustible. The thing to do was put all the negative thoughts away and visit him as if nothing else mattered.

NICHOLAS LOOKED out onto the pathway and smiled. Diana was coming his way. Her visits over the past month had become routine. He looked forward to chatting with her every day — and her buying yet another ring or two. He was managing to keep his guild afloat.

"You look a little distracted." he smiled as she arrived in front of his blanket. "Going to buy some more rings too, I hope."

"Yes, I am," Diana said. She pushed unpleasant thoughts away.

"Ah, yes, the demons in our minds," Nicholas said. "Sometimes, they are worse than those who appear in the flesh. I have them as well."

"And your demons are?"

Nicholas hesitated for a moment, then decided to rush on. "Well, perhaps it is better to talk about it a bit." He held out one of his arms. "See the color of my robe? I am a neophyte magician. Tomorrow is my second and last chance to be promoted to an initiate."

He waved his hand over the trays of rings. "Instead of this, I should be studying even more. Preparing as hard as I can for my oral examination. It will be my last chance to pass." He shook his head. "Each day, I review the texts before I come to the market. It feels like I have memorized them all.

"But, deep inside, I know the outcome will be as before. When I take the test, my mind will be blank. I will not be able to recall a single thing. Remember a deduction that has not been reasoned out. I wish — I wish I knew a master sorcerer, one who would make me feel and think as if I truly were a magician."

Diana smiled at Nicholas. "Sorcery is not like that at all," she said. "Part of the myth. I don't think the craft gives one a power they does not already possess."

"So, what am I to do?" Nicholas's frustration bubbled out before he could stop. "I must look like a pitiful fool."

"Well," Diana began slowly, "I do know a little bit about the workings of our minds."

"Like what?"

"One thing you could do immediately before your exam is to spend time in a place you are comfortable with. Do something else rather than focusing on your challenge."

"The place where I have the most comfort is here," Nicholas said. He hesitated. "Especially talking with you."

Diana smiled. "Well, the bustle here might be a bit too

distracting. Where else?"

"At my guild. It is housed — temporarily, of course — on Honeysuckle Street, in what was an abandoned apothecary. The exam is there, too, but the masters usually will not stir from their quarters until just before."

Nicholas watched Diana ponder. He imagined he could almost hear the gears turning in her head.

"I will be there in the morning," she said at last. "We can chat about other things for a while."

"You would do this for me?"

"It is no imposition. My…work does not start until late afternoon. And these rings help me in…in what I do. I am only returning the favor."

Nicholas smiled. Diana's words were enticing. He wondered. Could this be the start of something deeper?

Diana said nothing more for a while, then finally broke the silence. "Practice is good, too. Practice giving answers aloud that you have already prepared."

"I have tried memorizing many of them, but when the time comes, I find that I can think of none."

"Start by echoing back the question first. While you are doing that, it will give your brain time to search simultaneously for the answer."

"How do you know all this?"

"Take deep breaths," Diana rattled on. "Project confidence through your body language."

"You didn't answer my question."

"Well, a long time ago," Diana said, "I, too, had to prepare for an examination such as yours." She stifled a sudden choke in her throat. "My mother was teaching me, but, but she —"

Impulsively, Nicholas reached out and touched Diana's arm. "I didn't mean to pry."

Diana wiped away a tear, but she did not withdraw her

arm. Stop feeling sorry for yourself. The unspoken thoughts scolded her. Think of something positive.

She glanced at Nicholas. His problems were now, not about the past. She looked quickly around the market. No passerby was paying them any attention. Then, without any preamble, she looked him in the eye and began chanting a charm she had never tried before, one that was reputed to enhance self-confidence.

Encounters

IT WAS almost dawn. Nicholas sat at his desk in the makeshift vault, trying to follow Diana's advice of yesterday. Think of other things instead of his upcoming exam. He stretched and yawned. It looked like the guild could keep going for a while longer if the sale of magic ring blanks remained as high as it had been. He could count on two a day for Diana and even more than that from other passersby. But as always, the long-term result was the same. The masters needed to come up with something else to make and sell sooner rather than later.

Inner thoughts bubbled. Why was he doing this? The answer was always the same. He was not adept with his hands. No craftsman would accept him as an apprentice. And the fate of his two brothers could not be his as well. Employing his mind was the only way with which to strive.

A sudden crash came from outside the vault. If the strongroom had been truly magic, no noise would have penetrated, of course. It sounded like the front windows had shattered. Then, before Nicholas could react, a second concussion blew a hole in the vault wall. Three sword-wielding men burst through it.

"Okay, boys, step lively now," Izzy said. "Gather treasures we can carry and then get out of here before the city guard arrives. Make Diana proud of you. And didn't I tell you over and over that it was worthwhile to hang out with the nighttime guard until he spilled everything?"

"Where is he then?" Intrepid asked.

"Back at the tavern. I gave him enough coppers to stay away for a while. Look around and spot the most valuable items we can nab. This will be the last heist we will ever have to perform. The very last one."

Nicholas bolted alert. His heart raced — just as it had before his failed exam. What had the first intruder said? Something about Diana?

He took his thoughts inward, and surprisingly a feeling of calm washed over him. The trio was not rushing at him. Instead, they waved their swords and gawked. There were only three of them. Why, he could handle that number by himself. He blinked about what he had just thought.

Nicholas looked around for a weapon. There were no magic swords in the vault, of course. Such things were difficult to produce and often took on minds of their own. His guild never dabbled with such things. He spotted the crate of mirror blanks and lifted the one on top.

It was difficult to hold, and he had to use both hands to keep it from slipping out of his grip, but at least it would not shatter. Then, swinging it rapidly back and forth, he charged at the tallest opponent.

"Glass?" Claymore laughed. "That's not a weapon. It will explode into shards, and then you will be undone."

Claymore relaxed his guard momentarily, and Nicholas plunged the end of the blank into the warrior's ample gut. Startled, the giant backed off a step.

"Stand aside, mouse," Claymore croaked. "You have no chance against the three of us. Tell us where the gold is, and you will continue to live."

"Gold?" Nicholas laughed. "We have none here."

"Don't tell us that. Everyone knows magicians are

wealthy from selling what they produce.”

“Look around,” Nicholas said. “What wealth do you see?”

“You probably have another vault around here somewhere, perhaps underground.”

“Did any of you bring a shovel?” Nicholas shot back. Somehow, he felt his confidence growing stronger, although clearly it should not be.

Intrepid lowered his sword and began walking around the vault. He kicked at one of the hemisphere stacks and the half-spheres clattered to the ground. He noticed the cash tray next to Nicholas’s bed and scooped up a few of the coins that were there. “This troll is right. Look at how bare this place is. Not a brandel in sight.”

“Yeah,” Claymore said. “Why would a guild use an apothecary lab anyway?”

“It’s a bust,” Intrepid concluded. “Another of your schemes gone bad, Izzy. Come on, let’s get out of here before city guardsmen come to investigate the noise.”

“Sorry about the hole in the wall,” Claymore looked at Nicholas. “I know a guy who does plaster work. If you like, I can get you his name.”

Nicholas waved the mirror blank a few more times, and none of the trio responded. Shoulders slumping, they left through the apothecary entrance portal without saying another word.

Nicholas stood dumbfounded in the middle of the vault. Had he really vanquished a gang of thugs with a glass mirror blank? He gawked at the hole that had been blown in the wall. Yet another expense. What would he tell the masters? How would he garner enough to pay for the repair?

Surprisingly, none of the masters had been aroused by the noise of the blast. None had come to investigate. Nicholas decided that they all must sleep in exhaustion after trying to solve the mysteries of magic without cease day after day.

And what about his exam? Would it be postponed because of the piercing of the vault? Would he ever become a true magician?

But most curious of all was how he had acted. Holding off three brigands with only an unsharpened blank of glass. That was so unlike how he thought of himself. Where did he find the strength to do something like that? If called upon, could he do it again? He shook his head. Too many riddles. No matter what, he should get some sleep. Diana would be here soon enough. He huddled himself as comfortably as he could, but slumber did not come.

IT WAS late morning. Diana struck out onto one of the rutted streets bordering the hovel. Thoughts of yesterday's predicament could not be totally suppressed, but helping Nicholas was a welcome distraction. It felt strange without the familiar tread of Listen Up and Pay Attention behind her.

Following Nicholas's instructions, Diana crossed one of the river-spanning bridges into the finer side of the city and continued her journey towards Honeysuckle Street, the location of the city apothecaries. As she climbed the slope, her feelings lifted. The paint on the buildings became brighter and fresher. There was less litter and even some uncluttered vacant lots.

Nicholas, she thought. She was going to see Nicholas again. What was it about him that made him interesting to her? He was no great warrior physically. But then, his manner felt comfortable to her. He treated her as an equal rather than a wench he was trying to bed.

Suddenly, she saw a squad of guardsmen dressed in their leather jerkins and headed by an armor-clad leader marching with purpose on one of the cross streets she passed. The image of another squad leader sprang back into her head. Yes, the one she had enchanted. What was it now, a month ago? The one who pledged he would help her if ever she asked. Diana shrugged the thought away. It was because of her spell, of course.

Without her planting the seed in the noble's mind, he would not have spoken to her as he did. Still — it was quite pleasant to daydream about him, about being a true lady with a gallant lord at her beckoning call. She glanced down guiltily at the frock she had bought with some of the protection money. Not a regal gown, but so much better than the worn and patched sorcerer's robe. She had managed to slip it on while Izzy and the others were still asleep. She touched her hair and refixed one strand back into place. What would the encounter be like if she were to meet the lordling again?

Nicholas and Lionel. Two so very different men. She shook her head to clear her thoughts. There really was no reason to think any deeper about either one.

LIONEL GRUMBLED as he dressed. The messenger had been insistent. The lead guardsman for the day shift had reported in sick. There was no one else besides himself to send and investigate the dawn disruption other than himself. He made as much haste as he could to get this task taken care of. Soon, he stood in front of the apothecary door and rapped on it soundly.

"Who is it?" a voice from inside called out.

"I am the Captain of the Guard," Lionel said as he entered and strode over the broken glass from the blown out front windows. "I've come to investigate a report of an explosion on this property. "When did this happen? Who did this? Where did they go? Were you here? Did you see anyone suspicious before the blast?"

"One question at a time," Nicholas snapped back.

"Shouldn't you first ask if anybody was killed or hurt?"

"The sooner we can get on the trail of the perpetrators, the more likely they will be caught," Lionel said. "Do you want the aid of the queen's city guard or not?"

There was sudden motion in the doorway.

"Diana!" Nicholas said. "Thank you so much for coming."

"My…my lady," Lionel said.

(5)

A Meeting of Three

DIANA LOOKED from one man to the other. Nicholas, she expected, but the other, her fanciful knight, was here as well!

"Is it that late already?" Nicholas asked her. "I did not spend much time preparing myself yet." He pointed at the gaping hole in the vault wall. "As you can see, much as happened here. And, and," he stammered. "I have caused them to flee."

"You need not concern yourself," Lionel said. "My lady, I am here to serve you."

Diana blinked. She looked at Nicholas and could not help smiling about what she saw there. The charm she had laid upon him in the marketplace had helped. It had enabled him to discover something that had laid hidden within. Another application of the charm, and who knew how self-confident the neophyte would feel then.

She held out her hands, palms upwards. "Here, Nicholas," she said. "Place your hands in mine. Look into my eyes. I think a more potent booster will work wonders for you."

Nicholas hesitated.

"What?" Diana asked. "This is not going to hurt."

"No, no, of course not, Diana," the neophyte managed to say. "It is merely that — "

"Finish up with it, knave," Lionel interrupted. "I have other duties to which I must attend."

Diana swung her head back to the lordling, the one about whom she had thought about as she traveled across the city. It would be easy to enhance the warrior's interest in her as well. And he should be her first enchantment before the remnants from what had endured for a whole month before completely faded away.

She looked at Lionel. His expectant look made her heart flutter.

"Please, sir," she said. "Focus on me for a moment. Concentrate on my words."

"As always, your wish is my command, my lady."

Diana stared into the guardsman's eyes. The first words rolled into her thoughts. She opened her mouth to speak, then hesitated.

Wait a moment, she thought. For the first time in her life, she was about to use her gift for her own personal gain. This was so different from enhancing hopes of wish fulfillment in exchange for a few coins. Her mother's words from so long ago had suddenly surfaced in her mind.

'Most who practice our craft do so for selfish reasons. See how much they can make others dance like marionettes on strings. That is why we are so feared and shunned. Misused enchantment is an abuse of the power given to us. We must use it gently or not at all.'

"No, this is not right," Diana mumbled. "Enchantment is but a façade that papers over underlying manipulation."

"What?" Lionel said. "Your words were not loud enough for me, my lady."

Diana inhaled deeply to banish her thoughts about what might be. "Here, sir knight, my wish is this," she said. Then carefully, she spoke the words that, rather than intensifying, released Lionel from the remainder of the charm to which he had been bound. She knew her head would throb for hours afterwards, but this had to be done.

"My lad —" he started, then slammed his mouth shut, suddenly confused.

Diana then looked back at Nicholas. He, too, was still under her influence. She sighed. Best to get all this cleared up before some real harm is done.

Nicholas was still clasping her hands in his. He dipped his head. "In Brythia, where I am from, holding hands across from one another is an old tradition. It means…it means that a couple is betrothed."

Diana rushed to reply, "But we are in Procolon, are we not? I shall not hold you to a vow that only has meaning in the South."

Before Nicholas could say more, Diana started the first recital and smiled at the neophyte. Her head started to pound, and tears came to her eyes. "There, that was not so bad, was it?" she managed to ask when she was done with the third recital.

This was a new experience, she thought to herself. Yes, reversal charms were not as head-wrenching as their original counterparts, and somehow the targets' memories fogged about what had transpired.

Nicholas shook his head. "Bad? Bad, you say? What are you talking about? I don't … understand what you have done, and now, somehow, I don't feel quite the same as before. At least, I don't think I — "

"I am the Captain of the Guard," Lionel interrupted. "My day is always full. As far as I can see, there was no damage to anyone here. Isn't that correct?"

"Yes," Nicholas scowled at Lionel. "My guild did not ask for you to come. So, you can be on your way and pontificate to the next on your list."

Suddenly, a crack of thunder rattled the apothecary windows. It did not sound as loud as the one Nicholas had heard at the market, but still strong enough to draw the trio's attention. They all stood still and said nothing for a dozen heartbeats. Then, the sharp sound vibrated again.

"I had better attend to that," Lionel said. He stepped towards the door, then paused and pointed at the hole in the vault wall. "No loss, therefore no harm, right?"

"Nothing was taken," Nicholas shrugged.

Lionel opened the front door, peered out, and listened. He cupped his ear and turned it towards the center of the city. After a third rumble, he said, "I think it is coming from the direction of the queen's castle." Then he bolted off.

Nicholas squeezed his grip on Diana's hands. She did not pull them away. Together they waited for more booms, tensing for them to come.

There was a fourth, and then a fifth window rattle, both like all the others.

The pair held their breaths for what felt like a millennium, but then no more disruptions occurred.

Nicholas gently removed Diana's hands from his. "I need to go as well," he said.

"What? Where?" Diana asked.

"The explosions," Nicholas said. "That is what they are. Something even less understood than lightning."

"Why? It might be dangerous."

"One disturbance is bad enough, but five evenly spaced can mean only one thing."

"What?"

"Magic is involved. An even cadence is a common aspect of our rituals. But more importantly, one of the surviving masters in my guild might be behind this. The one who is deceased caused enough damage and sorrow with what he has already attempted."

Diana grabbed Nicholas's arm. "Wait, don't do that. Your feeling of bravado is merely that all my charm has not worn off."

"What?"

"I — I enchanted you when we last met in the market. Something light. Only enough for you to tap inner courage. I apologize. I wanted you to have a clear head for the exam."

Nicholas's eyes widened with wonder. "You're a sorceress, aren't you?" He took a step backward. Diana stood silently in front of him, not sure what to say.

After a moment, a small smile crept onto Nicholas's face. "How can any of the tales be right about someone like you, Diana," he said. "I don't care what you are." He looked around the wreckage caused by the erstwhile robbers. "There won't be an exam here, at least not for a while. All this mess has to be cleaned up first." He took a deep breath. "And I am not going to be the one to do it. I, too, must go and investigate."

"No, no," Diana said. "I must not have completed the disenchantment correctly. Stand still for a moment. It will only take me a little while to say the words."

"No."

"Then, at least let me accompany you. Hope for a chance to change you back to — to normal."

"Normal?" Nicholas said. "I like the way I feel now. This is the new normal for me." He put his other hand on top of Diana's. "Let's go."

(**6**)

Bold, Brazen Robbery

DIANA AND Nicholas joined a crushing throng racing up the hill towards the queen's castle. The pair held hands to ensure they would not be separated. There were no more explosions.

At first, as they raced and jostled, Diana was preoccupied. She looked across at Nicholas and wondered. What had she done? Had her charm-casting been flawed from the start? Was he still under her thrall, or, once his inner courage was tapped, it could not be returned to sleeping? Perhaps her mother's instructions had not been precise? Would what she had done going to cause him harm?

If the charm on Nicholas was not absolutely correct, then what of the one on Lionel? Perhaps some of his feelings for her she had engendered still remained. Perhaps having a knightly lord's interest in her had not gone away completely. She glanced at Nicholas, and at the same time thought about Lionel.

And, as the pair grew closer to the castle, other voices made their way into her thoughts.

"An attack by the king of Ethidor. One of the kingdoms to the south finally is showing some nerve."

"The barbarians of the north. Vendora's consort has united them in demanding that he assume the throne."

"Arcadia across the great ocean has had enough of, what are they called, tariffs — "

115

Diana sucked in her breath. Focus, she told herself, focus. A coup? An invasion? Her little world was but a mere flea on the back of what could be a tiger.

LIONEL APPROACHED the castle's barbican. It had not been changed since it was constructed half a millennium ago. The structure was part of the wall encircling the entire bailey. Between its two small flanking towers stood a gate of crossing iron bars that could be raised and lowered in times of peace to allow traffic to enter and exit.

Each tower was manned by royal guards who approved or denied entry. When enough were accepted, the portcullis would be raised so that ingress was possible. Inside the gate, a cadre of six additional guardsmen stood armed and ready to quell any disturbance that might arise while the gate was open.

A large crowd had already formed on the side facing the city. Lionel pushed through the spectators. He yelled at the guardsman behind the small grill in the left tower. "I am the Captain of the City Guard. Let me pass!"

"No one is to enter."

"I said I am the Captain of the City Guard. I pass freely in and out of the castle whenever I desire. Do you not recognize me?"

"No one is to enter. By direct order of Wandred, the Wary."

Wandred? Lionel thought. Surely, if there was a problem within the walls, the curmudgeon would welcome help in restoring order. Many of his city guard ate and slept in the armory.

"What is going on here? Are the queen and her consort safe?"

"I have my orders, sir. They are quite explicit. No one is

allowed to enter."

Lionel fumed. He put on his most intimidating face. "You recognize me, right?"

"Yes sir. You, indeed, are the Captain of the City Guard."

"Outside the castle, I am the one who is in command, right?"

"Yes sir."

"Don't you want this crowd to be dispersed?"

"That has been accounted for, sir."

"Accounted for! What do you mean?" Lionel's frustration grew.

"Please step aside, sir, so I can serve the next person in line."

Lionel exhaled deeply. He would have to wait until the end of the shift. That was when his troops returned from patrol, and his evening squad formed on the other side of the gate, ready to go out into the city.

IT HAD taken most of the morning, but Nicholas had been insistent. He kept Diana near as they pushed their way through the crowd. As the day wore on, it became easier and easier. Nothing was happening at the barbican gate, and many were giving up and melting away.

"There's Lionel," the neophyte said. "Come on. We have to talk to him."

"Why?" Diana asked as they maneuvered past a woman weary from holding one child to her chest and clinging to the hand of another.

"As simple as a geometric proof," Nicholas said. "He is going to need my — our help."

MORNING WORE on into noon. Lionel, peering into the bailey as best he could, saw that Wandred's troop of gate guards had become alert. Leather vests were tugged into place and swords withdrawn from their scabbards.

The portcullis chains rattled, and then the gate rose. When at its full height, Lionel heard orders being given, and the troop guarding the barbican marched out and onto the city street in front. An instant later, the gate fell shut again. The guards took up positions in two rows, three on each side of the rutted roadway leading away from the castle. What little of the crowd that remained gave way without any protest.

Nicholas and Diana spotted Lionel, but before they could come close to him, he raced to the closed gate. With Wandred's troop out of the way, he got a better view of the bailey. Was anything at all happening at the armory? His own men preparing for the second shift of city patrol should be visible there, getting ready. Stooping to get a better view up the castle hill, Lionel tried to make out if anything was happening at the long, thatched-roof structure, but he saw nothing — only two of Wandred's royal guards lounging around the armory entrance.

While he pondered, a double-brace of horses pulling a heavily laden wagon came into view and approached the rear side of the barbican. The wheels creaked and the wagon bed sagged between the two axles. The load being carried was covered. More men mounted on horseback followed. Lionel recognized some of them. They were the palace guard's most recent recruits. It must be at least a dozen royal guardsmen who were involved. Wandred was in the lead.

The wagon exited and moved into position between the two rows of Wandred's other men already there. Those on horseback split into two smaller troops and blocked off the front and back. Then the armory doors burst open. Lionel saw the rest of his own city guard spew forth. Somehow, they had been surprised and confined. Now there was no one left to impede them. Their swords were drawn as they raced down the slope towards Wandred's formation.

"Stop them! Stop them!" the city guardsmen shouted. "They have looted the treasury!"

The treasury! Lionel's thoughts whirled. The so-very-well guarded treasury? How could that be? Then, the number of explosions clicked in his mind. Five guard doors and five explosions. Lionel frowned at the impossibility of his thoughts. Somehow, each door had been blown open. This turmoil was not about an invasion or coup, but simple theft!

And Wandred was involved! The old man must have decided that wealth now was worth far more than a meager pension from the queen later.

Several hundred-weights of powder were needed to cause such damage to any of the treasury doors. But, for sure, the sentry on guard would have seen so much powder being lugged into the tower that an alarm would have been heard much sooner. And after it exploded, there would be only splinters left and no one left standing to tell the tale.

Nicholas caught up with Lionel. As if reading the guard captain's thoughts, he shouted, "Magic. I don't know the ritual for how it is being controlled, but somehow the explosions are the result of magic."

"Magic?" Lionel spun to look at Nicholas. He recognized him from being at the apothecary. "What do you mean? How is this done?"

"I, I am not sure," the neophyte said. "Tell me, have any large spheres or hemispheres been brought into the castle recently?"

Lionel shook his head. "There is a daily inventory of new additions. I look at it at the end of every day. I do not recall any such things described as 'large.'"

"Hmm, something else then," Nicholas said. "Anything else seem unusual?"

"The only other things were the little, what did Hector call them, 'binding guards' ... for the record books, But the accountants and their records are far removed from the treasury tower ..." He paused, "Wait! After those were accepted, Wandred told me about other devices purchased and then delivered by the magician Hector as well. *"Alarm disks* he had called them.

"Alarm disks?"

"I was told they resembled tiny apothecary pill boxes. One of the tower guards was curious and unscrewed the cap on one. It was empty. Nothing inside but air."

"What was it made of?" Nicholas asked.

"Hmm, copper, I believe."

"That's it!" Nicholas exclaimed. "Hector has somehow worked through enough of Garavak's notes to reproduce his ritual! Not with a big sphere but small squat cylinders instead. Smaller container and smaller result."

"Magic, you say!" Lionel agreed. "He thought for a moment. "I think that might explain it. A little sticky disk was attached to each of the five barrier doors. But they were not alarms at all. Instead, Wandred's men must have descended the passageway, and destroyed the doors one by one."

The wagon started down the road surrounded by the royal guardsmen. Lionel glanced back at it, began to withdraw his sword, but then stopped. He glanced at his own guards who had shown up. At the moment, there were too few of them. All he could do now was report what had happened to the queen — something he did not look forward having to do at all.

A Train of Logical Thought

THE CROWD that remained broke into small clusters, jabbering questions. But, like melting snow, they all soon vanished back into the city. None were anxious to be brought to attention and questioned.

Nicholas pondered. What had just happened? Had it really been gold under the cowhides covering the wagon? Was that why there were so many armed men?

Lionel ordered one of his guardsmen to enter the barbican and raise the gate. The others he directed to search all the buildings in the bailey for more of Wandred's palace guard. "Challenge their allegiances. I do not suspect any more traitors will be found," he explained as he gave his order, "Nor anything else stolen, but it is far better to be sure."

He did not protest when the neophyte and Diana tagged along with him to inform Vendora. "The more eye-witnesses, the better," he had said.

Nicholas scowled as the trio hurriedly walked from one part of the bailey to the next. He watched the sorceress's eyes widen as Lionel assumed control of the castle activity. What was so difficult about what the lordling was doing? Someone like him, a neophyte could accomplish as much. It was mainly about knowing what was located where, a commanding attitude — and the garb that one wore. He shook his head; the robe of a neophyte did not bring forth such awe.

Nicholas's thoughts continued churning. First, Hector must have understood what Gavarak had accomplished. Now, evidently, more than one master magician could produce an explosion.

Second, the shape could be, well, most anything. Alarm disks were very short cylinders, not spheres.

Third, the greater the container's volume, the stronger the resulting explosion.

Garavak's had been huge. The blast in the market was much smaller. No one had noticed it anything out of the ordinary before it happened. Perhaps that explosion was a test, a calibration of what damage would happen from a small disk pasted onto a door. It was to be just large enough to break its target into manageable pieces so that the barrier could be passed, but not so large as to obliterate his guild's original palace of magicians.

Fourth, the most important of all. Why was Hector doing this?

AFTER ALL Lionel's men and Wandred's remaining ones had reported to him, he left the bailey and climbed up a staircase in the portion of the castle that contained the apartments of the queen. Diana and Nicholas scurried to keep up with his demanding stride.

Without a preamble, the trio streamed past the unarmed servants in a series of anterooms and entered Vendora's innermost domain.

"My ladies-in-waiting have been in a flutter all morning about the loud noises. Where is Wandred?" the queen asked as soon as the trio entered. "He should be the one reporting what has happened, not you?"

"Alas, he is a scoundrel," Lionel said. "The mastermind behind the pilferage of your treasury."

Vendora's face distorted into a combination of astonishment and disbelief. "My treasury!" She closed her eyes for a moment, and then stood tall and straight.

"Not Wandred," she shook her head. "He is one of my favorites. That cannot be. And as far as taking from my treasury, there is more there than he or anyone else could carry off. Was there any other damage?"

"The explosion also rocked the dungeon. One of the walls collapsed. Some of the prisoners escaped."

"All this accomplished by a single man?"

"Wandred was not alone, my queen," Lionel said. "A portion of your royal guard also was part of the plan."

Vendora was silent for a moment. Her forehead wrinkled in thought. Then she quickly ran a smoothing hand over it and spoke as if giving commands for an afternoon tea. "For now, assume command over all those who remain. Root out any more traitors who might still lurk among them."

"As you know, I am the Captain of the City guard," Lionel said. "I know little of the workings inside the castle."

"So now, you will have to learn. That is my command."

A scowl of irritation started to form on Lionel's face, but he quickly replaced it with a more neutral expression. "As you wish, my queen," he managed to say.

The room lapsed into silence. The trio waited for Vendora to speak again.

"How much then?" she asked at last. "How much was taken?"

"Reputedly, a wagonload highly piled," Lionel regained control of his speech.

Vendora laughed. "Only a single wagon-load? My wealth is much greater than that."

Nicholas spoke up. "Forgive me, ah, my liege, but probably what is more important is perception, not the truth."

"What do you mean?"

"What will everyone now think about the scrip?"

"What about it?"

"At the least, now there is no clear correspondence between what is written on a scrap of vellum and the golden brandel it represents."

"But the value on the scrip clearly states — "

Vendora stopped speaking. Her eyes widened.

Nicholas glanced at Diana. She was not moving, probably as overawed by her surrounding as was he. "It was not clearly certain that golden brandels were in the wagon that exited to the street," he continued. "Perhaps the thing to do is remain silent about what was stolen. It was a heavy wagonload to be sure, but it was entirely covered as it exited the barbican. Maybe only one chest of gold and the rest deceptive surroundings."

"And you are?" Vendora asked.

Nicholas steeled himself. "A neophyte magician, my queen," he blurted. "I also was a witness to what transpired. And besides me is Diana, the sorceress, yet another who observed."

Lionel blinked in surprise. "A sorceress?" he exclaimed. He gawked at Diana. "I did not suspect!"

"I have had many at my court," Vendora said. "Some of the illusions they provide have been quite amusing."

Nicholas rushed on. "I think — ah, I suggest the thing to do is to remain silent about what was stolen. Scrip will continue to be used, just as it was before."

"What about the lower classes?"

"There is enough coin in circulation now. That will not change."

"Word will get out eventually," Diana spoke up. "The thing to do is locate where the trove is now. It probably is still together, not broken up yet or stashed for safekeeping."

"And how is that to be done, my pretty one?" Vendora

brushed back one of her own curls and glanced into a full-length mirror at her side. It stood next to a vanity crammed with beauty salves and lotions. Evidently, the queen was a frequent buyer of Honeysuckle Street's latest products.

"Merely sitting on a guarded stockpile of gold is worthless to Wandred and his men," Lionel said. "They will want to spend their newfound wealth. Otherwise, what was the point of taking it?"

"There is bragging to be done," Diana agreed. "What is needed is a way to tap into the gossip of the street."

"And we do that how?" Vendora asked.

"I have some, ah, connections who might be useful," Diana replied. "They could keep their eyes and ears open."

"That sounds iffy." Nicholas frowned. "The real risk is more explosions. The treasury robbery may have been another test. Much more is at stake here. I just know it. Magic has to be fought with magic."

"A well-planned search of the city," Lionel said. "Look everywhere. In a methodical fashion. Find the gold before it is broken into smaller lots. That is the first thing to do, and it must be done quickly."

"Even moving slowly, a single wagon could be well away soon," Nicholas said.

"Seek what is under your nose before going on a wild pigeon wander," Lionel shook his head. "It is in the city that we must begin our search first. I will start formulating the plan now and present it to you as soon as I can."

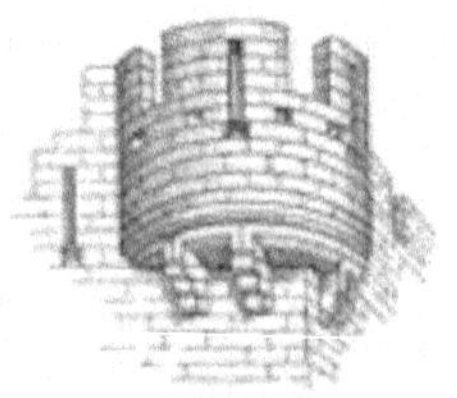

8
Nicholas's Reward

NICHOLAS ENTERED the made-over apothecary. Nothing had changed. The gaping hole looked the same. He looked inside it. Neither Antron nor Randolph was in the vault. He sauntered slowly back to the solitary compartments and studied the shut doors. The nearest was Antron's and the other, Randolph's.

Antron was his first choice. Both masters might be even better, but he was unsure how the two would work together.

He knocked softly on Antron's door and put his ear to it. He heard nothing stirring. How much time was proper to allow a master to wake and make himself presentable? Nicholas did not know. He counted to one hundred slowly, then tried again, a little louder this time. And again nothing.

Randolph then. Nicholas shrugged. Did it really matter which? He tapped Randolph's door even a little louder than he had Antron's, and almost immediately heard a voice from inside.

"Yes, what is it?"

"Master Randolph, you must come out. The queen and the city of Ambrosia need you. Already, too much time has passed. They need you now."

Almost immediately, Randolph's door sprang open.

Nicholas blinked. The master was dressed in a nightshirt, adorned with the same logo as on daywear robes, but otherwise made of a flimsy weave.

"The queen needs me!" Randolph smiled. "Come in neophyte. What compelled her to ask?"

"Well, not you specifically. But what is important is that the evidence suggests that Hector has gone rogue. He provided the means for looting Vendora's treasury."

"Hector!" Randolph's expression transformed into a snarl. "I suppose everyone in the city is now mouthing his name."

Nicholas did not like the way the conversation was starting. What was important was to act. Do something, not argue about who should get credit or blame. "Yes, Master, Hector probably is famous — I mean infamous already. Didn't you hear the explosions that took place this morning? Wandred, the head of the queen's personal guard, and his men caused those. They did the actual stealing."

The neophyte rushed on. "But Lionel, the lordling in charge of peace in the city, says the explosions were created from five tiny disks, I guess you call them that, stuck to passage barriers. They were supplied by Hector. Each not as potent as — "

"Smaller volumes! Of course," Randolph said. "That sounds like what Hector would do. Don't worry about understanding the steps of the ritual at all. Don't try to reason out how to modify a few to reduce to a desired potency. Apply it to a lesser quantity of air and see what happens. The disruption a few evenings ago was a first test."

"Master," Nicholas said. "Please, with all due respect, let's remain focused. Your knowledge is sorely needed before there is any further disruption. Hector has become dangerous. How do we stop him?"

"*We* stop him? You speak boldly for one who is but a neophyte."

Nicholas stopped talking. The words hit him like a

hammer. With Hector gone, the palace now had only two masters. Without a third, there could be no candidacy examination, not as planned days ago, not soon, never.

"About my exam," he began slowly.

Randolph's eyes brightened. "Of course, of course. I see your concern." He stroked his goatee. "Hmm. Over the years, this is not the first time such a shortage has happened. When it does, a temporary visiting master — "

"Then it can be done!" Nicholas exclaimed. "Thank you, thank — "

"Calm down, neophyte. It is not simple for such a thing to be arranged. And, of course there is the consulting fee involved." Randolph was silent for a few moments. "No, no, I think Antron will agree," he finally said.

"Agree to what?" Nicholas ventured.

"Neophyte, what is the product of seven and twelve?"

"Why, eighty-four, of course."

"Correct! Now open my wardrobe on the wall to your left."

Nicholas did as he was told.

"See the initiate's robe hanging there? Not as deep a blue as my master's one next to it. I have saved it as a fond memory for many years."

"Yes."

"Shed your own and don it instead."

"Yes, Master." Nicholas's heart began to race. He was actually putting on the robe that he had yearned for so long.

When he was done, Randolph spoke again, "You are now hereby ordained as an initiate of the Palace of the Setting Sun."

"But, but," Nicholas sputtered and then stopped. He could not help looking at himself in Randoph's full-length mirror.

"What will Master Antron say?" he managed to ask after a moment. He could not believe it. Was this all it took? Some sort of secret handshake that had nothing to do with becoming proficient in the lore? The ritual of the formal examination was merely for — for what?

"I will handle Antron when the time to do so comes," Randolph interrupted the train of Nicholas's thoughts. "For now, as an initiate there are some things for you to do. Things not normally entrusted to a neophyte."

"Like what?"

"You will be my sounding board. I propose a conjecture, and you either extend it or explain why it is false."

"But there is still Hector to be dealt with."

"Do you want to be an initiate or not?"

9

Diana Triumphant

DIANA FANNED the smoke from the smoldering incense in the alcove out into the meeting room. Help to deaden the senses. Bossman's imps had been efficient. They had the message out to all her underlings yesterday. She glanced at the sprites who were gently fanning the flames in the fireplace to glow. Not too hot, but enough to make everyone feel comfortable surrounded by air slightly warmer than outside.

Diana focused inwardly, hoping her plan would work. Two days had passed, yet there were no rumors on the street about stolen gold. But, merely waiting for a lucky break that led to the hiding place was not going to work. Instead, more methodical searching must be used.

They were all assembled, nearly two dozen of them. Protection collectors from all sectors of city life in Ambrosia. From the one with the gilded leggings to the three or four shrouded in capes and hoods.

She had expected a steady stream of suggestive remarks and masculine barbs as they assembled, but none came. Diana could only speculate that word had come down from higher up to treat the new boss with respect.

She cleared her throat and began speaking. "Yes, I'm the new one in charge of protection," she said. "You might not know it, but over the past month, I have performed better than any of you. There have been no complaints in my territory. Bossman decided that I am an improvement over the 'screwup', as Bossman called him, before me. If you have trouble with that, see me personally after this is over. I will ensure any disrespect you might still have is dealt with immediately."

She took another breath, a shorter one this time so it would not be noticed, and waited. There was a shuffling of feet and then what seemed like too long of a silence. She steeled herself to remain quiet. Her mother had taught her that the one who spoke first was always at a disadvantage.

Finally, a thug in the first row, the one with the fancy tunic, asked, "What makes you so special?"

Diana was ready for this. She slammed down a fan onto the desktop. It made a satisfyingly large thump. Fancy-pants eyes flinched, his eyes widening in surprise. She rushed through a simple charm at break-neck speed, the fastest she had ever performed it.

"So, I was starting to say — " His eyes widened. He tried to shape his mouth to complete his thought, but all that came out was "Baa, baa, baa!"

"Anyone else?" Diana looked from one side of the room to the other. She had to act quickly. Some of the simpler charms faded soon after they came on. Thank her mother for taking time with her training rather rushing on to spells that were useful.

"All right, then. Now, listen up, there is something in addition I want you to be alert for on your rounds, starting now."

"Wha — baa, baa, baa."

Everyone except for Fancy-pants laughed. Diana relaxed a little. Having all the rest focusing on his misfortune made the next charm a lot easier to get right.

"First, we are going to have a go-around. Each of you report how your territory is going. You there on the left, begin"

The first collector started speaking. Diana wafted more of the soothing incense out into the crowd. After the first two had finished reporting, several were already slumping into their seats, nodding. What could be more boring than listening to others talk about their own accomplishments and problems? In a soft voice, she began adding her own words to the recitals, speaking the charm she really wanted to be the one taking effect. One that produced loyalty, and willingness to suppress one's own desires to those of the enchanter.

As she slogged through the three recitals, a nagging thought kept bubbling up about what she was doing. From the start, her mother had emphasized using the craft only for good. And, well, yes, this was for the good, wasn't it? 'The destination justified the trek', the old saw said. What would happen if it became well-known that a vellum of scrip did not correspond one-for-one to a coin of gold, then what would happen? To all the commerce that kept Ambrosia alive — the markets, the craftsmen …

Worse still, one of the southern kingdoms might well decide now was the time to strike. Ethidor most likely, but perhaps Laudia, Samirand, and Brythia as well.

Diana shook her head. That was not the real reason for doing this. Be honest with herself. It was so she could keep the attention of Lionel, have him see that she was more than just a pretty … Well, she didn't know if she were pretty or not, but surely helping him restore order as seen in the eyes of the queen was worth the effort.

IT TOOK half an hour before the last report was completed. By then, all the protection leaders had settled into a gentle twilight zone — warm and drowsy, ready to do whatever she said. Diana gave them their instructions to report to her any sudden appearance of wealth and dispatched them back to their designated territories. She felt exhausted. Her head and throat hurt more than ever before, but it was something that had to be done.

After the last collector had departed the meeting, Diana turned her attention to the stack of vellums on her desk. The accounting sprite who had brought them hovered near her head and had explained she would get such an update every day.

"I will walk you through them," the sprite said and then chuckled. "Get it, walk you through them. It is what my boss tells me what I should say to a new leader. Make you feel at ease. But it is so hard to do without a grin or two.

"First of all, your human idioms are so much nonsense as any idiot can see. Sprites like me fly about, not walk. And we certainly are not going to somehow pass through one page onto another."

Diana sighed. Best to get through this. Maybe catch a short nap before having to make the collection round in the tents later in the day.

"Each territory has its own status sheet," the sprite said. "It lists the total submitted daily and on the side an update of the running average for the month."

A bolt of alarm suddenly pierced Diana's fatigue. She had been so busy preparing for the meeting to establish her control and task the other collectors. She had dismissed Listen Up and Pay Attention from attending her two days running so she could prepare.

Diana riffled through the packet and found the leaf for Saddar's territ — no, not Saddar's, what was now hers. There, she saw the numbers she feared. Zeros on the last two lines. Word would go up the hierarchy. She would be brought to the attention of …

Like a brick smashing into the side of her head, Diana suddenly understood. There was no cause for alarm after all.

She was the one to whom the daily reports were sent, the one who meted the discipline when a territory started falling short of its goals. "That is my own territory," she told the imp. "I am well aware of it. Any problem with that?"

"I don't mettle with how you run your business," the sprite said. "My job is only to make sure the numbers add up to the totals correctly."

Then, there will be no complaints, Diana thought. Certainly not from the tent occupants. They were not going to mouth a protest that their protection fees were no longer being collected. When they were no longer being collected going forward at all!

No, that was not quite right, Diana corrected herself. She shifted through the sheets and found one more. It listed the total collected daily from each of the territories. That total was something that surely was reported upward.

Glancing across the rows, Diana saw that what each territory brough in varied widely. The 'Tents' was the lowest. The one for 'Fancy Pants' twenty times as much. Evidently, the protection racket extended far up Ambrosia's central hill.

"Wait a moment," she said. "Ten territories, right, but eleven columns on the vellum."

"Ah, not as dull-witted as most," the sprite said. "The eleventh shows your cut. It is deducted from the total going up the chain."

"Only the total is important? Not the details of how it comes about?"

"Of course not. Bossman does not rock boats that are steady."

Diana's thoughts began to race. "I see my personal total from all the territories is greater than what is usually collected from the tents. I could transfer some funds from my take into the total going upward to cover what is missing."

"Your game, your fame," the sprite said. "Tell me how

you want things set up, and I will take care of it."

Diana felt a warm feeling start to fight it way through the fatigue. Those in the tents no longer having to pay for any protection at all. Not Izzy. Not anyone! Not ever!

"Alright, I understand now," she said to the sprite. "That is the way I want things to be. You can take care of all this, right?"

DIANA WOKE from her nap feeling refreshed. She opened the small window shade behind her desk and looked out. It was barely past noon. She savored again the structure she had set up. The other collectors were not a problem. They all were under her sway. It was true the protection continued in Ambrosia, but at least those least willing to pay would be spared.

All that remained was to show up at dusk each day, give Listen Up and Pay Attention what they expected, and provide Izzy with a few coppers for her share of the expenses for his little group. But, for the first time in her life, she was almost totally free.

Until meal time, each day, she could go on another shopping spree and — no, not a wise thing to do. Her blankets now could barely cover the trinkets and pieces of clothing she had already bought for herself. It was only a matter of time until her cache was discovered by Izzy or one of the others. There would be too much to explain.

So, why not rent a room at an inn? The thought sprung to her out of nowhere. Keep all her hidden things somewhere else, a place with no prying eyes. Yes, withdraw a few — what, maybe brandels, from the account Bossman's imps had set up for her. Travel uptown and get someplace better — better than trying to find a soft spot under a lumpy blanket.

IT TOOK Diana a surprisingly short time to sign the rental agreement. After the first two stops, she was able to judge from the surroundings what were the going rates. She spun herself around happily in her newly acquired room. *Her* room, one she herself had picked.

It was not much. A bed with fresh linens next to a small table holding a daily ewer of water and, on the far wall, a four-drawer chest. A room with a tub, down the hall. Even a window overlooking the city street below.

For the first time in her life, Diana felt free. Her spell kept the other collectors in line. The sprites took care of all the finances. All that remained was each day to bring a few coppers to Iz — .

Diana stopped. She did not like where her thoughts were taking her.

A Question of Respect

LIONEL WAS back in Vendora's private chambers three days after the explosion had passed. There still was no word about where the treasure was being stored. He waited patiently while the queen paced back and forth in front of him. "Four able-bodied men from every fiefdom, you said, right?"

"Yes, my liege. This must be accomplished sooner rather than later."

Vendora shook her head. "You are too young to understand. My position is not set in stone. I rule by the pleasure of those who have sworn fealty to me. That keeps the peace. But the oath is not binding unconditionally. If enough lords decide my actions are too extreme, they will rebel. Pick one of their number to assume the throne."

"I have not heard of any discontent, my queen," Lionel said.

"And you would not. There could be secret meetings."

"Do you really suspect something?"

Vendora sighed. "No — but that does not mean there is no trouble brewing. The absence of a demon does not mean he does not exist."

Lionel clamped his jaw shut. He had stayed up half the night three days running, putting together a plan — trying to balance the requirement on each fief by its ability to respond. There were barely enough names on his list to scour the city in six days — what he had set as a goal. Any longer than that and the search degenerated into a game of whack-a-sprite — moving the treasury wagon around from one site to another before any inspectors came to visit.

He had expected praise for what he had done in so short a time, but the queen did not seem to have taken notice. Instead, she seemed preoccupied with phantoms — things that would not happen. He gritted his teeth.

"Things are what they are, my liege," he said.

"What about wizards?" Vendora ignored the comment. "They boast of controlling many types of demons. Ones larger than the imps and sprites we employ everywhere. Ones with special powers to, say, sniff out gold from where it has been hidden."

"I have looked into that — the very first thing I thought of. But as you know, wizards are a cantankerous lot. Babbling on about the risks they take. I found none willing to help for less than a fifty percent share of what was found."

Vendora sighed. "Very well, then. I will call for an assembly of the peerage." She stopped and looked Lionel up and down. "You are but a shadow of Brak in his prime. His mere presence snuffed out any embers of sedition before they burst into flame." She shrugged. "You are not quite up to what I need, but I guess you will have to do. The last thing I want when the peerage assembles is to suggest that one of the fiefholders should take command of the search."

'Not quite up to what I need' Lionel fumed silently as he tried not to show a reaction. How did the queen know anything about him. He felt his resolve quicken. He would show her what he could do, her, and anyone else who might wonder.

"An assembly to set up first?" Lionel asked as smoothly as he could. "How long would that take?"

"Relay mirrors work quite well. The call will go out today for an emergency congregation tomorrow." Vendora paused.

"I wonder. Perhaps your father should be the one to request help. He has endured enough years that he will not be suspected ."

"Suspected? Suspected of what?"

"Suspected of greater ambition," Vendora shook her head. "You have much to learn, scion Lionel. Going forward, be sure to have loyal swordsmen at your side at all times."

"I will do my best, my queen." Lionel bottled up the rest of his thoughts, bowed, and left the chamber.

ANOTHER DAY passed. It was evening. Lionel sank wearily into the ornate chair in the armory. The assembly had gone well. The fiefholders all seemed to understand and appreciate what was at stake. The first of the volunteer searchers were pledged to arrive the day after tomorrow by no later than dusk. They all understood that they would take their direction from him.

He looked out through the slit window of the armory that faced west. The, what was it called, watch, that Hector had given him had been flung aside. There had been no time to recall the timing imp he had discharged. His father would arrive soon to give him his performance — how he had conducted himself.

Lionel flexed his shoulders, trying to remove some of the stiffness from his back. He felt more tired than he did after a full afternoon training raw recruits. I could take a small nap right now, he thought.

He adjusted his position in his chair, scooting backwards a tiny bit, and trying to find a comfortable orientation for his neck. As he did, his eye caught circulating dust in the air drifting lazily in a beam of light — a shaft that came from the setting sun and streamed through the western window. He surveyed the length of the beam back to where it entered the wall, and then blinked in surprise.

The beam also illuminated something else, a thin, vertical rope stretched taut. Tracing it upward, Lionel saw it loop over a hook in the high ceiling and then attach to some webbing wrapped around a large stone.

With a start he pushed himself backwards, tipping over the chair. The stone crashed into the upraised legs, barely missing his head.

Lionel scrambled to his feet, as his father entered the door. "What was that," Tetris cried out, and then stopped, eyes wide at what had happened.

"Who would want to do this to me?" Lionel seethed. "I am not part of the petty taking sides the other scions pass their time with. I make a point of not being involved."

"You *are* involved, my son," Tetris said. "I came to warn you right away."

"Involved how?"

"It is obvious. You are now not only in charge of the city guard but also in command of the protection within the castle. At the moment, who else has such power within his grasp?"

"Yes, and it has already started to weigh on me. I have to keep order in the city and cater to the queen's wishes as well."

"Exactly!"

"What?"

"No better place to be. So much independent power. No one else in the kingdom has such an ability to usurp."

"Usurp? I have no thought for such a thing."

"No, I believe you do not — at least not yet. But consider. Consider how it looks. Once you are married, you will be in position to rule over not one fief, but two. On top of that, you control the city both inside and outside the castle walls. How can a new dynasty not be far behind?"

"Father, I don't want that! I want, I want — time on my

own."

"You are not listening to me, my son. From now on, above all else, make sure only those with proven loyalty come close to you. This attack will not be the only one."

Lionel wondered. Whose path was he on anyway, his own, or his father's?

⑪

Symmetries of Reality

NICHOLAS RAN his hands down the sides of the initiate's robe — *his* initiate's robe. A full week had gone by since the robbery. Still no idea where the treasure wagon had been hidden. No sudden appearances of wealth. No rumors on the street about scrip being worthless.

Although thankfully, there were no more explosions, he felt guilty about having acceded to Randolph's demand to focus on other things. Maybe the amount of Hector's loot had satisfied the master. Perhaps he would retire to one of the southern kingdoms or even to Arcadia across the great ocean. Let others handle what to do with a magician who had access to great disruptive power.

No, that was not right, Nicholas shook his head. Sooner or later, Hector would reappear. Probably no amount of wealth would satisfy him.

Randolph displayed the same focus on his passions. The goateed magician never once asked for any details about injuries or deaths from what had happened. Instead, he had wanted to know more than once what people were saying about Hector's feat.

Nicholas slapped himself on the cheek to disrupt his train of thought, but it did not distract him from where they were going. Not hard enough, he grimaced. He did so a second time, almost losing balance and scattering the notes he had prepared fluttering onto the floor.

"So, what new do you have for me?" Randolph said to Nicholas's back as if nothing unusual had happened. "What in our library have you found out about symmetries?"

"How long have you been standing there?" Nicholas asked. He felt he must have looked like a complete idiot. "Why symmetries?" he rushed to say.

"Yes, symmetries," Randolph answered, completely ignoring Nicholas's first question. "Gavarak's notes are very unclear, but I am beginning to suspect that we have been focusing on the wrong thing — the size of the enclosing container."

"But the larger the enclosure, the greater the effect, right?" Nicholas asked. "Our guild was destroyed by one of Garavak's spheres. Hector used smaller cylindrical disks to break through the treasury doors."

"Perhaps there is some size effect, but it might very well be secondary. That is where symmetries come in. Gavarak's notes are not clear, but I am beginning to suspect that the amount of power released depends on what is the shape of the ritual's target."

"Like what?"

"Ah, my initiate, indeed that is the question. You see, Garavak's ritual in itself looks to be quite ordinary. One starts by — "

"Wait! You know what the steps of his ritual are?"

"Oh, yes. Nothing remarkable about that. All magicians of any worth carefully record the steps to be taken to achieve a magical result. A simple one might be able to be remembered, but anything of worth can take thousands of discrete actions."

Nicholas's jaw dropped. "If we have the documentation of his ritual, then where is the mystery? What is so special about what Gavarak has discovered or deduced?"

"Ah, initiate, you bring back memories of when I first

donned the robe of sea-blue myself. Yes, as even a neophyte is told, magical objects are ones that have been transformed by a ritual — words and actions aimed at a chosen target. The more complex the desired result, the longer and more intricate are the ritual steps.”

“Yes, yes, I remember all of that,” Nicholas said.

“So, the mystery here is what are the characteristics of the ordinary object that is started with. What is it that is transformed into something that explodes with so much power.

“As the saying goes, ‘No one has ever figured out how to magically change a dragon’s tongue into a bottomless purse.’”

“So that is why, Garavak’s notes are so important?”

“Yes, therein lies the solution to the mystery of these great explosions. Hopefully, together we will solve it.”

Nicholas exhaled deeply. He could hardly believe what he was hearing. Evidently, he indeed was being treated as an initiate — something more than a drudge. He felt a great weight lifting from his shoulders. For the moment at least, he was conversing with someone he could relate to. Not an equal, he was no master yet, but the tightness in his neck was dissolving away. He felt his thoughts begin to soar.

“So, what now?” he asked, excitedly.

“The target object of Gavarak’s ritual has to satisfy special conditions. They have to be symmetric in some way or another. And I think that perhaps the explosion then might be quite precise. The degree of symmetry of the target object determines that. In fact, perhaps, it even might not need to be an explosion. That is what Gavarak sought to figure out.”

“And maybe there was nothing inside his sphere but air.” Nicholas was somewhat surprised at how assertive he was becoming. Conversing with a master magician on a, well, an equal footing. He looked at his initiate’s robe and took a deep breath. He was exactly the same as he was a week ago — or was he?

"An assumption, initiate." Randolph shook his head. "We do not know that for sure. An assumption that has built a barrier to our thought. Maybe Gavarak's sphere was merely a safety precaution that proved to be woefully inadequate. We do not know what he placed inside, but whatever it was must be very important."

"So, Nicholas said, "you — we, want to investigate symmetrical objects — things that look the same after we have rotated or moved them. Place them in containers like the ones Hector used and see what happens when — "

"No, my initiate, our research will not be so clumsy. No trial and error. That is Hector's way. We will study symmetries from the first fundamentals. Use my — our intellects to deduce the formulas for what a target object should be. Exactly what, so that precisely a desired amount of energy is released."

Randolph paused for a moment. "Garavak's notes about symmetries are cryptic. We need to understand them in depth. So, what have you learned so far?"

"Yes, Master. Ah, as you probably already know, there are five simple symmetrical three-dimensional shapes."

"Let me recall," Randolph said. "There is the cube and the pyramid — "

"And what the texts label as the octahedron, the dodecahedron, and the icosahedron," Nicholas finished. "Rather than experimenting with a smaller sphere, we could construct tiny target objects of these five."

"No!" Randolph almost shouted. "No experimentation! That is how Gavarak went wrong. How Hector is diddling. Yes, size is important, but I suspect not as important as *form*. To be safe, the magnitude of the energy outcome for a given symmetrical target must be *predictable* first.

Nicholas was silent for a moment, then summoned the courage to speak again. "*So, where* does the energy come from?" he blurted. Even if we can predict how big an explosion would be, don't we need to understand how it comes about?"

"What do you mean?"

"Well, I have been thinking. Alchemists deal with explosions, too. From the little I have read from the reference volumes of the craft in our vault, they think that the bonds that hold small bits of matter together, molecules they are called, can be somehow broken and the binding energy released."

Randolph shook his head. "A step at a time, initiate. First, walk me through how symmetries are described and catalogued."

AFTER HE had been dismissed by the master, Nicholas' thoughts began to wander. Randolph was right, of course, but Hector's way seemed much more straightforward — and faster. And if the container were small enough, then whatever explosion came from it probably did not matter. Surely the first step in researching an advance was to reproduce whatever had gone before.

He looked at the stack of coppers in the secret compartment in the cash tray. Obviously, the correct metal and very small. How large were the alarm disks that had broken through stout doors in the keep, anyway? A thumb's joint at the most — yes, they must be.

So, if he scraped out some of the central parts of two coins and then glued them back together ... all that remained was to exercise the ritual himself. Randolph had given him a copy of it without any hesitation. He looked at the new robe he was wearing and smiled. Even Diana was going to be proud of him.

Diana and Izzy

DIANA WAITED uncomfortably inside the tent. Nine days since the explosion and everything else in the world continued on its expected way, although not quite the same as before. Trade kept happening. No sudden spending sprees. No rumor about a wagon of gold was being hidden. Scrip was still being accepted as a medium of exchange, but now, for no obvious reason, it required six pieces of scrip vellum for five brandels of gold.

There was still some light left in the day. No one else had shown up yet. She opened and shut her hands, waiting for Izzy to return, hopefully before Intrepid and Claymore did. Just as she was about to give up hope for the day, her uncle stumbled in through the flap.

"Diana!" Izzy exclaimed. "You are here first for once, rather than the last to straggle in."

"Yes, I want to — "

"No need to offer an excuse. All of us have a bad day every once in a while. You know that. Your recent lucky streak has been long enough that having no sales in a single day does not matter. Tomorrow, you will see. You will do better. Besides, no one who replaced Saddar has even shown up yet."

"Uncle Izzy, I need to know your answer to a question very important to me."

"And what is that?" Izzy cocked his head to the side.

"First, I want you to know how grateful I am for looking after me for all these years. Without your help, I would not have survived. It is something I can never repay."

"Well, ump, about that, Diana. Since you bring it up, I guess now is as good a time as any. You are no longer a little lost waif any more. No longer a mere girl. Any man who looks at you now easily can tell. I am sure you are aware of that, right?"

"Yes, I agree. I feel — well, empowered now, more able to make my own way."

"Please don't interrupt, girl. This is not easy to say."

Izzy cleared his throat. He did not look Diana in the eye. "Surely, you have seen enough about the things that go on in the tents — throughout the entire city in fact. Am I not right?"

Diana blinked with surprise. She was totally innocent. And if this was a 'facts of life' lecture, it was coming years too late.

"Uncle Izzy, I can guess what you are talking about."

"You can? Then it is settled! How wonderful! I have already made arrangements with Macros — you know, the one who has the house you were so curious about when you were much younger. He said he will have a room ready for you in a day or two. I will get ten percent of everything you earn."

Diana's jaw dropped. This was a total surprise. No, worse than that. It was betrayal! The family bond he had professed for her all these years was merely an investment for a bigger payoff later.

"I am not going to be such a woman." Diana tried to keep her voice level and firm. "Uncle Izzy. I am — I am better than that."

"It will not be so bad, my sweet. Your daytimes will be entirely your own to spend as you wish. No more casting charms in a small sweaty tent." He kicked at Diana's pile of blankets and then frowned at the clanking that resulted. "And you would be resting on your back far more comfortably than you do now."

Diana straightened her posture. "Uncle Izzy, listen to me. I — I have decided to move out to a place of my own."

"No!" Izzy suddenly raged. "Out on your own? Totally unacceptable. Not unless you agree to give me the going share from what you earn. Ungrateful wench. For years, I sheltered you, and yet you expect to give me nothing back from having done so."

Diana felt the tightness in her chest grow. All her tender thoughts about how her uncle cared for her after her parents had been slain vanished like windswept smoke. "How could you harbor such a fate for me for all these years?"

"Life is a series of business propositions, my sweet. There is nothing else to it. Yes, I did shield you from your 'calling' until it could no longer be kept from you. Thank me for that, and now make up your mind to do as you should."

Diana ripped aside her blanket and exposed what she had collected. "Here, take all this," she spat. "Get whatever silvers you can from what you find there. I never hope to see you again." She stood and marched out of the hovel, pushing aside Intrepid and Claymore as they ducked their heads to enter.

DIANA HURRIED up into the better part of the city as fast as she could. Her legs began to cramp from the effort, but she did not care. Things were going to end this way, no matter what, she kept telling herself. It was not her fault that circumstances had so conspired against her.

She reached the inn in which she had decided to make a home for herself, her mind churning over the things she still wanted to do. Visit the market and buy a few things that would make the place — what was the phrase — lived in. Perhaps a small sketch for one of the walls. A half-dozen hangers for her frocks so their wrinkles would hang out. A matching comb and brush set to display on the small table beside her bed.

Then, tomorrow morning, give Listen Up and Pay Attention enough coins for a fortnight bender. Enough time to think through what she should do in the long run with them. Time enough for Lionel's attention to be garnered. More pep talks for Nicholas — although it might be he no longer needed them.

Diana climbed the stairs and reached up to grab the pull-string that opened her door. When she did, a wadded-up piece of vellum fell to the floor from the jamb. She reached down to get it and with curiosity smoothed it out to read the words. When she did, her heart skipped a beat. It read:

"I still know where you live. *S*"

13

A Little Experiment

NICHOLAS PUSHED away the thought about how much to pay for tonight's meals for the masters. More than a fortnight after the robbery, there still was neither general panic nor clues as to where the gold was being hidden. The only change was that now it required twelve pieces of scrip vellum in exchange for five brandels of gold.

The initiate sighed. There was no point in putting things off any longer. He reviewed the logic that had brought him to this point. It certainly was not as elegant as what a master like Randolph would come up with, but it was the best he could do. Either the ritual worked or it did not.

Gavarak's notes had made clear to him that the stronger the symmetries involved, the more explosive the results. But what was a strong symmetry as opposed to a weak one? The notes did not explicitly say.

When one thinks of symmetries, crystals immediately come to mind. Was there a particular shape that was the best to insert into the outer container?

Crystals — there were 230 different types of them! Nicholas had found out from his reading, 230 possible shapes for a crystal structure. He looked at the array he had purchased from scouring the jewelry shops in the city. Orthorhombic sulfur, hexagonal quartz, cubic galena, and tetragonal zircon. These samples were tiny and not perfect — far from it. They were small, scratched, and chipped, discards from those placed into sellable jewelry, but maybe their interiors maintained the different symmetries they represented.

What was most important was their size. They were small enough to fit inside the cavities Nicholas had carved out of the copper coin containers. If there was going to be an explosion, it would be a small one. He selected the piece of crystal-clear quartz, sealed it in the makeshift sandwich, and then backed away to the far side of the vault to begin enacting the ritual.

For the first few steps, he had nothing to say, nothing to chant. Merely sit down on a chair and after a count of seven spring up again. Next was the business of sticking his thumbs in his ears and wagging his fingers back and forth. The instructions said to do this for one-third of an hour to someone close by or else the ritual would fail. Or if no one else was present, for a full hour without pause.

Nicholas glanced at the remaining height of a clock candle flickering on the floor in front of him and impressed in his mind how it looked. Its alternate bands of white and black were quite distinct. Each one represented one hour. He waited patiently for when the flame was beginning to melt the next ring of ebon before he began the ritual he had committed to memory.

He followed exactly as he could what Gavarak had recorded. Like all rituals, there was no rhyme or reason to it. Rituals just were. Reasoned out logically from ones formulated before. The only thing constant from one to the next was the Maxim of Persistence — 'perfection is eternal.'

Nicholas had pondered about that for quite some time. If magic items last forever, did that not mean there should be no explosion at all from what Gavarak performed? Obviously, there was a basic flaw in what the magician had done. But how else were Randolph and he to figure out what was wrong without repeated testing and retesting to isolate the flaw? And once that was done, what would be the result? Something of value approaching that for a magic mirror or merely an elbow pad that never wore out?

Time slowly passed while Nicholas contemplated. Minutes slipped by and then two groups of ten. Still with his thumbs in his ears, Nicholas arched his back. It had started to get stiff. The instructions had been silent about whether he had to stand or not, and he had decided to take the choice which was the more difficult to execute. The more strenuous the journey, the greater the reward, he had reasoned.

A few moments later, his wiggling fingers also began to tire. The pointer on the left hand started to cramp. Nicholas took a deep breath and steeled himself. Gritting his teeth, he summoned the resolve to continue. A ritual broken off in mid-performance could cause consequences no one could foretell.

Two more fingers began hurting and could barely be moved. This was not fatigue, Nicholas decided. His other hand felt perfectly fine. Instead, he suddenly realized, there was something else going on, something every magician feared. Negative feedback, it was called.

The ritual was fighting back. A part of its nature was too far off-kilter. Either his timing, his precision, or the objects he had decided to use were not correct. The ritual could not go forward.

Nicholas stomped his foot with frustration and then immediately regretted he had. His leg twitched and lurched forward. He took a deep breath and tried to remain motionless but he could not. His other leg moved in front of the first. Involuntarily, he had taken a full step. Somehow, an overwhelming feeling of loss of balance swept over him. He felt he was about to fall.

His rearward leg responded as one would almost expect. It swung forward again in an effort to maintain himself upright. But it did not help. The second leg staggered to be back in front. He tried to stop moving but could not. His pace increased, each step trying vainly to get his out-of-control forward motion to end.

'Festination! That is what it must be. He had heard of it from the initiates when he had originally joined the guild in the south. What he was attempting was so wrong that however magic worked was impeding him. He had to stop thinking entirely about the ritual and instead concentrate on saving himself.

But he could not. The rapidity of his steps accelerated until he could hardly stand erect. He was out of control. He slammed into the front door and bounced back to fall on the floor.

He lay there for a moment and finally the twitching stopped. Cautiously, he put one hand on the door handle and pulled himself to standing. But as he did, the need to continue moving returned. He needed help. He needed to get his brain stop what it was doing.

His brain. His thoughts. Diana, he suddenly realized. She was the one, the one who could do something. Change his thinking. Remove the ritual thoughts. Get the feedback to stop.

Nicholas flung open the door and felt the incessant urge to shuffle forward, to regain his balance again. He lurched into the street, and as he did, he pulled the scrap of paper out of his pocket he had received a day ago. It had her new address on it. He would have to go there, but as slowly as he could.

Like a wayward tumbleweed, he careened into the street. Other wayfarers scrambled to the sides to stay out of his way. No one tried to grab Nicholas and force him to stop.

SOMEHOW, THE initiate managed to get to Diana's street. He

stomped up the stairs to her door and collapsed. His legs kept twitching as he lay on the floor.

"Nicholas, listen to me," a voice penetrated his dismay. It was Diana. She had opened her door and bent down to him. She grabbed him by his shoulders and face to face, looking him in the eye, she began chanting.

Nicholas looked back at her, into her kind, gentle face. He felt her words wash over him. Each one like a lid forcing downward on the violent thoughts frothing in his mind.

How long the two looked at each other, Nicholas could not tell. All he knew was that the longer they did, whatever was consuming him was fading away. Slowly, he calmed.

"Wait, don't stand up yet," Diana said after a few more moments. "Give yourself time to heal."

"I don't understand how this came about," Nicholas said. "I have heard about the danger of feedback but never experienced it before." He paused, "Well, but then, I do understand. I was in too much of a hurry. Do some real magic and impress Randolph about it."

He looked into her eyes and slowly shook his head. "I am such a fool. I do know that every sorcerer has only a certain number of spells they can perform in a lifetime. I used up one of yours."

"All I did was cast a simple charm," Diana said. "One that is the beginning of others more complex."

"That could be useful in a lot of ways," Nicholas said. "From time to time, everyone needs help in — well I guess one would say 'help in calming down.'"

"My mother never mentioned such a use." Diana smiled.

Nicholas shook his head one final time to clear it. "I am so lucky I have found you."

"I just was going to see Lionel," Diana said. "I, I now feel foolish that I have ventured out alone and unescorted before. But one of my — ah, associates has reported where some brandels have been appearing."

She dipped her chin as her cheeks reddened a bit. "It is a clue to where the queen's stolen treasure might be stashed. And, well, there is something else more personal I need to talk to Lionel about, too."

Nicholas barely comprehended what Diana was saying. He looked into her eyes and felt his pulse quicken again. She had not enchanted him at a deeper level, had she?, he wondered.

After a moment, he shook his head. No, that was not it. The growing feeling he felt for her was entirely his own.

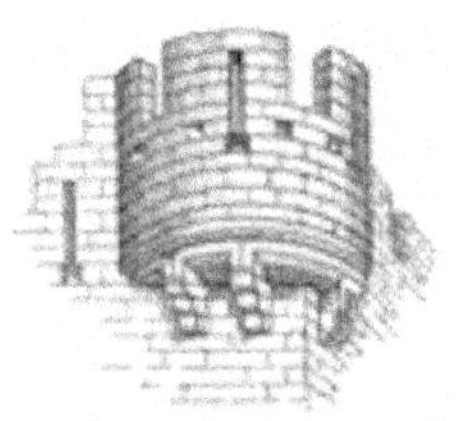

14
Searching

"I HAVE news," Diana said immediately as she and Nicholas were escorted into Lionel's office in the armory. She blinked at how the scion's appearance had changed. His eyes sagged and his shoulders slumped. It was clear he was not getting enough sleep.

"I can cast a light enchantment on you that will help," she blurted. "No side effects. Only the ability to fall into slumber once your head touches a pillow."

Lionel smiled grimly. "It is not more sleep that I need, but more waking hours instead. Is *that* something you can provide?"

"Well, yes, but I do not recommend it." Diana shook her head. "Sorcery does not repair bodies. It only alters thought. And Nicholas and I are not here for that. I have something more important to relate."

"Yet additional problems to solve," Lionel scowled. "You don't have a solution to the shortage of poultry products, do you? The queen continues to insist on at least three eggs every morning for breakfast."

"Diana has a clue on where the stolen treasury is hidden," Nicholas burst out. "She did not come here to bother you with a personal whim."

"Well, actually, there is something else — " Diana began.

Lionel managed a smile. "Excuse my manners," he said. "Responsibility is a heavy load. I am — I am glad to see you. A welcome break. What is it you have to say?"

"You have been searching in the wrong places," Diana smiled. "I have learned something from — from an associate. The gold is nowhere in Ambrosia. Instead, it lies in the summer villa of one of the outland lords from the south."

"Where precisely?"

"Near Carmela-by-the-Sea."

"Carmela!" Lionel frowned. "It couldn't be at a more worst place."

"I am told that the gold is lightly guarded," Diana said. "But as long as it has not been recovered, the value of scrip will continue to get worse."

"Being hidden in Carmela presents another concern." Lionel shook his head.

"What?" Nicholas asked.

"Carmela is too close to the border with Ethidor to the south. The boy king there, Quilson, has ambitions. Prove he is a monarch to be reckoned with. If he also learns of the gold, he might mount a raid to capture it for himself."

"Lionel, we must — "

The lordling stopped and frowned. He pointed at Nicholas. "Wait a minute. You're wearing the robe of an initiate now. How are you allowed to do that?"

"Because I am one," Nicholas said. "Master Randolph has seen fit — "

The rest of his words were cut off by a loud explosion.

"The keep, the keep!" someone shouted from outside. "It is under attack again."

"More of Hector's disks," Lionel growled. "Must be. I told everyone to be on high alert for anything new that looked suspicious. Somehow, he must have managed to camouflage them so they went unnoticed."

"How did this happen," he yelled at the messenger. "My instructions were quite clear. As soon as any brigand was spotted, I was to be informed."

"Dozens of them. Disguised as city dwellers in the queue waiting to exchange scrip for gold. Their weapons were concealed."

Lionel began buckling on his chest plate, then stopped and cast it aside. "Too much time," he growled. "Proper direction and instruction are the more important things now." He grabbed his scabbard and rushed out the door.

Lionel's minions emerged from their dormitory, strapping on their armor just as he had tried. A second explosion ripped through the air. He looked back in the direction of the portcullis. The entrance gate had shattered and lay on the ground in billowing dust.

"Stay here out of the way," he said. "I have to go out and command our defense."

DIANA LOOKED out of one of the window slits of the armory. She gasped. There were too few defenders and most were already down. The path to the keep was completely unguarded. "What should we do?" she asked. "Where can we hide?"

Nicholas was silent for a moment. He looked about the office. "No place to do so here," he said. "There!" he then pointed to a corner. "No, not hide. We can help. See the megaphone there. Use that."

"How?"

"Project one of your charms on the invaders."

"*Project* my charm. I've never tried something like that. I am not sure such a thing will work."

"We will have to find out." Nicholas positioned the sound amplifier through the window slit aimed nearest to the entrance to the keep. "Start chanting now."

Which charm to use; which one? Diana thought. Then she realized there was no time to select the best. Simple sleep, a lullaby, would have to do. "Acumen stratus eronomus…" she began.

Nicholas kept the megaphone steady as he could with one hand, placed his head firmly against the wall, and covered his exposed ear with the other. Diana's words still filtered through to him, not loud, but enticing nonetheless.

He felt the beating of his heart begin to slow. A gentle peace began to fall over him. Why was he doing this, he managed to think. Did it really matter? What concern did he have about gold stashed away in a vault far underground anyway? That was not important, not important at all. Except for jewelry, gold was quite useless. Yes, shiny and did not tarnish, but, really, who cared?

After a time that he could not measure, Nicholas became aware that Diana had stopped speaking. He looked at her and was surprised to see her slumped to the ground. Her face sagged. She rubbed her forehead as if trying to smooth the wrinkles away.

"Are you all right?" he asked in alarm.

Diana waved away his concern. "Yes, yes, the charm must have gone well enough. I hear nothing more from outside. But there were so many of them. I am surprised that projecting my words into a large area worked."

Nicholas pushed the megaphone aside and peeked out the window slit. What he saw reminded him of the toy warriors one played with as a boy. Attackers and defenders alike sprawled on the ground. A look at their faces told which were which. Most of the defenders showed the agony of impending death. The attackers wore vacant smiles on their faces. Lionel slept with the rest, his sword laying at his side. He too had survived.

And then an additional movement caught Nicholas's eye. He saw a solitary figure stride through the portcullis with his hands on his hips to survey the scene. It was Hector, silently observing what had happened! Nicholas could not tell for sure, but it looked like disbelief was on the magician's face.

In the stunning silence, more people cautiously approached the floor of the bailey — cooks and maids from the apartments in the castle wall carrying brooms and cutting board knives at the ready. Slowly, they inched forward — the last line of royal defense. Evidently, the queen still commanded respect in her own little domain regardless of what might be said elsewhere.

Hector saw them coming and bolted to the portcullis and vanished into the street, evidently frowning that he had not stolen even more.

"THANK YOU, thank you," Lionel smiled at Diana as he slumped onto the chair in his office. He shook his head from side to side in order to remove the last vestiges of her charm.

"If not for you, more lives would have been lost. And more of Vendora's treasure as well. Confidence in her rule would have suffered another blow. But because of the help of the castle staff, all of the brigands have been secured. Our own men are being well fed as they recover."

"The effects of the charm were only temporary," Diana said. "It was Nicholas's idea for what to do."

"Yes, yes, of course, the neo — initiate, too," Lionel replied. He grabbed the megaphone and moved to the slit window. "But now, a minute of silence for the slain."

When he had finished, the lordling turned his attention back to his two visitors. "Now there is more work to be done. Thanks also to you, Diana, for helping us learn where the results of the first raid are stored." He looked at her with a beaming smile. "Not one great achievement but two. You are — you are quite an accomplished woman, my lady."

Diana could not help herself from blushing. The words she was hearing were not the result of one of her charms. They couldn't be. Lionel's praise sounded so sincere. Unbidden thoughts began to surface in her mind. Was a real ladyship such an impossibility? She pondered. Perhaps — perhaps there was a chance after all.

Lionel rushed on. "Nevertheless, time is of the essence. We now know where the queen's purloined treasure has been hidden. We must seize this opportunity to attack and get it back before it is moved elsewhere."

He sighed. "But, alas, with what? Many of the fighting men in this castle were slain before the sleeping charm took effect. The cooks and maids are to be praised for their loyalty to the queen, but they will not suffice against toughened brigands."

"You asked for help from Vendora's fiefholders before," Diana offered. "The ones who helped search Ambrosia but did not find any hidden gold. And now we understand why."

"The queen is leery of dipping into that well too often."

So why not another spell? The thought rushed into Diana's mind. She felt her feelings soar even higher. "I know how to contact and, ah, control men of less savory reputations. With enchantment, a squad of followers can be directed to serve in the queen's cause."

"How many men?" Lionel asked.

"A dozen or so captains," Diana answered. "They each probably have a score of helpers each."

Lionel rubbed his chin, then frowned. "More than two hundred. A start perhaps, but I don't think that will be enough. We must overwhelm the loot defenders, not merely engage in a battle whose outcome could be in doubt. And we will have to contend somehow with Hector's magic. We need more than a few, perhaps a thousand."

Diana pondered again. What she had done with her own protection lieutenants had worked well to root out the location of the queen's stolen treasure. Perhaps she could do a repeat performance with the Bossman and all of his lieutenants. With all the city gangland enchanted, maybe that would prove sufficient.

She smiled at Lionel. "Leave it to me. I will see what I can do."

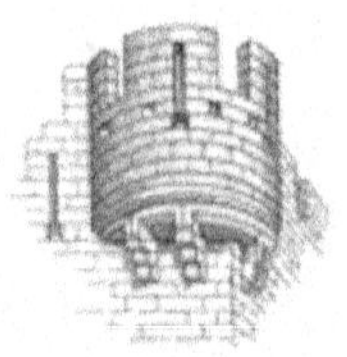

15

Diana and the Bossman

DIANA CHECKED her preparations one last time. The regularly scheduled meeting with the Bossman and his lieutenants would begin shortly. The setting was different from the one she conducted with her minions before, but the basic elements were the same — smoldering incense and a glowing fireplace to make the setting warm and comfy.

Diana wiggled in her seat next to Bossman. Eventually, he would begin to wonder why the low number of complaints in her own territory had not been replicated throughout the city. The sudden unbidden thought jarred her confidence. She squirmed and tried to cut off the alarm-inducing possibility as the other lieutenants entered. Now was not the time to have her attention going down the wrong path.

The top-ranked ones began to file in, exchanging boasts and barbs with one another. None said a word to Diana. She was not yet regarded as one of the boys. But then, that is what she wanted. The less attention paid to her, the better it would be.

Bossman entered last and plopped into his chair. "I am going to shake things up a bit this time," he said. "We are growing stale, and not everyone is paying full attention." He glanced at Diana. "Let's go clockwise. Protection first and extortion last."

Diana sucked in her breath. Her heart skipped a beat. She had not counted on this! The spell she needed to cast was not a simple lullaby to sleep. It needed encouragement from the surroundings. The time before with her protection thugs, the incense, drowsy warmth, and mind-numbing reports had served her well. After the first had droned on for a while, her chanting blended in unnoticed.

She faltered. Always being last, she had been intent on making sure her chant was correct. She did not even bother to prepare a report. It would not have been needed.

"Sweetcakes?" Bossman frowned at her hesitation. He reached out and patted her hand next to his. "It happens. Sometimes the take is good, others not so much. Go ahead and give your report." He stroked her hand again, and his stomach jiggled as he laughed. "Come on. I am not going to bite."

Diana's mind almost blanked. She did the only thing she could think of. Leaning toward Bossman, she cupped her hands around his ear and began another chant, this one like those she had used to get a few coppers from strangers on the street.

"Wait! What's going on here?" Embezzlement cried out. "No favorites! That is not the way things are supposed to work."

"The dame was a bad idea from the start," Arson said. "One gets to be the boss by consensus — but only as long as he shows the wits and judgement to do so."

Bossman slapped Diana's hands aside. He glared at her, but only for a moment. "All of you are forgetting," he bellowed to the others. "Forgetting the reason why I was able to take over in the first place." He raised one hand above his head and snapped his fingers.

The sprite near the ceiling began to glow brightly in front of a reflector as it had before. It illuminated the four armored behemoths standing there. Bossman snapped a second time, and the warriors woke up. In unison, they withdrew their swords and took a first menacing step forward. "Arson, as you were saying?" Bossman asked.

Diana stopped chanting even though she knew that nausea would follow. She slumped back into her chair. Her target was too aroused, too focused on what was happening. Her words were not having any effect.

Bossman shook his head at Diana. "You disappoint me, my dear," he said. "Yes, ambition is good. How else does the best rise to the top when the one already there starts to stumble? But too soon, far too soon." He shrugged. "And too bad. I was really looking forward to seeing how my experiment turns out."

He motioned one of the enforcers forward. "To the dungeon." Two of the nearest lieutenants sprang from their chairs, seized Diana by both her arms, and forced her erect. She stumbled, losing her balance. In a heartbeat, they dragged her away into the surrounding gloom.

"I will have to think a bit about how to deal with her." Bossman pondered for a moment. Then back to the remaining lieutenants as if nothing had happened, "Where were we? Oh, yes. Going clockwise this time. Robbery, you are up first."

LIONEL DRUMMED his fingers on his desk. He glanced at the magic clock given to him by the traitorous Hector. How long had it been? Too long. Too many hours. No lady of any refinement should be traipsing about the city looking for hulking brutes who wanted work. He should not have let her go out unescorted.

But Diana had been insistent. She would take care of things, she said. No one needed to accompany her. Lionel shook his head. He had relented — because she was so unlike all the others. The corners of a small smile formed on

Lionel's face. At least he had the good sense to have her followed.

One of his remaining guardsmen burst into Lionel's chamber. "A poor part of town," he panted. "I finally decided to race back when, after several hours, she did not reappear."

"There are many poor parts of Ambrosia," Lionel snapped. He blinked, surprised by the intensity of his feelings. "Where?"

"The worst of places. One that none of our patrols even dare to go. I was afraid for my life the entire time I waited at a discrete distance from the door."

"What door?"

"An entrance to a building with no windows, no signs at the top. Only blank walls. About a dozen visitors, but none arriving together. A tap on the entrance. Some words exchanged, and then admission. The lady was the first to go in."

Lionel scowled. His troop had been decimated by Hector's attack. His goal was to bulk up the ranks again before storming where the queen's treasure had been hidden. Risking more to rescue a single person first was folly. And yet…

"How many did you say entered?" he asked.

"I did not count," his pikeman stammered. "You never trained any of us to do things like that."

"Yes, yes. Another of my failings," Lionel snapped. "Something to be remedied in the fullness of time. But for right now, what is your best guess on how many are in the structure into which Lady Diana has disappeared?"

"I have no idea. After a couple of hours, all the men exited, one after another. I waited a while longer, but the lady did not. Ah, and to be truthful, my captain, she does not comport herself the way one expects of a lady. No posturing and nose high in disdain when she walks about."

Lionel felt taken aback. He was the one at fault, the one who did not think things through. What was his reasoning? Sending Diana into what turned out to be absolute peril. Lionel slammed his fist onto his desk. One failure to do his duty today was enough. "Assemble all the able-bodied men we have left. Today's lesson will be on conducting an assault."

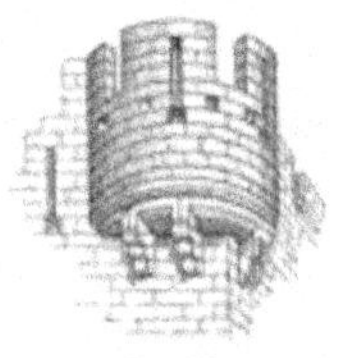

16
Rescue

LIONEL PEEKED out onto the street from the crossing alley. It was deserted. Everyone knew to stay clear of this part of the city. He looked back over his shoulder at his men. Only seven of them; all who remained after Hector's attack. The building across the street was as his pikeman had described — dull rusty brown with no windows, no signs in the middle. A blank wall with a slab door without handles.

"What is the plan, Captain?" one of Lionel's minions, Morton, whispered. "Even with a crowbar, we won't be able to pry open that door without raising an alarm from within."

"Yes, only idiots charge into an unknown lair," Lionel answered. "We will need more information first. Observe and learn."

He pulled a book out of a backpack and opened it to the page with the end of a bookmark sticking out of it.

"There are instructions for this kind of thing?" another of Lionel's men asked.

"Quiet," Lionel snapped. "The queen's vaults contain more treasures than only gold. And luckily, Bovine had cataloged them before he passed." The scion turned to the marked page and cracked the book open. "Awake," he said softly. "There is work to be done."

The bookmark seemed to wrinkle. Four tiny limbs shot

out from its sides. Eyes blinked open above a mouth not apparent a moment before. A soft but high-pitched hum filled the air.

"Lower," Lionel commanded. "We can't hear what you are saying the way you are configured now."

The mark widened, filling the page upon which it lay. The mouth expanded in scale.

"How about now?" a tiny voice was now faintly heard.

"What is that thing?" another of the troop asked.

"Quiet, I said. I will explain more later. This is an imp from the realm of demons. Not all of them have the same basic shape that we do."

"But — "

"Think of — what do the wizards call them — plasmodia in our own realm. This is much the same."

"What good is it?"

"For the last time, silence," he whispered as he turned his attention to the imp resting on the open book page. "I want you to slither into the small gap between the door and its jamb. Explore inside and return to tell me everything you observe."

"The ways of your realm are quite strange to me. What I learn may not be of any value to you."

Lionel did not answer. He looked both ways and crossed the street. He held the open book to the jamb and watched the imp ooze into the narrow crack between it and the door. Then, he returned back to his men and said, "It moves very slowly and might not be able to explore all that it finds. And at some point, it will want to rest for many days. For now, we will have to sit and wait."

AFTER SEVERAL hours, the imp reappeared and pasted itself

on the entrance door. Lionel scooped it up and returned to the other side of the street. "What is your report?" he asked.

The imp created a larger mouth again and started talking in its very-high pitched voice. "The place was mostly empty. Only six humans were there."

"Six?"

"Four were quite large. In a room by themselves, eating and drinking. They performed strange rituals with small rectangles they held in their hands and passed between one another. Each had a pile of round copper tokens that they exchanged from time to time."

"Who else?"

"Only two more. One was elder, corpulent — well all of you are that way, but this one more than most. He appeared to be in the trance-like state you fall into. Eyes closed, a loud racket from the mouth, but otherwise not moving."

"What about the last? Male or female." Lionel tried to keep his voice calm but feared the worst.

"Can't tell. But the clothing was different. No leggings that I saw. Instead, large pieces of cloth wrapping all the way around."

"What is immediately behind this door?"

"An empty passageway. Without light. All of the humans are in rooms to one side or the other."

Lionel exhaled. "You have done well — "

"I am called 'Unrelentless avenger,'" the imp said. "In your language, my friends use what translates to 'Hey, you.'"

Lionel grunted acknowledgment and returned the imp to its place in the book. He pondered for a moment and then motioned Morton forward. "You were a carpenter by trade, before you enlisted, right?"

"Preparing to become a journeyman thaumaturge, sir, but that did not work out."

"Still have your tools? Brace and bit?"

"Yes, sir."

"Return to the armory and fetch them. Use your tools to create an opening in the door that we can use. But be as quiet about it as you can."

"There is no way to avoid the noise one makes."

Lionel slapped one of the utensils he had strapped to his belt — a small atomizer filled with a yellow-orange liquid. "Squirt this ahead of where you plan to cut. But be careful about it. Alchemists call it royal water."

Morton took the atomizer and his other tools with him and crossed the street. With a brace and bit, he drilled four holes in the door that defined the corners of a large square — one big enough that a full-grown man could stoop and crawl through.

Then he aimed the atomizer along the path from one hole to the next and squirted its bulb as he went. As he did, a fuming yellow liquid began eating through the wood and softening it. Finally, with a hole saw, he cut through the plastered door. He only had to slow down when a crossing beam on the other side got in the way.

Lionel fidgeted as he waited. Was Lady Diana still unharmed? How long would it take to find out for sure?

ANOTHER HOUR passed, and Lionel and his men grew increasingly restless. Finally, Morton completed the cutting and removed the opening in the door. Lionel instructed everyone to check that their weapons were in good order, and then the troop crossed the still vacant street and ducked to enter. It was pitch black inside. Not a single candle glimmered. No one was there to oppose them.

All eight managed to enter without any loud noise. Lionel stood silent for a minute waiting for his eyes to adjust to whatever dim light there might be. There was some. A row of glowimps in a string of globes high along one wall marked a central passage farther into the building. And there were sounds as well, the voices of the cardplayers.

Lionel tiptoed down the passageway quietly as he could, cursing the noise made by his leg armor at every step. It was not loud, but in the surrounding silence, it sounded completely out of place. He reached the door behind which the game was being played and paused. What were the odds everyone could sneak past and continue searching?

The scion did not have long to ponder. The door burst open and the first of the warriors inside emerged. Lionel gasped. He was huge, a full head taller than himself or any of his crew.

"You were right, Peewee," the first fighter called over his shoulder. He opened his eyes wide to take in the feeble light. "Looks like more than one, but nobody of any challenge. Go and wake the Bossman. I can take on these by myself."

"You are outnumbered." Lionel waved his sword. "Surrender now and you will not be harmed."

The fighter threw back his head and laughed. "So be it then. I have yearned for some exercise for a long while." In a flash difficult to follow in the dimness, he withdrew his own blade and swung it in a wide arc at Lionel's chest.

The lordling spun aside. He was familiar with the maneuver from his training sessions. Despite the great height, perhaps this giant would not be such a challenge after all. He thrust his sword forward aiming directly at the behemoth's lightly guarded throat.

The giant shifted slightly to the right and dodged the blow. He laughed again. "Ah, more of a challenge than I first thought. Very well then."

Lionel pressed his attack. He cocked back his arm for another slash.

But before his blow struck home, the giant extended his other hand and grabbed Lionel's wrist.

The scion blinked at the sudden rush of pain. His hand spasmed, and he dropped his sword. The giant was not only strong but incredibly fast for one his size. Lionel winced as he thought of the expected blow he would receive on his other side.

But the stroke did not come. Instead, the giant roared much louder than before. "See this, you scum huddling behind. Watch what will now happen to your leader. In a moment you will be next."

"Circle behind him," Lionel gasped. "He can't take on all of us at once."

None of Lionel's men moved. They stood transfixed.

"Get it over with," another of the giants mumbled from behind. "I was going to win the last pot, and you are merely stalling for time."

Lionel started to feel light in his head. In the dimness, he could only make out the rough outline of the other three warriors who now formed an impenetrable barrier behind the first. He thought for an instant to grab his dagger from his belt and groped to unmount it. His hand bumped into the atomizer affixed in the next belt position — the one filled with the royal water.

It was not manly. It did not observe the accepted protocols of battle. It was not honorable, but what else could he do? As his knees began to buckle, he somehow was able to pull the atomizer from his belt and squirt some of the liquid into the giant's eyes.

The colossus roared in pain. He released his grip on Lionel and with both hands tried to clear his vision.

The other three titans lumbered to their comrade, two on one side and one on the other. But Lionel was ready. With three more well-aimed squirts, all four of the goliaths were sent stumbling back to the cardroom looking frantically for towels, paper, water, anything to wash away the sting.

Lionel did not rejoice in his victory. It was what a base coward would do, not one of the noble class. He shook his head. Something to reconcile with himself later. Instead, he flexed the fingers on his sword hand. The numbness was receding. Now there was still a rescue to be made. He directed three of his men to find the snoring fat one.

He and the rest methodically examined the rest of the building. It took more than an hour, but finally Diana's cell was located. The door was locked, but in an instance bashed into pieces. Diana lay curled into a small ball in the back corner of her cell.

Lionel gently lifted her to standing and wrapped his arms around her as she started to weep. "Hush, my lady," he said. "It is over now. You have been saved."

17

A Full Circle

LIONEL LOOKED critically at Diana as she sat up from her bed. Color had returned to her cheeks. He scowled at the memory of the other inn lodgers wagging their tongues as he had carried her up the stairs to her room. Such goings on were common place among the nobility but evidently, the lower classes had more rigorous taboos.

There was a knock on the door, and Lionel crossed the room to pull it open. Nicholas was standing there with alarm etched into his face. It had not taken long for the message to have been delivered.

Diana sat up from the bed. "I am going to be fine," she said. "Now that I can see the sun again through my window, I realize I was imprisoned only for a few hours." She frowned for a moment. "Of course, at the time, it seemed much longer. A lesson in perception that is good for one who dabbles in sorcery to know about."

"How in the world did you get involved with such thuggery?" Lionel asked. "What were you thinking?"

Diana blushed. "I don't really want to go into that now," she said. "What is important is that we still need more help if Hector's hiding place is to be stormed."

Lionel blinked. "It is not so simple, my lady. Had we delayed longer, who knows what could have hap —"

"I might have a solution to our problem," Nicholas broke in. "I was conversing with Randolph when your message arrived. Sir Lionel, the master has agreed to drop all his other research and help us."

"Why?"

Nicholas smiled. "Don't look a gift sprite in the eye," he said. "The master wants to defeat the one who is creating a bad reputation for all who ply the craft."

"Yes, that is good news," Lionel said slowly. He caressed the small goatee beginning to grow on his chin. They had been the fashion in his father's time, but now all the nobility was clean-shaven. "But in the end, it will be blade against blade that will cause Hector to taste defeat."

"It was not sword arms that defeated the recent attack on the castle," Nicholas disagreed. "Have you already forgotten? It was by Diana's sorcery that you were saved."

"Actually, it was you, Nicholas, who did the saving," Diana said. "You were the one who came up with the idea of projecting my voice with a megaphone. Without that, we surely would have failed. I am sure the lord has not forgotten. You are worthy of much of his praise."

"No, no, not me," Nicholas answered. "You are the savior, Diana. Remember, you were the one who broke me out of the cycle of my thoughts when I could not do so by myself. Without you, I would have continued to who knows where. I can see myself marching into the river until I drowned."

There was silence for a moment. "So yes, you saved me, Diana," Nicholas said. "But consider, Lionel has saved you as well."

"And you have saved Lionel." Diana completed the thought.

Lionel looked at Nicholas. Nicholas looked at Diana. Diana looked at Lionel. Simultaneously, the trio started laughing.

"I conclude that each of us has within ourselves part of the makings of a hero," Nicholas said after a moment. "But together, we have brawn, brains, and …" He looked sheepishly at Diana.

"Heart," she said. "It is the cornerstone of my craft. One cannot succeed without being able to tap into the feelings deep within others." She looked from one man to the other and smiled. "Yes, together we will figure out a way to stop Hector, and who knows, in the process, create a place for ourselves in the sagas.

"Well, perhaps only Jason, the metamagician is worthy of something like that," she continued softly. "All we can do is strive to be the best we can."

The trio was silent for a moment, letting Diana's words sink into them.

Lionel felt the disenchantment with his lot in life drain away. He looked at Nicholas, then Diana, and smiled. Yes, this was perfect. For the first time in his life, he felt a twinge of fulfillment. He was the one who saved the queen and her throne. And his reward would be the one who had struggled with him at his side. Diana, the sorceress. No wonder it had been so easy for her to enchant him when they had first met.

Diana wrinkled her brow at where her thoughts were taking her. She had already been rescued not once but twice by her knight in…how did the phrase go…by her knight in shining armor. Side by side, they would work together to save a kingdom and then join in united bliss.

Nicholas pictured himself wearing the robe of a master after Hector had been thwarted. How every magic guild in the city would open their doors to fete him for what he will have done. His victory, too, would be complete.

He looked at Lionel's smile and then Diana's as well. The initiate's thoughts suddenly clouded. Perhaps his victory would not be quite complete. He started to grimace but held his feelings in check. He recalled how she had first met him in the marketplace, and how straightforward and unassuming she had been. No ladylike airs. A woman, an extremely smart and caring one that he wanted to share time with when all this was over as well.

The knight and the lady, yes, that was the logical outcome, sure. But, to be honest with himself, Diana's heart was something he desired as well. Maybe the future was not so perfect after all. What was he going to do about that?

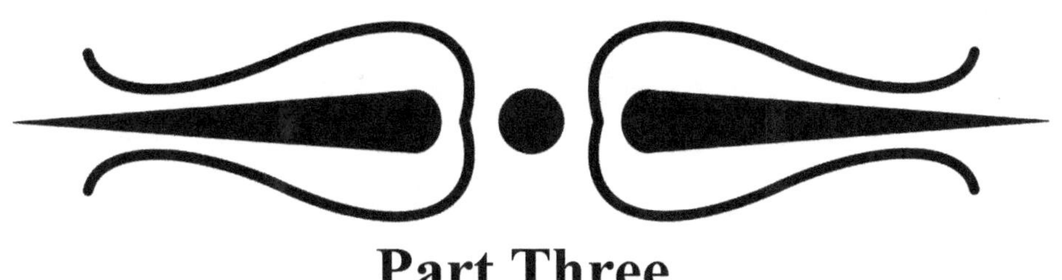

Part Three

Resolution

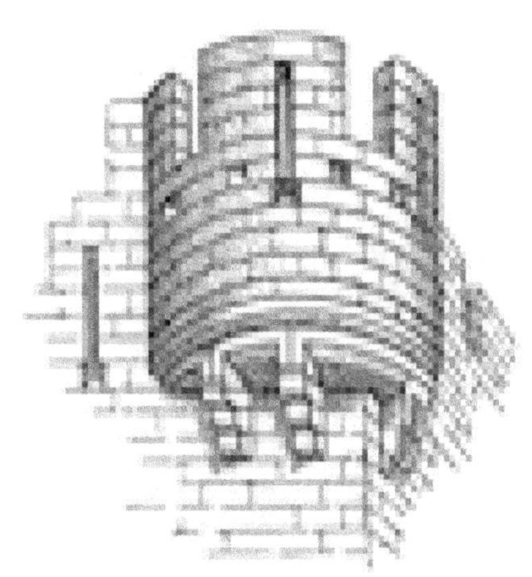

1

Randolph's Proposal

THERE WAS a knock at Diana's door. Nicholas moved to open it, but Lionel cut him off. "Caution. For all we know, it might be this Saddar character. Let me handle this."

Nicholas bristled but said nothing. So long as there was only a single version of Diana, how could things end well?

Lionel opened the door and accepted a note from a page standing there. He unfolded it and started reading quietly. Nicholas's scowl deepened. He glanced at Diana. How could she be attracted to someone who has to whisper aloud the words to himself when he reads?

When he finished, Lionel crumpled the note and tossed it aside. Another mistake, Nicholas thought. The warrior's essence was now on the thrown-away. The initiate shook his head to clear it of what he was thinking. It was wasteful to be doing so. But, if he were the better man of the two, then surely Diana would realize it. Better to prove that by focusing on the tasks lying ahead.

"It is from the queen," Lionel said. "She summons me to give her council." He looked at Nicholas critically. "It seems as if the initiate is correct. A master magician named Randolph has told her that he can remove Hector's threat before he can do more harm."

He looked at Diana. "And of course, my lady, you must accompany us. We cannot leave you alone by yourself."

THE QUEEN'S attendants had to exchange the small divans in the private reception chamber for larger ones. The smaller ones each could have accommodated two side by side, but not comfortably.

"It all comes down to the application of the correct ritual, my queen," Randolph said. "Hector's display of fireworks was child-play." He glanced at Nicholas sitting at his side. "Even an initiate could mount a presentation like those that — "

"But no true initiate would attempt such a thing," Nicholas interrupted.

"And with good reason," Randolph said. "None would have the sense to tinker with forces he did not understand."

"You claim, then, that this cognizance is what you have?" Vendora asked.

"I do indeed, my queen," Randolph said. "It is all a matter of containment. A different magic ritual all together. A power stronger than another that releases unknown forces. I have thought of what can be achieved — "

"Hector is not going to submit meekly, whatever it is that he is exploding, to be placed within confinements before he does more harm," Lionel interrupted.

"Please hear me out, my queen," Randolph said. "I realize that all this talk of rituals and mathematics, ah, strains your thoughts, but you must be patient until you hear the end of what I propose."

For a moment, there was complete silence. Randolph smiled and then continued speaking to the queen as if there were no one else present.

"All magicians are vain," he said. "I must admit, that to a slight degree, so am I. Evidently, it is part of what it takes to be a master."

"Get to the point," Lionel growled. "There is a formidable schemer at loose. The queen does not have all day to ponder the motivations of a rogue."

"The trap must be one Hector cannot resist," Randolph continued as if Lionel's words were not worth acknowledging. "A grand challenge to prove who is the greater master."

"And who would that be?" Vendora asked. She looked Randolph up and down. "I think I can guess."

"Quite so, my queen," Randolph smiled. "When it is all over, there will be no doubt who is the greater."

Lionel looked at Nicholas. "Does your schooling include listening to droning such as this?"

"We understand your distrust, Lord Lionel," the queen said before Nicholas could speak. "You do not wish to be bettered again."

"I was not the one who agreed to let Hector find out how your treasure vault was secured," Lionel said. "The business about preventing ledgers being tampered with by using little magic disks was merely a ruse." He exhaled deeply to calm himself.

"So then Master," Diana spoke up, "what is it that you propose?"

"Offer Hector a challenge," Randolph smiled. "I prepare a confinement that I state can withstand Hector's greatest forces whatever they are. He gets a single chance to prove me wrong."

"Why would he agree to something like that?" Nicholas asked.

"Well posed, initiate," Randolph said. "Of course, the stakes do matter."

"So, if Hector wins?" Lionel asked.

Randolph smiled again. "It should be worth his while. If Hector wins, then the entire content of your treasury, my queen, becomes his, not a mere single wagon load."

"I am not crazy," Vendora spat out. "Why would I ever agree to something such as that?"

"Because the temptation must be too great for Hector to resist," Randolph said. "He would not only have almost unimaginable wealth. but everyone, yes, everyone in our entire world, would agree he is the greatest mage of all."

Randolph paused. Everyone hung on his words. "But if Hector were to fail, my queen, the agreement would be that he would be subject to whatever punishment you propose." The magician shrugged. "What that would entail is secondary, really. The important thing is that he will have been bested. I, Randolph, will be the one heralded as the greatest magician in the world."

"You prattle like a drunken wizard," Vendora said. "If Hector wins, I lose everything, and all you get is a dent in your reputation."

"Believe me, my queen, were that to happen, I would end my life because of the shame." The magician's face took on a distant look for a moment. "But my reputation is too dear to let something like that happen."

"Which would do nothing at all to bring back my treasure."

"Perhaps there is a modification," Diana spoke up.

"Like what?" Nicholas asked.

"Well, the rest of the queen's treasure need not be placed at risk," Diana answered. "I gather from all this talk that gold is not the central element at all. Between magicians, it is merely one reputation against another. A single brandel could be the prize just as well."

Before anyone present could reply, the queen's secretary burst into the room. "I beg your pardon for the interruption," he said. "But I have a message from the remains of the portcullis gate. A crowd is gathering. They are all demanding gold in exchange for their scrip.”

“There always is a crowd,” Vendora shrugged. “Give them what they want.”

“It takes some time to satisfy even a single note holder,” the secretary said. “An entry must be made in the accounting books for each transaction.”

Another page entered, out of breath. “The beef provisioner refuses to unload. He demands real gold in payment, not scraps of vellum.”

“A panic,” Diana nodded. “It is starting.”

Then, a man in leather staggered into the chamber.

“Lionel, you are slacking in your duties,” Vendora said. “Wandred would never have let the security protocol get this sloppy.”

“My report is important, my liege,” the man panted. “I overwhipped three horses to get it here.”

“What?” Vendora snapped.

“It is Ethidor,” the messenger said. “The king there, Quilson, has launched an attack northward. He has announced that his troops are marching towards Carmela-by-the-Sea.”

“Ethidor,” Vendora spat. “It has been a thorn in Procolon’s side for as long as I can remember.” She glared at Lionel. “Summon your father, Tetris. We must assemble an army and punish Ethidor as quickly as we can.”

“MY QUEEN, we all knew that sooner or later, Quilson’s ambitions would become clear,” Tetris said.

“Prophecy after the fact is always easier than before,” Vendora snapped back.

“The thing is — and I speak for all the fiefholders — the thing is, this, ah, rumor, that scrip is worthless is spreading throughout all Procolon,” Tetris said. “There is growing unrest. No one wants to direct his men-at-arms to serve on a foreign adventure right now. And the fiefs have already serviced your search of Ambrosia for hidden gold."

"A search that revealed nothing," Vendora said. She breathed deeply, then spoke again.

"Then I will conscript more common men into an army. Promise them ample rewards if they serve me well."

"To convince me and the other lords will be impossible," Tetris shook his head. "Such an army needs a charismatic leader. Brak is drunk more often than he is sober. He must have a slate somewhere where he marks off how many ladies-in-waiting, he has seduced."

He looked at Lionel and smiled for a moment. "No, even you, my son would not be enough. Not that popular with most of my peers. The recent attack on him proves that."

Lionel scowled. Even his father, he thought. What kind of wastrel did everyone think he was? Hadn't he already proved his worth?

Vendora also reacted, but with much more passion. She bored into Tetris. "I am still your queen, not a puppet to do your will. I command you to do my bidding."

"This problem is your doing, Vendora, not that of the peerage." He took a deep breath and rushed on. "It is for you to prove that you still deserve to be queen."

"Out of my sight," Vendora yelled. "I will deal with you weaklings later."

Tetris blinked. Then with a perfunctory bow, he left the chamber. No one spoke. Everyone facing the queen began to shift uncomfortably on their feet.

Vendora wrinkled her head in thought. She looked Lionel up and down. "I am decided," she said. "You command what remains of my personal guard, that of the city, and the pledges sent from my fiefs to help in your city searches."

Lionel felt stunned. He did not like the way Vendora's

thoughts were going. "But I would have to recruit mercenaries," he said. "And it sounds like scrip will not suffice to pay them."

"Do you want my help or not!" Randolph roared. "A wagon full of gold, two wagons, it does not matter. Hector has the means to bring you to your knees, my queen. Do not let petty squabbles detract you from your salvation."

"Yes, I am your queen, ruler of you all," Vendora said. "My word is law, and I have decided." She looked around the room deliberately from one to the next. "Lionel, yes, dispatch yourself to the south as soon as you can. Take with you as many fighters as you can muster. Defeat Ethidor. After that, we can reconvene and decide what to do about the magician, Hector."

"I cannot believe this," Randolph stormed. "A single wagon load of gold is not important. The question is who will wear the crown after Hector attacks again. By your own devices, you have no hope of defeating him. Come begging back to me then — if you are still alive in order to do so."

The master magician swirled his robe around himself as if he, too, were wearing a cape. With majestic steps, he strode out of the chamber.

$\bigcirc\!\!\!2$

Thought Conjectures

"WAIT, MASTER, wait!" Nicholas called after Randolph as the magician trod to the portcullis exit. "Your help is needed. I know it is."

"Imbeciles," Randolph growled. "I can save the throne for a queen, and she is too dense to realize it."

"There are many things on Vendora's saucer, right now. There probably always is. Let your proposal sink in for a while. Perhaps later, she will be more receptive."

Randolph halted his rapid pace and eyed Nicholas critically. "So, initiate, what do *you* think? I assert that the meager supplies in our vault are sufficient to contain one of Hector's explosions. True or false?"

"Ah, our store of magical items is quite small, master. You know that as well as I. What can we possibly possess that will be more powerful than these explosions?"

Randolph laughed. "It is obvious, initiate, once one attacks the problem from the proper perspective. We have all that we need here in our vault.

THE PAIR arrived back at the apothecary a short time later. Again, Antron was not about. Nicholas frowned as he thought about it. How long had it been since he had even seen the elder master, let alone exchange a word with him?

"Fear not, initiate," Randolph said over his shoulder as he disappeared into his private abode. "After another of Hector's attacks, the queen will come to her senses. What I foresee will all come to pass. I have deduced what should be done. I will triumph. I will defeat Hector. And when that happens, your loyalty will be rewarded. But for now, make yourself useful. Do a little more organizing in our vault. Make sure the workmen who are going to replaster the wall will not make off with anything."

Nicholas fumed. He was sick and tired of whiling away hour after hour in the vault. He could not yet understand all that was contained in the volumes stored there, but he had sampled each and every one at least once. He *did* know more than he had when he failed his candidacy exam.

Nicholas closed his eyes for a moment. He would much rather be in Diana's company again right now. Thinking of her comforted him, relaxed him, gave wings to his thoughts. He looked about the familiar surroundings. Nothing inside the vault should have changed since the last time he looked. Although it would take almost all their remaining cash, the repairs must be made.

He shrugged and opened the vault door rather than scramble through the hole in the wall. His cot, the tray of coins, and another array of rings looked unchanged. The stack of mirror blanks standing next to the flasks of resin needed in some of the more elaborate rituals were undisturbed. Garavak's hemispheres along the far wall next to the shelves of scrolls and books were the same.

There really was nothing more he should do, Nicholas thought. But, he had to spend at least some time here before leaving. Perhaps take a peek at one of the manuals he had not had mastered yet. Maybe something that could start him thinking. How had Randolph phrased it — with a new perspective.

"Basic forces and how to use them," Nicholas mumbled as he pulled the volume from one of the shelves. He made himself comfortable and started to read.

'Everyone thinks that there are four basic forces in the world: mechanical, gravitational, electrical, and magnetic, but that is incorrect.

'Yes, gravity is one, but electricity and magnetism are merely different aspects of the same thing.

'Consider a small particle fixed nearby with what we call a positive charge on it. We approach with another that is charged negative. Even a neophyte knows that the two attract one another. The closer they are, the more powerful the attraction.

'We think of magnetism as something different. It deals with currents rather than charges. But what is a current? Is it something special or merely a charge that appears to be moving past us?

'And as for mechanical forces, levers, inclined planes, pulleys and the like. Are they not merely positive and negative charges bound together tightly in some sort of fashion?

'No. In terms of fundamentals, there are only two types of basic forces in the world: gravity and, what will be called herein, *electromagnetism*'.

Nicholas put the book down. It seemed highly speculative. And clearly it did not help him in any way for the problem of how to stop Hector's explosions.

He took a deep breath and then let it out slowly. Stop this, he told himself. No negative thoughts. Focus instead on the possible. He smiled wistfully. If Diana were here, maybe she could give him a light enchantment that would open his thoughts to new possibilities.

New possibilities? He should think outside of the backpack. Remove unconscious assumptions that were inhibiting his thoughts. Nicholas glanced again at the book.

All right, agreed there weren't four basic forces after all. But rather than fewer, maybe there were *more*!

His pulse quickened. Yes, he should keep his mind open to the possibility that there was an entirely *new* force heretofore undetected that could release energy and cause explosions. Something not suspected, something called perhaps *dark* energy.

The term had sprung into his mind. He had no idea what dark energy meant. Still, maybe, just maybe, this dark energy was something that was *everywhere*, permeating everything. Perhaps hard to detect, perhaps normally gentle with its push. And … and … the magic ritual that Gavarak stumbled across accidentally did something to it — releasing its power into our world all at once in a big explosion.

Suddenly, the puzzle became almost completely solved!

1. Uttering a specific magic ritual focused upon a particular nearby target. That was standard magic.

2. This focus enabled the release of some strange, unknown form of energy contained within the target.

3. The larger physical size of the target, the greater was the amount of energy released. Small disks shattered doors. Whatever Hector used demolished walls.

4. But in addition, there was something in particular about the target. Some characteristic it had also influencing the result.

5. Describing this characteristic was the remaining challenge.

Nicholas felt his excitement rise. His thoughts were taking

him to the heights of nonsense, but the thrill of wondering 'what if' propelled him on.

So, if the magic ritual was responsible for the release of the dark energy in the target, then there must be a way for magic also to contain it. Not mere boxes of stout metal, but boxes built of things *magical* in themselves … things like the blank slabs for magic mirrors!

Nicholas sprang up and ran to where the slabs were stacked. Each was about half the length of a human body — from head to just below the waist. He had learned that much somewhere along the way. If any shorter, you could not get a reflection from head to tail when looking into one. Each exactly twice as high as it was wide.

Still, what use would a slab be for containment? Nicholas continued to ponder. After another few moments, another rebel thought popped into his mind. He could use more than one! Almost instantly, he visualized the geometry that would work. First, two slabs lying side by side on the ground. Then four more standing erect around the border of the two. And finally, a pair more for the top and bottom.

What was such a thing called? A cube? A box? He remembered, yes, the technical term — a parallelepipped, a box of pure magic that could not be broken apart! It could contain an explosion no matter how strong it was!

Nicholas's thoughts continued to race. What would bind the blanks together? An explosion inside could escape through the seams where one blank touched another.

But then, Randolph had said he could build something to contain Hector's explosion using materials in their vault. Something else was needed.

Nicholas looked around. What could that be?

Almost instantly, he saw the answer. He ran to the flasks of resin and fixers. Mix them and they would create a bond impossible to break. They were magic, just like the blanks.

Oh, my stars! he thought. So simple! He had to tell Diana

about this! Here in the impoverished salvage from the guild was the solution to what Gavarak was trying to accomplish in the first place. Had the master known the risks, he might have used the mirror blanks, resin, and fixer himself. And their guild would not have been destroyed. And Filicia would have liv —

Nicholas's thoughts tumbled to a halt. Felicia … Diana. He suddenly felt himself become completely confused. No, not a good idea to tell Diana about this yet. Not until he had sorted out all his feelings first.

To do that, he needed a distraction. Let the back of his mind ponder while his more conscious thoughts focused on something else. He picked out another book at random, Basic Principles of Attack and Defense, and started reading more.

$$\textbf{3}$$

A Bold Step

THE NEXT day, Nicholas climbed the stairs to Diana's room in the inn. Yes, he would always remember Fiona forever, he rationalized to himself, but she was gone now, a memory fading into the past. Diana represented the possibilities of the future.

He was anxious to tell her what he had deduced. A magic box that could contain *any* explosion no matter how powerful it was. She could not help but be impressed. An initiate magician, well, really still a neophyte in skill, had figured out the means to thwart a master!

If that had occurred in one of the fictions scribes were writing about currently, Nicholas would have flung the book across the room in disgust. A totally unbelievable event. And yet, what he had come up with did happen. Why? What was different about this problem of thwarting Hector?

Nicholas stopped and considered. The difference was that Randolph had said that he had a solution. No hint about what it was other than that gear in their vault was sufficient to produce it. And somehow, knowing that single fact unlocked the barrier that one erects in their mind when pondering hard problems. It removes the burden of being the trail blazer who does not know if there is an answer or not.

The initiate shrugged. No matter. He could hardly wait to tell Diana. He knocked, did not wait for an answer, and entered. He discovered Lionel sitting on the edge of Diana's bed with his eyes closed. Diana sat in a chair beside him, slowly speaking a string of gibberish. Nicholas clamped shut his jaw before his feelings burst forth.

When Diana finished the last repetition of the charm, she glanced at Nicholas and put a finger to her lips. "He needed some encouragement," she explained softly. "Recruiting an army is not going well."

Nicholas nodded, not trusting himself to say anything he would regret later.

"Tell me, Lionel," she returned her attention to the lordling. "What is the essence of your problem?"

"Scrip!" Lionel spat with his eyes still closed. "Already, there is too much panic in the streets about it. Bad news travels fast. The queue outside the portcullis to exchange the slips of vellum for gold continues to grow rather than contract. In a single day, throughout the city, metal coins are being demanded for almost every transaction. Bartering is becoming the norm. The queen continues to accept all requests for redemption. But, to be an example for everyone to follow, she insists I continue to use scrip for mercenary recruits. The result is that as yet, I have not found a single fighter willing to sign on for the expedition south in exchange for paper."

"I understand now," Diana said. She quickly rattled off the counter charm that brought Lionel out of his trance. "My plan to get you hundreds of followers did not work," she said when he fully recovered, "But I still can produce — maybe several dozen."

"Who?" Lionel asked. "I am talking about the lowest rung of our society here. How would you ever have had any contact — "

"Well," Diana replied. "First, I guess you might call them my — bodyguards."

"Bodyguards? What do you mean? Where are they from?

Who are they?”

“I don’t know their real names. But they respond to ‘Listen Up’ and ‘Pay Attention.’”

“Hmm, they sound like they will fit my purposes perfectly, my lady. Anybody else?

The recent painful memory returned. Diana had resolved never to see her uncle again — wash him from her memory. She looked at Lionel and melted as she saw the strain in his face.

Diana steeled herself and continued. “I resolved never to visit him again, but my uncle is also associated with two warriors.”

“Four fighters and perhaps five then.” Lionel shook his head. “That will help, but far, far more are needed.”

“Finally.” Diana rushed on. “There are the ones who managed to find out that Hector’s hoard is near Carmela. A several score more altogether.”

“Who?”

“The followers of the, ah, captains I control.”

“Controlled, you mean.” Lionel shook his head.

“No, control,” Diana persisted. “Bossman probably will choose one of the captains to be my replacement.”

“So?”

“So, I failed to get all of Bossman’s criminal empire under my sway, but at least the protection captains still do what I tell them. The thugs they command, in turn, will do whatever they are told — well, mostly.”

Lionel sighed. “The remains of Wandred’s palace guards, the city patrol, and a few score of criminals more. Thank you, my lady, but that hardly will constitute an army.”

“Ethidor is not large, is it?” Nicholas burst in. “Do we have any estimate of how big of a force the king will march with — how many men he could recruit?”

“There is no way of knowing,” Lionel said. “It could be

thousands."

"Thousands?" Nicholas shook his head. "In the sagas, maybe. But a border skirmish with a minor kinglet is nothing like that. Isn't marching even a hundred men, or maybe two, over many leagues a difficult proposition?"

"Yes, yes, it is," Lionel agreed. "But victory favors number more than valor." He stood up and began to pace.

"From what I have read," Nicholas said, "a battle favors the defenders if they fight from places that are shielded. It is the attackers who must rush pell-mell over intervening open ground to face them. To overwhelm well dug-in positions, the attackers have to outnumber by at least three to one."

"How do you know all this?" Lionel scowled.

"There are more books than those about magic rituals in a guild's library." Nicholas shrugged.

Lionel furrowed his brow, mumbled indistinct numbers for some moments more, then decided. He looked at Diana. "Not a sure thing, but if we get there in time to fortify ourselves, it might be possible. Tell me, my lady, how do I contact these men you know of. Give me directions to them and some token of yours so that they will know that I am speaking in your stead."

"But I intend to go with you," Diana protested.

Lionel shook his head. "The battlefield is no place for a lady." He pointed at Nicholas. "I will let the initiate accompany me because of what he might know, but that is all."

Lionel looked at Diana wistfully for a moment, then swooped her into his arms and kissed her for a long while. "To remember me by," he said softly. "Fortune does not always favor the brave." Without saying anything more he strode out of the room.

Nicholas studied Diana. She clearly had been stunned. But then, gradually, a small smile began to creep onto her face.

This cannot go unanswered, Nicholas thundered to himself. If Lionel made known his growing feelings, then, by the laws, so shall he!

He took a step towards Diana, looked up into her face and then halted. Diana was tall. Lionel was taller still whereas he, himself … It would be so awkward. He should just say farewell and …

"No! By the most sacred of all the rituals, no," he said. "I will not give up so easily."

He looked about the room and spotted a small stepstool in the corner. Without thinking more, he raced to it and planted it at Diana's feet. Scampering upon it, he, too, took Diana into his arms. She did not resist, and let herself be pressed against him.

"The brave make their own fortune," he whispered, kissing her as gently as he could.

An Unexpected Visitor

AFTER NICHOLAS left, Diana sat down slowly on her bed, idly groping for a comb behind her back to smooth her hair. She smiled. It was a reminder of how far she had come — the newest rage, not teeth on both sides but a single row with a slim handle by which to hold it.

She sighed. What had just happened? Her fantasy about a shining knight was being fulfilled. Lionel, tall, handsome, resourceful, defender of no less than the queen. She should feel overjoyed …

Well, I guess I do, she told herself. But, there also was Nicholas to think about. She remembered how good it had felt to reason with him about what to do with the magic rings. How her problems seemed as important to him as to her. And he was brave as well. Brave enough to share about his own shortcomings and fears.

Outside some sort of ruckus was starting. Shouts about swindles with worthless paper rather than real coin. A city street was no place to be. And Lionel and Nicholas, her thoughts rushed on. Things were even worse. Now, both of them going off to put their lives in peril for —

The door to her room suddenly slammed open. Had one of her — suitors, dare she call them that — returned?

"Alone at last, my sweet. You can't imagine how much I have waited for this day."

"Saddar!" Diana exclaimed as she stood. "How did you find me?"

The brigand was in rags, with long stringy hair and an unkempt beard hanging from his face like moss on a tree. "The explosions in the keep, my pet," he said. "Collateral damage, I believe it is called. More than a dozen of us were able to get away. And talk on the street is cheap if you ask enough questions with a knife in your hand."

He shut the door behind him with a rearward kick.

"You chose a good place in which to reside, my lovely. Thick walls. A street outside bustling with noise."

Diana backed into the bed. She could retreat no farther. Saddar matched her step for step.

"Every day while I ate the slop and slept on the cold, hard stones," he continued speaking, sounded like it was something he had rehearsed over and over again. "I savored what I would do when I was again free. Word travels almost as quickly in a dungeon as it does outside. Not only did you cause my arrest, but as a final insult took over my livelihood as well.

"I am going to take my revenge on you. The city is in an uproar outside. It will only get worse. No one will care about another silly girl until long after. I am going to take you, woman. Take you now, over and over until I am tired. And then …"

Diana's heart began pounding like it never had before. Her only way to escape was blocked. She started to scream, but then stopped. No one outside would hear. She had to handle this herself.

She returned Saddar's stare with one of her own. The words came back to her in a rush. Speaking as quickly as she could, she started the first rendition of a charm.

For a moment, Saddar hesitated. He put his hands over his ears, staring at Diana in defiance. But soon after, he relaxed with a grin. "It will take some time, won't it, my pretty one?

Not a simple 'abra pocus' or whatever it is. Three times through to complete a charm."

Without further warning, Saddar reached out and, with one savage sweep, tore Diana's fancy dress away. "Of course, a pretty shift underneath, like one for the lady you pretend to be," he said. "That comes next." He readied for a second grab.

Diana stopped speaking, choking on the words. He was right. There would not be enough time. Instinctively, she reached behind herself and found the comb with the long slender handle. She grappled for only a heartbeat to grab it by its teeth.

With an unthinking whirl, she whipped the comb around herself and plunged the handle into Saddar's eye. The metal handle did not break.

The scoundrel opened his mouth to cry out, but no words came. For what seemed like a decade, the pair stood facing each other like statues in a park. Saddar finally sagged to the ground. A few last pulses of blood emerged from the wound, but then they stopped and all was still.

Diana began to pant. She looked down at Saddar and could not will the image away. To make sure of what she had done, she stooped and pushed the handle in harder, feeling it twist in his brain.

What have I done? she thought as she slowly rose again. Killed a man. He deserved it yet, but what did that make her, nonetheless? What had she done? How could she have?

Diana sagged back onto the bed. She closed her eyes trying to burn what had happened away.

"HOW DID this come about?"

Familiar words brought Diana out of her swoon sometime later. She sat up from her bed and then tried to stand, but a steadying arm gently pushed her back. There was a crowd of people in her room.

"Better to take it easy for a little while longer," a familiar voice said.

Diana focused and then exclaimed. "Listen Up," she said. "It has been a long time."

"Too long, boss," Pay Attention answered. "The 'vacation bonus' you gave us. Well, we have used nearly all of it on … vacation. What does that word mean, anyway?"

"Get to the point," Listen Up said. "Doesn't matter what it means. What is important is that we were getting bored." He pushed a thumb over his shoulder to behind his back. "Then this high-brow found us, just now. Gave us some story about glory and loot. Said it was because of your recommendation. Recommendation, whatever that means, too."

He looked at the ground and spat. "Saddar," he growled. "Good riddance."

"Yes, I am the one who pointed you out to Lord Lionel here," Diana answered. She looked down at her shift and blushed. "Just a moment," she said hurriedly as she raced to the tall cabinet that held her dresses. "He is assembling an army to go south and defend — "

"Army!" Pay Attention looked over his shoulder. "We are the best of the lot, and that is not saying very much."

"I will take on both of you with one arm tied behind my back." Diana heard another voice from before. With more effort, she waved the restraining arm away and stood.

"Claymore!" she said.

"Yes, me. Intrepid, too. Your Uncle Izzy is waiting on the street below. He didn't think that you would want to see him."

"Well, I — " Diana began.

"Time is of the essence." Lionel pushed through the crowd. "How are you feeling?" He pointed at Saddar's body on the floor. "I recognize him from the first time we met and will take care of things. The important question is, 'After this, are you well enough to travel?'"

"Travel? You said I was to stay here."

"Obviously, not now, my lady. There is rising unrest in the markets. With no city guard, looting and rioting could start. If one brigand can find you, then so can others. You will be much safer with me."

Diana cleared her thoughts as best she could. "With you — and Nicholas — right?"

"Yes, my lady. Now. We must hurry."

"Don't push her," Listen Up said. "She's the boss. Whatever she says goes."

"*I* am the boss, your commander," Lionel said. "You may as well get used to that now. Whatever I order must be followed unquestionably. Otherwise, we are not an army at all, merely a mob."

"And if we do become a mob?" Pay Attention asked.

"Disobey me at your peril," Lionel said.

Pay Attention frowned. He looked at Diana. She nodded her head, and he said no more.

"All right then," Lionel said. "It is settled. A triple destiny stands before us. For the glory of the queen, we will secure a victory in the south and rescue the gold."

"That's only two," Claymore said.

"And somehow defeat Hector so he cannot do something like this again," Nicholas added.

⑤

In Service to the Queen

NICHOLAS LEANED against a tree and panted. It was hot. It was humid. Lionel's troop of less than one hundred had started marching from Ambrosia two days ago. They had continued without letup during all the daylight hours.

"Everybody could use a little rest, Lionel," the initiate said. "None of us ever had a chance to build ourselves up for all-day trekking."

"First of all, call me 'Commander'," Lionel said. "I've told you a dozen times already. Morale is undermined if the troops think that I have favorites."

"Diana's thugs don't seem to mind what I call you. They are quiet and do whatever she tells them."

"Yes, perfect. Everyone should be that obedient."

Nicholas started to rebut, but then pushed the thought away. A good result is what mattered, not how it was achieved. "How much farther then?" he asked.

Lionel snapped his fingers. A boy no older than twelve scampered to him with a rolled-up map in his hand.

"Tomorrow evening," the lordling said after a brief examination of the vellum. "We will reach Carmela by then."

"What about Wandred's men?"

Lionel shrugged. "I don't know. But their number is small compared to what we have assembled ourselves. Perhaps they all have returned to Ambrosia while we were busy getting ready to march. We have encountered no one on our trek so far. Far more important is to learn how near are Quilson and his army."

"Don't we have three horsemen in our troop? Perhaps they can scout ahead and find out exactly how close the Ethidorians are."

"Hmmm," Lionel answered. "I will think upon that."

DIANA STRETCHED herself by the fire. It kept the evening chill away perfectly. What was the attraction of such blazes? Was it true what the wizards say? 'Inside each enticing flicker is a demon wanting to cross over into our world.'

Lionel stood to address those who had been designated squad leaders and now surrounded him. Nicholas shook his head in admiration. Somehow, the lordling had a knack for accomplishing organizational tasks, even while everyone was on the road marching.

"It has been confirmed," Lionel said. Our scouts have verified that the wagon loaded with gold is in a barn a short distance to the south of Carmela's last building. It is lightly guarded. Only a half-dozen men inside. Our very first task tomorrow will be for some of you to secure it for the queen."

"First task?" someone shouted from the ranks. "Isn't that all we came here to do?"

"As important as that is," Lionel continued as he began to strut with his arms entwined behind his back. "It is not our only objective. Quilson, the king of Ethidor, probably will be arriving from farther south almost as soon. He must be thwarted as well."

"How many warriors will he have?" someone in the surrounding circle asked.

"We don't know for sure," Lionel replied. "He may have twice as many men as do we."

"Gold is no good if you have an arrow through your gizzard," another squad leader said.

"Splitting our forces into two smaller pieces is a lamebrain idea," another shouted.

"Let's get possession of the gold and start on the road back with it now. Torches can provide whatever light we need."

"A closely followed retreat while being outnumbered never works." Nicholas stood up to speak.

"And everybody understands that we are the ones outnumbered," one of the squad leaders said.

"Yes, that is why it will be better to fight than show our backs," Nicholas answered. "We all need to understand what will be our formation of battle and why it will work."

"Sit down, initiate," Lionel said. "I am the one conducting the meeting."

Diana frowned. She did not like this bickering between the pair. It only made her feelings harder to untangle. A distraction was needed.

"Hear me," she commanded. "Look me in the eye. Listen to my words. In your mind, imagine the future you want to have."

Without waiting for any protest, Diana started the visionary enchantment. It was a standard one, used by sorcerer entertainers the world over for paying audiences. Easy enough to get through the words three times, especially when everyone was exhausted. Each listener imagined their own vision of achieving their heart's desire.

Afterward, Diana told herself, with warm comforting memories still fresh in mind, everyone would be much more willing to work together and decide what should be done.

IT WAS the early morning of the following day. Nicholas pushed aside his last reservations. He probably should not have been as vocal the previous evening in suggesting what to do. But In the end, it had been decided. Lionel and his army would stay almost entirely in one piece and confront Quilson whenever the Ethidorians appeared. Meanwhile, he, Diana, and a squad of four warriors would retrieve the stolen gold.

Nicholas pushed aside the door suspended by pullies over the barn opening. Two guards sprang alert from where they had been dozing and unsheathed their swords.

"Easy," Nicholas said. "Easy."

"Whatya want?" one of the guards demanded.

"See my robe." Nicholas tried to convey a calm he was not really feeling. "I am an itinerant initiate magician."

"So what? If you know what's good for you, you should vanish now."

"Ah, what's good for you," Nicholas answered. He hoped there was no quiver in his voice. "A worthwhile question." He held out six magic ring blanks in the palm of his hand. "I see that your beds are no better than straw on the hard ground. What you need is the means to achieve deep restful sleep."

"I told you to — "

"Yes, yes. I will be on my way in a moment. But before I go, what harm is there in trying on one of my dream rings."

"*Dream* rings?"

"Here try one. Feel the tingle. That will calm your mind. Bring good dreams for the entire night."

"Lemme see," the one nearest to Nicholas said. He grabbed one of the rings from the initiate's outstretched hands and thrust it on his finger.

The thug's eyes widened. "This guy is right!" he called out to the others. "There is something, something — "

"Something magic," Nicholas smiled as he nodded. "For

only one brandel apiece, each of you can ensure — ”

The thug grabbed the remaining rings from Nicholas's hand and offered them to his accomplices who were now wide awake.

“But, my payment,” Nicholas began.

“Your payment is your life,” the first brigand snarled. “Now, get out of here!”

“Hey,” another said. “I can't get this thing back off. It's stuck to my finger.”

“I believe that might be caused by a dab of what we magicians sometimes call supergoo,” Nicholas said.

Two of Lionel's men burst into the barn from the rear door with swords drawn. The other two appeared behind Nicholas. A couple of the men guarding the gold tried to wave their swords, but the uncomfortable feeling in their hands and the soothing thoughts buzzing in their heads made them hesitate. Meekly, they surrendered.

In the blink of an eye, the wagon of gold was secured. Minutes later, horses were hitched, and it was headed back north towards Ambrosia. Diana enchanted the driver and guards to ensure there were no second thoughts about returning the loot to the queen.

⑥

Prelude to Battle

NICHOLAS WAS tired of all the arguing. It had taken hours for Lionel to have accepted his reasoning. Their location was not perfect, but it would have to do. They were camped south of Carmela. Looking east, the ocean was only a few hundred paces away. To the west stood a bluff demarking the end of a range of small hills that disappeared into the morning gloom.

No one had had much sleep the night before. Except for Lionel and, of course, Diana, everyone had helped create a trench and berm stretching from the water's edge to the high ground. There was no way to be outflanked by Quilson's army. What they had to do was to repel its charge.

Nicholas shook his head as he looked at the sprawled men. Digging the trench and using the dirt to create the berm had been exhausting. He hoped that Quilson would be cautious enough to spend all the daylight hours today with reconnoitering rather than attacking.

It was this last part that Nicholas could not drive into Lionel's skull. The lordling was emphatic that the two forces should meet on the plain. The side desiring victory most would emerge as the winner. That was the way recorded in the sagas.

A trumpet fanfare broke Nicholas out of his reverie. Quilson had arrived.

Nicholas scrambled to look out over the berm. There was

no mistaking the king's location. In the center of the field, he stood in a light chariot pulled by a single horse and holding what looked like a compound bow. Next to him was the driver, reins in one hand and a shield in the other. The chariot wheels were of the latest design, spoked instead of solid in order to lessen the load propelled over the ground. It was pulled by a horse covered with a cloth over thick padding — barded for protection.

On either side of the chariot were arrayed Quilson's troops. Nicholas smiled. It was as he had hoped. Rather than cluster together in one place to penetrate the defenses, warriors on foot were spread into a row matching the length of Lionel's own. Nicholas counted. They were outnumbered two to one.

He blinked. Someone else was near the king. It was a wizard! Yes, the flame emblems on the robe made it clear. The man was old. He had once been tall but now could not stand straight. At his side, on a wheeled stand a massive bird rested. It looked like a condor.

Wizards dealt with demons, creatures from another realm. Everybody knew that. But maybe the skills one needed for dominance were similar to those employed for ordinary animals — far less risky than challenging beings of great power.

Lionel hopped up onto the berm. "Nicholas, and you there — what is your name again?"

"Claymore," the giant said.

"The two of you will be my escort," Lionel said. He wore a coat of mail over his chest and a flared helmet on his head. "Let's see what this kinglet has to say."

"Wait," Nicholas shouted, but it was too late. He sighed and joined the other two scrambling out onto the field.

Quilson motioned to his driver, and the chariot wheeled to meet the trio at middle ground. The wizard lumbered forward, pulling the stand by a rope and trying to keep up.

"Well met," Quilson said when the two groups faced one another. "I hope I am in conversation with a man of reason. There is no need to shed any blood over this at all."

"I will not surrender the gold," Lionel said. "We will defend it to the death."

"Yes, yes, duly noted," Quilson answered. "Of course, you are brave. All your men are brave. Et cetera, et cetera." He waved his arm at the berm and then the condor. "But with my eye in the sky, I have counted the heads you have, just as easily as you can estimate the number with me. Face it. You are outmanned. Back away, and let us have the gold, and then all of you will manage to live."

"No," Lionel said. He turned away and started back to the berm.

Quilson nodded to the wizard, and the great bird took wing. Nicholas noticed that at the last second the master had thrust a fairly large-sized rock into the bird's claws. Everyone watched the majestic climb of the condor into the sky — everyone but Lionel.

"Now," Quilson commanded the wizard. The old man cupped his hands around his mouth and shouted something into the sky.

The rock hurled earthward. It was well-targeted. It hit Lionel squarely on the top of his helmet. The lordling immediately fell to the ground, unconscious.

"You there, the one with the initiate's robe. Perhaps you have more sense. Convince those around you of the futility of your situation."

Nicholas did not answer. Claymore picked up Lionel's unmoving body and slung it over his shoulder like a large sack of potatoes. "Come on," the giant rumbled, "before any more surprises are placed on us."

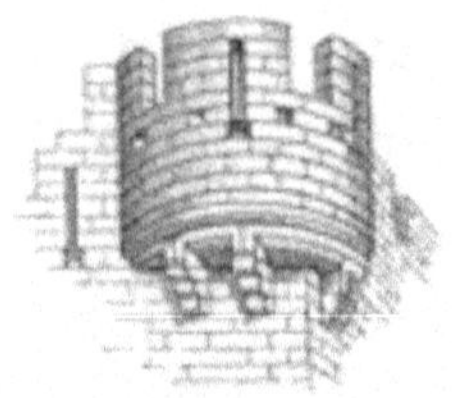

7
The Spoils of War

"LET ME up, let me up." Lionel strained against Claymore's grip to hold him steady as he awoke in the trench behind the berm. Diana stroked his cheek and Nicholas huddled close. There was yet no movement by either of the two small armies.

"Patience, my — my love. Lie still. It is too soon to move." Diana blinked at what she had just said. Was that really true? Why did she say that? Did she really mean it, or was it merely what was expected in the sagas?

"We must attack," Lionel said weakly. "Down the slope in a line. We have the greater valor. We will prevail. I know we will."

"No, no," Nicholas shook his head. "Don't you remember a word that I have told you?"

Before anyone could respond, one of Quilson's trumpets sounded. With a ragged hurrah, the king's warriors began jogging across the field.

"Over the berm. Meet them," Lionel said weekly. "Be true to our worth."

Nicholas stiffened himself. He could not merely remain standing idly by. He pushed Lionel back down onto the hastily erected cot. "Only to the top of the berm," he called out. "Only that far. Let them have to struggle to reach you while you smite at them from above."

Some of the squads started to follow Lionel's original command. Others held back as Nicholas directed. In a few heartbeats, Quilson's men covered the distance to the berm and began to ascend all along its length.

They were met with the sound of swinging swords clinking against shirts of mail. Along most of the dirt wall, the surge stumbled and then stopped. Launching offensive blows while trying to guard against the swipes aimed at them from above was difficult. Most of Lionel's men squatted down on their knees, swatting aside upthrusts that barely imperiled them. The air rang with the curses of men and the high-pitch noise of metal against metal.

AS THE battle raged, in ones and twos, men staggered back to where the makeshift triage site had been set up at the trench's center-rear. Diana huddled next to the alchemist there who administered sweetbalm to the most grievously wounded.

"That was the last of it," he whispered to her. "I will have to brew up more."

Diana looked at the man sagging to his knees before her, blood pulsing from a deep cut to his scalp. "How long will that take?" she asked.

"Probably too long," the alchemist replied. "What is important is the will to live. Those who do not possess it, those in more pain than they can bear will expire before they can be helped."

Diana looked into the pleading eyes of the man collapsing at her feet. "I can do something about that," she said. Immediately, a charm that lulled one to sleep began rolling off her lips.

AS IF he too had been enchanted by Diana, Nicholas felt the outside world fade away. He had read about this being described in the sagas many times. In battle, time stopped. There was no tomorrow, only today, only right now. Every sense focused on what was immediately happening. No thoughts of wondering if one would survive the day.

After who knew how much time, Nicholas managed to look about. He let out his breath. His plan was working as he had visualized! Perhaps the mental exercises for a neophyte to picture how rituals were to unfold had other benefits as well.

He glanced to one side and then the other, then sucked in his breath. The results were not the same down the entire line. In two places to the left and one on the right, despite everything, Quilson's attackers had managed to pierce the defense and jump down into the ditch.

"Reserves," Nicholas shouted. "Ganfold, to the right. Artimis, your squad to the left. Engage them. Protect our rear."

"You two there." Lionel propped himself up on an elbow and looked about. "Do as the initiate commands. Aid those defending our backside."

"We are," Listen Up responded. "Pay Attention and I are making sure no one will get close to our boss."

Lionel whirled his head from one side to the other. "Yes. Yes, defend my lady. No, wait. To the left. You must obey my command." He grabbed his face in his hands and slumped back onto the cot where he lay.

Then, like a balloon suddenly releasing the last of its imprisoned air, the attackers backed down the berm's slope. Those who had reached the ditch and still remained alive scrambled to follow. Quilson railed at them from his chariot as they streamed past him, but no one gave him notice.

Several spat on the king as they hurried by. The attack had failed, and the cost expended had been too dear. Quilson was a man whom they would no longer follow.

After a few moments more, the king flung his helmet to the turf and directed his driver to turn his chariot around to slink back with the others to home.

"Too young," Nicholas mused as he watched. 'Et cetera, et cetera' indeed. Not enough gravitas to be compelling. Quilson had much to learn. A battle is settled after only a single assault only rarely. And somehow, a true leader would rally his troops to try again.

A FEW lookouts remained watching from the berm, but most of Lionel's forces were camped slightly north, relaxing and swapping stories of individual acts of daring-do. Nicholas felt himself relax as well, savoring the moment. There were few tales of battling initiate magicians in the sagas.

"Yes, yes," Lionel waved away any help and stood to face the troops. "The queen will honor her word. I am sure of it.

He turned and smiled at Claymore. "But do not dwell on that. There are some who have performed above and beyond. And this giant of a man saved me from being captured before the battle began. Double share for you, my warrior." He paused, looked around the assemblage and then frowned. "I, I do not recall. Who was it that brought this man to aid our cause?"

"That is me, your honorance," Izzy said. "I am the one who made both him and Intrepid, here, volunteer to aid in your cause."

"Did you engage yourself with the enemy as well?" Lionel asked.

"Well, you see, it's like this, your honorance," Izzy began. "My leg has not been steady this last few — "

Lionel frowned and glanced back at Claymore. "You both seem familiar," he said as his face clouded momentarily. "But no matter. All is well that ends well. What is your name?"

"Ah, my given name is Izzeance — "

"Kneel Izzeance — someone hand me a sword."

Izzy did as he was told, and Lionel tapped him on both shoulders with the offered blade. "By the authority granted to me by the queen while I am at war," Lionel said, "I dub thee *Sir* Izzeance, knight of Procolon."

Diana was aghast. Her uncle! She knew him far too well. Was there no honor in how the world worked? She looked at Lionel to protest, then halted by what she saw.

"You still are not quite well," she said. "Perhaps you should sit back down."

"One more thing," Lionel replied as he sagged to one knee. "Battle teaches how fleeting is life. It must be embraced as much as it can — and without delay while there is still chance. Seize the evening before it is gone." He took a deep breath and took Diana's hand in his. "My lady," he said. "Will you marry me?"

Nicholas's eyes widened. He gulped for breath. A stunned silence filled the air.

All eyes turned on Diana. For a long moment, she did not speak. *Wasn't this exactly what I have dreamt about all along?* she asked herself — a lady, a lady of the court, and not just one of many, but married to one who, no doubt, would be well-honored by the queen. But what should she say?

The silence seemed to stretch for a decade as Diana dithered. Yes, on the one hand she would be getting what she most desired. She could somehow slip out of her role collecting coins from those the least able to pay.

She glanced for a second at Nicholas, then turned away. Finally, she answered quietly, "Yes."

8

An Agreement

NICHOLAS PLODDED along with the troops returning to Ambrosia. Lionel no longer had any need for any of his council, and it was too painful to watch Diana ride on a pony next to the lordling, smiling at him as they rode.

Those around the neophyte were boisterous, shouting to outbrag one another about what they would do with their service reward from the queen. Nicholas felt none of that. The victory was ashes in his mouth. He could not join in.

He had not truly realized how much Diana had come to mean to him. They had only known each other for, what, merely days? But, now it was obvious. Nothing to do with the enchantments of sorcery, but the reality of life. And she was gone to him. Not everyone's tale ended up happily in the sagas.

The troops marching in front of Nicholas suddenly parted. A mounted groom led a pony through the gap. On the second horse was Diana! She had come to see him.

Diana dismounted and handed her reins to the groom. "I will walk a while," she said. "But please stay close by."

Nicholas restrained his impulse to run and hug her. "Lady Diana," he said thickly. "Er, congratulations to the one soon to be the baroness of — I forget what Lionel's fief is called."

"He is not the thane yet," Diana laughed. "And as I recall, his father still looks to have many years in him. But in any case, do not be so formal, Nicholas. I will always be Diana to you. Always, your friend. No, more than that. Think of me as a — as a cousin."

"When we embraced back in Ambrosia," Nicholas said, "I, I did not mean it like one with a cousin."

Diana lowered her eyes. "I know," she said softly. "And I must admit that what I felt was — "

"Was what?"

"Well, was unexpected." Diana looked back at Nicholas. "On another existence or perhaps on another world. But this is the one we are in and — "

"Never mind the 'dear Johnathan' words," Nicholas snapped. "Hector is still at large. Still a menace to be — "

"Please understand, Nicholas," Diana interrupted. "All my life I have yearned to leave the squalor in which I lived. A lumpy bedroll. Sometimes two days without a meal. Like many of the others in the tents, I dreamed the happy ending to the saga. Wealth to spend on extravagant things — gowns, jewelry. Each set new for the next royal ball. A handsome lord who did not deny my every wish. I — "

"Lord Lionel has given the order." Someone else broke into the ranks of the marching men. "There is word from the queen. Now, we must quick-march. No longer a leisurely stroll back to Ambrosia. Hector has been heard from again. He has issued an ultimatum. What he had done so far was merely an illustration of the power he commands. The rogue magician has demanded Vendora *abdicate* in his favor or face the full fury of what he can unleash."

THE REST of the return trip was a blur to Nicholas. His thoughts tumbled back and forth. Every one of Diana's words seemed permanently lodged in his mind. He strained to find a flaw as he played her logic over and over again, but it was as tight as any ritual's proof. Like a fool, he had aspired too high, and must live now with the results until they faded away.

The next day, numbly, he followed Lionel and Diana into the queen's chambers again. Lionel nodded briefly at his father, Tetris. Randolph, the master magician was already there — and Hector as well!

"As queen," Vendora said to Hector, "At this very instant, I could turn you over to Lord Lionel so he could thrust you into the dungeon."

"But, as I have explained, you dare not," Hector replied.

"You are bluffing," Vendora shot back.

"No, I am not. As you well know, Wandred's men are still at large. I have scattered them throughout all Procolon." Hector paused for a moment and smiled. "More importantly, I have taught them all how to perform the ritual that explodes the — bombs. Yes, bombs I have named them. If a single day goes by and they have not heard from me by messenger sprite. If even a single hair on my head is ever harmed, you will have chaos throughout the land, explosions everywhere. I — "

"This concerns all fiefholders, my queen," Lord Tetris interrupted. "Things are bad enough with having to convince our freemen to reap this falls harvest in exchange for paper instead of coin. I don't know for certain they will agree to that. There could be an uprising that we could not put back down." He pointed at Hector. "We must come to some sort of agreement with this man."

"What is it you want?" Vendora asked with the hint of command that came with being queen.

"I have decided you will not need to abdicate," Hector responded. "I merely shall be your *regent* — the one who actually rules all Procolon."

"What? Regent!" Vendora's eyes widened. "Absolutely not. I am still of sound mind."

"Why?" Tetris asked.

"Simple enough," Hector answered. "I have become tired of pretending. Pretending that eating the poorest cuts of meat and sleeping on a lumpy cot in an abandoned apothecary is the proper life for a *master* magician in a real, functioning guild. I have talent, and I deserve more because of it."

"Now that the missing gold is back, one would think the scrip redemption lines will shrink shorter," Lionel said. "But instead, they still are growing."

"Quiet my son," Tetris said. "Let me ponder this for a moment. Let me confer with the other lords who happen to be in Ambrosia at this time. I suggest that a short recess is in order."

SEVERAL HOURS later, everyone reassembled. Lord Tetris was the first to speak.

"Perhaps there *is* room for compromise here," he said. He turned to look at Vendora, dipping his head for a moment in respect.

"Age is the ultimate victor of us all, my queen," he began slowly. "Surely, that cannot be denied."

"I am perfectly fit," Vendora scowled. "You know that well."

"Yes, yes, all the fiefholders agree to that," Tetris responded. "But we must do more than live only day to day. Crises will occur. Planning ahead is something that must be done."

He paused for a moment. "So, to experience a regency — it would be temporary of course — is something that the other lords I have talked to have agreed."

Vendora's eyes widened in surprise, but only for a moment. "You will *not* do this. You cannot. I forbid it." She stared at Tetris as she scowled. "There should be no reason to remind you that I am your *queen*."

"What then are we to do?" Tetris asked.

"My offer still stands," Randolph spoke up. "Hector builds whatever he wants, as large as he desires. I encase it in a box that totally contains whatever happens inside."

He glanced at Diana. "We make the bet as suggested by the lady here. If Hector wins, he assumes his regency. If instead, I am the victor, he is confined in your dungeons, and you can do with him as you wish. For me, the single brandel is payment enough when I win."

Nicholas remembered his insight about using the mirror slabs to create the confinement. Magically unbreakable. "Perfection is eternal," he blurted. "Master Randolph would win such a contest. There can be no doubt about it."

Vendora eyed Nicholas' robe. "A bold statement from one so lowly placed." She could barely contain her rage as she stared back at Tetris. "Are your ears filled with wax? As I have said, I rule over you all. Every one of you has sworn allegiance to me. Rid your thoughts of such silliness now before I reconsider how Procolon's taxes are distributed."

Before anyone else could speak, a sharp roar like that from nearby thunder rocked the chamber. Mortar smoothed over the castle wall cracked and fell to the floor. A second blast followed the first and then another, each louder than the one before.

One of Vendora's pages ran into the room. "My queen," he shouted. "The curtain wall on the west of your castle. It has been pierced."

Hector grinned. "Merely a taste of what is to happen if you do not agree to my demand."

"Are we not defending the opening so that brigands cannot enter?" Vendora answered. "Lord Lionel, you are dismissed so that you can command your men."

"We have no other choice!" Randolph almost yelled. His face distorted into a frantic panic. "Hector *must* agree to accept my challenge. I admit we do not understand exactly what is the force that he is unleashing. Maybe it is from some other realm than ours. But in any case, the basic law of magic will protect us. After all, we cannot do better than perfection."

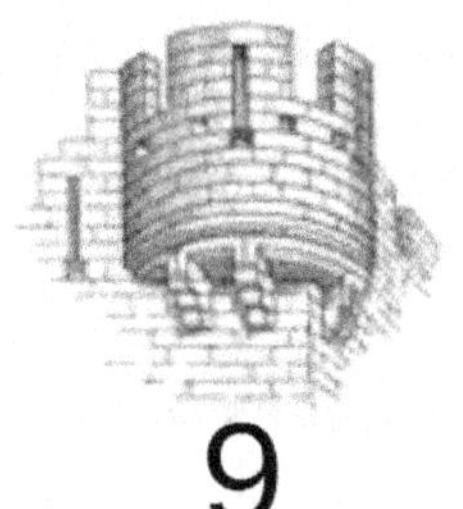

9

Rules of Engagement

AFTER A short break for Lionel to assess the damage and organize the digging for survivors, the group assembled again.

"With magic, there always is the matter of the *ritual* to be performed," Randolph said, ignoring the report of the numbers killed or maimed by the curtain wall collapse. He raised his voice as if he were lecturing a new crop of neophytes. "Magic does not happen on its own accord. A magical object of sufficient potency needs appropriate words or actions before it is activated — do what it is designed for. If one looks into a magic mirror without saying the correct litany, all you will see is your reflection."

"Magic rings don't work that way." Lionel held up his hand. "This gift from my betrothed tingles *all* the time."

"And that is the complete total of what it does," Randolph continued. "Additional ritual steps must be performed on it before it has any real use."

"I am not here for a beginner's lesson," Vendora said. "We are wasting time." She turned to Lionel. "Seize the villain now. My agreement for safe passage is no longer valid. It will not take much for my torturers to get from him how and what he communicates to his henchmen."

Lionel pushed himself forward from the others.

"Not so fast, my son," Tetris said. "We cannot be sure if you will act quickly enough. We must ponder this first."

"Approach me." Hector shrugged. "Do you all think I am an idiot? Come on, big man, approach me now."

Lionel hesitated for a heartbeat, then moved towards Hector purposefully. He almost reached him, but then halted. "There is some sort of a barrier, although I do not see one. I can draw no closer."

"Exactly," Hector said. "Algernon's cloak, it is called. Now, since all that has been settled, let us waste no more time and agree that I am to become regent of Procolon."

"*I* can stop him," Randolph insisted. "All magic can be thwarted, if one knows how."

"As wizards say," Hector replied, "The devil imp is in the details. Tell us all what you would do."

"I have spoken of this before," Randolph said. "A contest between the two of us. If Hector wins, then, yes, he does become regent of the realm." He paused for a moment and then raised his voice. "But if *I* win, then you surrender yourself to the queen, and *I* will be the one who receives all the accolades and rewards."

"Why would I agree to such a thing?" Hector asked.

"Are you afraid of what the outcome will be?"

"Of course not. I am the greater of the two of us."

"Words are valuable to a sorcerer. But they are cheap for a magician."

Hector sighed. "What is it then you propose? What will be your test? Determine who can create a sticky-pad the quickest?"

"No, it must be something bigger," Randolph said. "Something grander. Something symbolic so that there is no doubt who is the better magician."

"We will use the queen's heralds," Tetris said. "They can

get the results broadcast.”

“Words are slippery things. They are ignored or soon forgotten.” Randolph shook his head.

“*What* then?” Lionel asked.

Randolph’s brow unfurled and his face relaxed in peace. “Put one of your explosives, Hector, in — say, the first floor of the keep, a powerful one. State that you will detonate it at the end of one day — a full orbit of the sun.”

“Yes, and?”

“If the keep still stands after a day, then you submit to Vendora to do with you what she will?”

“And if it does not,” Hector said then as Lord Tetragon, or whatever he is call — ”

“Wait a moment!” Vendora shouted. “I refuse to be any party of this. An explosion in the keep might bring down the entire tower. The unrest is disruptive now. Think about how bad it would be if another blast did happen and no gold at all could be retrieved from the vault until after the rubble was cleaned away.”

“It will not happen.” Randolph shook his head. “I *guarantee* it. Hector will not be able to bring down the tower.”

“Hmm,” Tetris said. “There *is* a symbolic significance in what this Randolph has proposed. The keep still standing strong guarding the treasury — ”

“Hector will continue blowing things up until he is stopped,” Randolph said.

All eyes turned back to Vendora, expecting her to speak again. The queen’s brow furrowed while she spent a long time in thought.

Finally, she stared at Tetris. “If this manipulator of the arts is defeated, then there will be no more talk of regency, correct? I will still be your unfettered queen?”

Tetris sunk to one knee and bowed. “Of course, my liege.

Things would continue as they have before."

Everyone remained silent while Vendora pondered.

"You there, initiate," the queen finally said. "You know both of these magicians, right?"

"Ah, I do," Nicholas answered.

"Which side then would you choose?"

Nicholas felt the weight of the world seem to fall on his shoulders. He thought again of how a mirror blank construction would contain an explosion no matter how strong it was. It was so simple a design, wasn't it? Their guild had more than enough mirror blanks and plenty of resin and fixer as well. He took a big breath. "I would choose Master Randolph's proposal," he said at last.

Vendora's face hardened decisively. "So be it." She looked at everyone in the room, one by one and then pointed at Randolph. "I have decided that the contest will be as the one here proposed."

NICHOLAS WIPED the sweat from his forehead. There were more mirror blanks to load onto the rented cart than he had realized. And, as the sagas repeatedly reminded the reader, "Time *always* is of the essence." At noon tomorrow, Hector said he would detonate his explosive inside the keep, no matter if Randolph were ready or not.

"What are you doing?"

Randolph suddenly emerged from his room at the apothecary and saw what Nicholas was laboring with. For a moment, the magician breathed deeply, then calmed down. "Ah, yes, the cart *is* a good idea, initiate," the master said after a moment. "I can ride to the castle in a more befitting style rather than walk. But the only thing to carry is the little bell that I told you about. There is no need for mirror blanks. They will be useless."

Nicholas blinked. "Useless? But without the blanks, how can we — "

"Too difficult to explain now," Randolph said. "Later, after I have won, I will walk you through the details of the ritual I have deduced. As you might guess, it is a complex one. Spend your time now acquiring a seat for me in the cart. One benefiting my status. And get some bunting to drape on the sides that better disguise the crude workmanship." He smiled. "Think, initiate. By this time tomorrow, I will be famous throughout the entire world."

Randolph turned and walked back towards his room.

"Remember, initiate, a chair and decorative bunting," he said over his shoulder. "And, oh, I almost forgot, a small padded box for the bell to be used in my ritual. Let me know when you have obtained them all. For now, I must rehearse my words for when I am acclaimed."

Could it be? Nicholas thought after Randolph was gone. Was there more than one way to squelch Hector's explosions? He shrugged. Of course. There probably could be more than one. Randolph must have devised several. It was a nursery tale to assume that using mirror blanks and magic glue could also work. Certainly, containing the explosions was not something a mere initiate, well, neophyte really, could come up with.

Nicholas began pacing in a small circle. Why had he not spoken up and at least presented his idea about the mirror blanks? Without believing in himself, how would he ever become a master. He shook his head. For now, there was no sense in loading the cart with mirror blanks. Instead, he should go on the errand as Randolph had directed.

DIANA LOOKED at each of the five women sitting at the table with her. She was rueful that she had been shunted aside from what had to be of the utmost importance — affairs of state. Instead, she was expected to concentrate on the proper behavior of a true lady. There were rumors about some sort of contest between magicians, but as a woman, evidently, she would not learn of any of the details.

One was to carry on the same, no matter what. In imitation of the others, she carefully extended the little finger from her hand holding a dainty cup. "No, it all happened quite suddenly," she said as she tried to smile. "I, I appreciate you inviting me to a — a *tea*, you said it is called. A tea in the queen's afternoon alcove."

"Don't be so modest, my dear, one of the ladies said. "It does not become you. You have broken the heart of all our eligible daughters."

"Although, it means that becoming the heir apparent of the Alamain fief is no longer a possibility," another said. "Lionel will certainly inherit Talusan when his father dies. The lord of Alamain has no sons. Marrying the eldest daughter, no matter how young she is would make him perhaps the strongest lord in all of Procolon. I am surprised Lionel could make such a strategic mistake."

"Now, now, ladies," a third added. "Let us not judge the lordling too severely." She looked at Diana for a moment, then shrugged. "This could be no more than a fling. After the initial lust is satisfied, perhaps an annulment because no child is produced, and then everything returns to an expected path."

"I am *not* pregnant!" Diana slammed down her cup, sloshing its contents. She scowled because she could not conceal the blush starting to form on her cheeks. "We have not even — "

She slammed her mouth shut. Lionel had warned her how unwelcoming the other ladies of the Procolon aristocracy would be. Bloodlines defined an exclusive institution. No outsiders should apply to join.

"Well, give her a *little* credit." the first lady shrugged.

"She has accomplished what no one else at the court has been able to do."

"There is more to victory than winning the first battle," the fourth spoke up. "And I think this one is being deliberate with her attitude. Look at her. Putting us all on notice. Tossing down the gauntlet, as the men say. That it is time for a change. See what she is wearing? Her frock is three years old if it is a day."

Diana took a deep breath. The words of her teamates were malicious, but she was not going to be cowed this way.

"No, no," she protested. "I — "

"Ah, perfect." Lionel burst into the room. "One of the groomsmen said you would be here, my sweet." He bent down and kissed Diana on the cheek and then turned to address the others. "I fully understand that we are steeped in tradition. Something stolen, something green, a brandel in the shoe — all that sort of thing, but my bride-to-be is special. Whatever she desires for the wedding, then so shall it be."

"Well, Lionel dear," Diana began. "I certainly want to tap into the wisdom of traditions the wives of the other lords can give me. Information I need in very large doses. I — "

"Remember that now you truly are a lady." He frowned at the other women, one by one. "Whatever she desires. As does *any* lady of the royal court with all the privileges that imply."

He paused for a moment. "Oh, yes. The reason I have come. I wanted you to hear this from me directly first."

"What?"

"Two of the warriors that you recruited — "

"Listen Up and Pay Attention?"

"Yes, those two." Lionel shrugged. "I cannot tolerate their continued insubordination. Their stay in the dungeon for a spell should cure them of their incorrect thinking."

Lionel kissed Diana on the cheek a second time and then hurried out of the room.

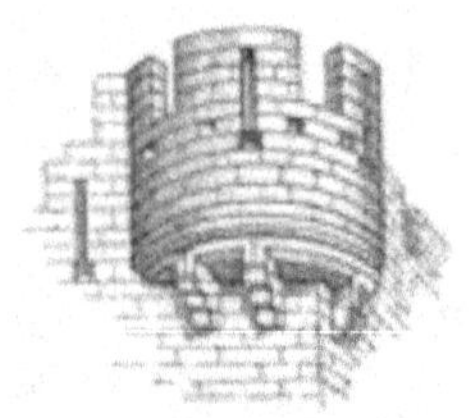

10

A Revelation

LIONEL WATCHED Hector closely as the magician's henchmen pulled a tarp-covered wagon to a stop at the entrance to the keep. They had appeared precisely at the agreed-upon time. The lordling looked about. The sun was not yet noon high but still blazingly hot.

If he craned his neck sufficiently to the left, Lionel could see Vendora's parasol that did little to block the light and heat from her fair complexion. She sat on her traveling throne placed in a clearing beyond the gaping hole in the castle wall caused by Hector's last explosion. Diana was waiting behind her with the other ladies of the court waving little fans rapidly back and forth.

Behind the queen and her attendants were the fiefholders of the kingdom. All were present, every single one. Standing with their backs to a remaining intact portion of the castle wall stood Nicholas and Lionel. Next to them was a squad of the city guard.

The lordling shook his head for the dozenth time. How could things have come to this? If Randolph were right, then in a little while this struggle would be over. But, what if, what if the glib magician was wrong? The central keep of the castle did become a pile of rubble? The path to the treasury completely covered for who knew how long? If a single wagonload of gold had caused so much disruption, what would happen if *all* of it was unreachable for a very long time?

"Enough delay," Vendora shouted. "Noon will come soon enough. Deeds determine who sits on thrones, not inflated gasbags of words."

"Now I will *assemble* what we magicians call a target," Hector called out so that everyone could hear. "It is the focus of an incantation I shall perform. "And then my once-colleague, Randolph, has until noon somehow to prevent it from exploding and bringing down the keep for all to see. The situation is simple. Either the keep is still standing at twelve or it is not. Everyone will see and know the result."

The magician paused. "And just to make sure that there is no argument when it is exactly noon, the queen will use the small timepiece I have here." He motioned to Lionel. "Take this eternal clock to the queen. You remember what it is, don't you? I had hoped to give you one when we first met as a small gift, but you refused."

"Go on," Hector continued. "The device is magic — minor magic but magic nonetheless. Whatever the outcome, it would not do if one side or the other complains because on their own timekeeper, twelve has not yet occurred."

A courtier scrambled to attention and took the little ticking device over to Vendora. "Having everyone agree on *when* the deadline is not important," Hector continued, but now, the chime of the device will indicate to all that it is indeed high noon."

Without saying more, Hector turned his back and grabbed a corner of the tarp covering the wagon's contents. With a dramatic gesture he pulled it away and flung it aside. Everyone strained forward to see what had been revealed. Some of those watching were flabbergasted, mouths open and silent. Others shouted.

"It is nothing but a collection of simple shapes," one of the observers yelled louder than the rest.

"These look like — like building blocks children play with," Lionel said to Nicholas. "How can they be the source of such powerful magic?"

The pair watched as Hector's henchmen began assembling the blocks together in the ground floor of the keep. As they did, Nicholas's eyes widened. "Look," he said. "There are just two kinds of blocks, tetrahedrons and octahedrons."

"You bookworm types are always coming up with fancy names. I would call them 'pyramids' and — and 'two pyramids glued together.'"

Nicholas's heart began pounding. He understood what Hector was doing. "Each block is highly *symmetrical* in and of itself. Together they can be assembled into bigger structures that completely fill a larger volume. There will be no pockets of air between any of them. Tiling, it is called. Tiling in three dimensions.

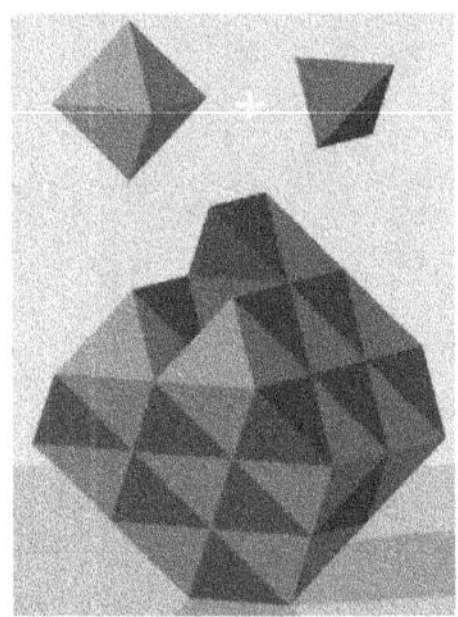

"Why does that matter?" Lionel asked.

"The more symmetries of the target object being manipulated by the magician, the more powerful the explosion will be. Look, Hector has begun performing the ritual that will make it happen."

"THERE IT is done," Hector cupped his hands around his mouth and yelled to the witnesses several minutes later. "The target has been triggered. No, I am not going to set off the explosion now. I have too much of a flair for the dramatic. But the ritual I have just performed sets the time of detonation.

"At one minute to twelve, the explosion will happen. The keep will fall. There is no way to stop it from occuring. The target is delicately triggered. Any attempt to dismantle it before noon will cause it immediately to explode."

"But Randolph somehow will be able to stop that happening?" Lionel asked Nicholas.

"I, I think so," the initiate said. "No. No, I am sure of it. Master Randolph has stated he can thwart Hector, and so he shall. I will go fetch him now."

Lionel looked up in the sun's direction. "Roughly two more hours until noon. Time to start evacuating everyone nearby just in case."

NICHOLAS'S FOREHEAD wrinkled with worry as he opened the front door when he returned to the apothecary. "Master Randolph," he called out. "Shouldn't we start loading the cart now?"

"There is time enough, initiate," the master replied. He held up two sample swatches. "Which decal do you think is better? The one on the left is simple and goes well with our logo, but the other has a certain flair that would distinguish the greatest magician of all."

"Master, the cart. It is still not loaded with the mirror blanks. We don't have all that much time."

"Mirror blanks?" Randolph asked. "I have already told you that I have no need for those."

"But Hector has boasted that the incantation he has cast will cause the explosion just a minute before noon."

"Yes, Hector has always been one for theatrics. Having the keep standing until the very last moment would have the greatest effect. He held the two samples of material up against his robe and considered.

"Yes, the one with the flair. It will stand out more. I will go back to the seamstress and tell her my choice. Continue as I have instructed you. I will return when it is time to set off for my grand entrance."

In an instant, Randolph was gone. Nicholas shook his head in both awe and disbelief. Was grandiose self-confidence one of the prerequisites to becoming a true magician?

He rubbed his chin and decided. He needed to hear wisdom from a master. Before he could change his mind, he went to Antron's door in the back of the apothecary, the one that had remained shut for longer than he could remember. He gave it a gentle tap and waited, just as he had several times before. And as before, nothing happened.

But Nicholas did not give up immediately this time. He knocked forcefully, surely loud enough to arouse the master even if he were asleep. Again, no response. He placed his ear to the door and listened.

Wait a moment! Did he hear something? It sounded like 'water.' Without thinking further, Nicholas put his shoulder to the door, and the latch-seat splintered open. He looked about quickly and recognized Antron reaching out with a shaking arm from his bed.

The bedside ewer was empty. Nicholas grabbed it, and hurried back to the pump near the front entrance to the apothecary and filled it. Tipping it slowly to the old man's lips, he saw some color return to his cheeks. When the ewer was empty, the initiate interpreted the master's nod, and rushed to fill it again.

"But, but, how is it that—", he began after the master signaled he had taken enough.

"It was a drug," Antron whispered. "At first, I attributed it to my ineviatble decline. But Randolph has been spiking my meals for some time. I should have suspected something when he offered to prepare mine when he did his own."

Nicholas's memory stirred. It now seemed like so long ago. His failed candidacy exam. Three stern masters probing for his weakensses -- well, of the three, Antron had been the most kind. Then, what the old master had just said hit him like a devil's dart.

"Drugged?" Drugged by Randolph?" He could not believe what he had just heard. "Why?

"I am not sure," Antron said as he strugged to his feet.

Nicholas was dumbfounded. He waited anxiously until Antron gathered the strength to speak again.

"As I am sure you have witnessed by now, Nicholas, pride is both a blessing and a curse in magicians. If I were not so decrepit now, I too would wrestle for…" Antron waved a gnarled hand in front of his face as if he were shooing away a fly.

"None of that matters," the master continued after a moment. "Hector and Randolph have always been at each other's throats. Bragging about who was the greater, the more proficient. And at the moment, it is Randolph who has been striving to outwit his peer."

"Evidently, he has," Nicholas said. "He has found the way to contain Hector's grand explosion. As Randolph says, he will be the toast of the world."

"No, my lad." Antron shook his head. "From time to time, when I was more coherent and Randolph had been away from here, I somehow found the strength to crawl to his chambers. I studied his notes, and deduced from them…"

"Deduce what?" Nicholas asked. "Randolph says he has found a way to prevent the effects of these Gavarak explosions from happening. Powerful magic indeed."

Antron shook his head again. "No magic by Randolph involved at all. Randolph's plan was to drug Hector as he has done to me before anything drastic occurred."

"But something drastic *has* occurred. I witnessed it. Hector assembled a target object for an explosion and — "

How it is done does not matter," Nicholas said. "If there is no performance of the ritual, there would be no explosion. All will end well."

Antron started coughing and did not speak for what to Nicholas seemed like a candidacy exam that would never end. Finally, the head magician regained his breath and continued. "'Two minds with but a single brain' as the old saying goes. Both of them, Hector, as well as Randolph, had rummaged through the residue of alchemical objects and supplies when we took up residence here."

"Master, I mean no disrespect, but the time until noon keeps getting shorter."

Antron tried to hold his breath, but that only served to start a coughing jag. Nicholas began to squirm. What he must do was beginning to bubble in his mind.

Finally, Antron rushed through the last. "Both of them had vials of a knockout serum in their quarters, but in addition, Hector had one more — the antidote to take if symptoms were to occur."

"So, Randolph did not plan to contain the explosion at all," Nicholas blurted. "Instead, he would dope Hector and thereby ensure that one never occurred."

"Yes, Hector would recognize the symptoms, give himself the antidote, and then continue as he originally planned." Antron shook his head. "And if I were a betting man, I would say that today the queen's tower is going to fall.

11

An Explosion in the Keep

NICHOLAS DITHERED. What was he going to do? If Antron was right, Hector would not be drugged as Randolph had plotted. The renegade magician had been alert enough to perform his ritual — the one exploding the three-dimensional tiling in the keep.

And then, would that mean that Hector would become regent?

With no accessible gold, Procolon's entire economy would collapse into barter. More than merely puny Quilson's, *all* the kingdoms to the south might unite and invade.

And what about Diana? What would happen to her? Lionel would be busy trying his best to preserve order. If the explosion was sufficiently powerful, would even she be far enough away?

Nicholas looked up into the sky. Noon was less than an hour away. He took a deep breath and decided. There was no other choice. He had to trust his instincts and hope they were correct.

He ran outside the apothecary to check. The horse had arrived and was hitched to an empty cart. There were no signs of Randolph. Hurrying back inside, Nicholas grabbed two of the mirror blanks, one under each arm. He did not have to be careful about them falling, but he had no idea how many to bring.

The simple box he had envisioned might not be big enough. To be sure, he needed a lot more of the blanks, maybe all. But how many, he could not tell. And the flasks of resin and fixer. Would there be enough of their contents as well?

Nicholas stepped outside and ran to the cross street. He dropped the blank he was carrying, and it caromed painfully off his foot. Looking up the road heading straight to the castle, he saw it became steeper and steeper the closer one got. Could the horse pull a fuller load or should he stop adding to it now? Was his scheme even going to work? With a struggle, he tried to focus his mind.

Back inside, he managed to juggle four more blanks, two under each arm. And then three more trips for a total of twelve so far. Trying not to think about what might happen, like a magician's automaton performing the same ritual over and over, Nicholas continued loading until his arms were spent.

He looked up into the sky. The sun was already quite high. How close to noon was it anyway? An eternal clock — that is what was needed! And Hector seemed to delight in making more of them in his spare time so that he could give them away in exchange for favor.

Nicholas burst into Hector's quarters and saw a row of them standing neatly on the top of a chest, each one clicking in perfect synchrony. He grabbed the nearest, raced outside again and studied the number of blanks he had already loaded. It was approaching eleven o'clock.

It felt like an eon, but finally, he decided. He did not want to risk the time it would take to add any more blanks. He gathered and loaded all the jars of resin and fixer that had survived. Climbing onto the buckboard, he flicked the reins and started the horse moving. The beast responded slowly, almost oblivious to the slap. He struck the nag with the whip, but then stopped and sighed. The horse was going to move at its own pace no matter what he did.

SEVERAL AGONIZING minutes later, Nicholas arrived at the portcullis. The gate was already raised. "Let me through," he shouted. "I have an important message for Lord Lionel."

The guard recognized the initiate and waved him to enter. Seconds ticked away as the cart slowly approached the keep.

"Stop, what are you do — " Lionel shouted. "Nicho — "

"No time to explain," Nicholas shouted back. "I must get a container built around Hector's assembly before it is too late."

"Randolph said he was the one to sto — "

"Later! Are you going to help or not?" Nicholas sucked in his breath when he finally reached the entrance to the keep. He leapt down from the cart, grabbed four of the blanks and hurried up to the door that was shut. "Damn!" he exclaimed as he let two of the blanks crash to the ground. With his free hand, he threw open the door — and gasped.

Hector's construction was even larger than he had remembered. It would take four mirror blanks to form a big enough base. The array of three-dimensional objects was as tall as Nicholas's waist. Nicholas looked closer. He glanced at the little eternal clock he had strapped to his wrist. It was just past eleven. Less than an hour to go.

Lionel raced into the keep and stopped. "Look at this thing. What a beautiful — "

"We will build a floor first," Nicholas commanded. "You take them off the cart and feed them to me here on the side."

Lionel hesitated for a moment, doing nothing. But then, he saw Nicholas's determination and decided to help.

"What are you two doing here?" another voice said. "Don't you know it is almost noon?"

"Diana!" Nicholas and Lionel shouted simultaneously. "Get out of here!"

But Nicholas's voice was firmer. "Never mind that. Open the flasks, Diana," he said. "Then watch what I am doing until you understand what more must be done. See? Apply resin to the edge of one of the blanks and fixer to the other I have placed next to it. Start bonding mirror blanks together down their longer sides and push the pairs together. Don't hesitate. The bonding occurs quite swiftly."

Diana raised her frilly dress to her knees, dropped to where Nicholas had pointed and began following the instructions.

Nicholas had no sense of how much time remained when a rigid slab was ready — one with a bigger footprint than what Hector had prepared. "Now we must slide Hector's device onto this foundation and then start building the sides. And once they are completed, we tip them up and glue them around the base."

He grimaced as he visualized the result he wanted. "The sides. Once three panels were completed, they would have to be pivoted to stand vertical and then be attached to the base slab. *Precisely* vertical. Otherwise, the top will not fit."

"So, what do we do?" Diana asked.

Nicholas shook his head in frustration. "There are no two ways about it. Back at the apothecary are some copper angle irons. They are bent exactly at right angles — sixty-four degrees. They can guide the orientation of the vertical walls. We use them in rituals all the time."

He looked at the eternal clock on his wrist. It was twenty to twelve.

"Keep assembling the sides," he said. "I will race back to the apothecary and get some of them."

NICHOLAS'S LUNGS ached when he returned to the keep. Physical exercise was not part of an initiate's regimen. All four of the walls had been built and dragged to lie next to the portion of the base to which they would attach.

"Alright now," he said. "I will glue angle irons around the periphery of the base. Diana, you follow by coating the edges of all of the floor blanks with resin. Then Lionel, you apply the fixer where they will touch the base. Finally, when each side is ready, the three of us will tip each side up and push it firmly against the base making sure we are flush with the angle irons. We will do this for all four sides, one after another. Hopefully, this will be accurate enough that the lid will fit."

In determined haste, they all continued working silently. Nicholas shook his head to clear away horrible thoughts. The design was simple. All they had to do was construct a big box, he kept telling himself. Either the trio were going to succeed in time — or they would not.

Nicholas and Lionel assembled the lid, and Diana coated its perimeter with resin. Fixer was spread on the top edge of each of the four vertical walls. Together the trio hoisted the lid above the tops of the vertical standing blanks and carefully positioned it so that the magic chemicals mated. Now only seconds remained.

For an instant, the trio did not move, dazed by what they had done. Now, one way or another, they would learn if Nicholas's idea would work or not.

"We are not safe yet!" Nicholas suddenly realized. "The mirror glass is transparent. The walls might hold but — "

He stopped speaking. He grabbed Diana's hand and bolted for the door. "Don't run straight away," Nicholas shouted back to Lionel as they burst back out onto the bailey floor. "Race to the side instead."

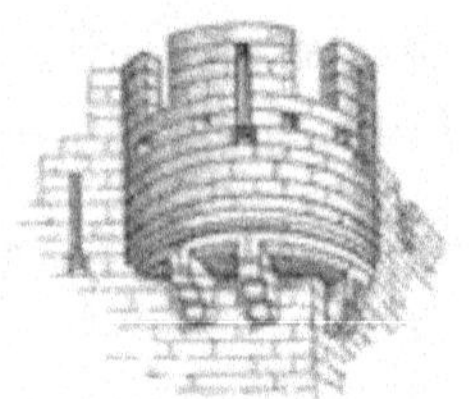

12
End of the Story?

"AND SHUT your eyes. Do not look back," Nicholas continued as the three exited. "The burst of light will be so strong that even the reflections from the other buildings will be too much to look at."

As he spoke, an intense light pierced his eyelids and shocked him into blindness. He stumbled and felt Diana stagger into him. "I cannot see!" she shouted.

"What happened?" several of the bystanders who had gathered exclaimed. "I'm blind! I'm blind!" shouted others.

"Maybe it is temporary," Nicholas said, although in his heart he could not be sure.

"What happened?" Lionel asked while feeling in front of himself. He raised his voice in order to be heard over the sudden outpouring of cries from others who had come to watch what would happen. "I thought the box was to contain the explosion."

"Most of it," Nicholas said. "We did not hear any crash of stone, so the keep does still stand."

"Then where did the blinding come from?" Diana asked.

"The mirror blanks did their job," Nicholas replied. "They confined almost all of the energy of the blast. But they are made of glass. The explosion had many, ah, aspects. It withheld the expansion of the air within it, but did not stop any of the light that was also produced. And all three of us saw were reflections from other buildings and the rest of the curtain wall that is still standing."

"Wait a moment!" Lionel exclaimed. "I think my vision is starting to clear."

"Me, too," Nicholas said. His lungs filled with relief.

IT TOOK almost a quarter of an hour for the eyesight of most everyone on the periphery to return. Those who had waited and watched directly in line with the door to the keep were now in the care of others. Some of the bravest approached the opening and cautiously looked inside.

"It's in a box!" some exclaimed. "Hector's intricate structure looks like it is still here, but now a pile of rubble within a box."

Lionel breathed deeply to catch his breath. He frowned at Nicholas. "Why didn't you tell me of this sooner? I could have made arrangements to keep order."

Nicholas shrugged but did not answer.

"Are you alright?" Diana asked as she gave the initiate a hug.

"Yes, yes. All's well that ends well," Nicholas said. His thoughts soared. He had done it! He was the one who was the hero of the day. And more importantly, for the first time in his life he felt good about himself. He was not a mere bumbler trying to fake the posture of a master magician. A thin shell with nothing inside. He had thought things through. He had deduced how to thwart the mysterious explosions when no one else had!

Nicholas looked up at the keep. It still stood, tall and firm as it had for hundreds of years, a symbol for everyone to see. Hector had lost. There could be no denial of that. A perfect ending for a tale to add to the sagas. Randolph would get his wish and become feted throughout the world …Wait a moment! That was no longer correct.

"Where is Hector?" the initiate exclaimed.

"The villain has fled," someone shouted over the buzz. "In the confusion, Hector has run away. Maybe the other magician was in cahoots with him all along."

"If I could have the attention of all of you," Randolph's voice boomed over the buzz of the crowd. "*I* did not flee. I was merely a bit delayed, because I had to *walk* rather than enter this bailey in triumph. But as you can see, the evil magician, Hector, has been defeated. It is *I* who have bested him. The keep tower still stands."

"I did not see *you* rush into the keep right before noon," Tetris shouted in reply.

"My initiate handled the details," Randolph said. "He carried out all my instructions to the letter — except perhaps for, at the very last, not providing the means for my triumphant entry. I had to walk just like the rest of you. and the time I spent looking for another cart was wasted."

Randolph paused, waiting for the crowd to quiet so everyone could hear what was being said. His eyes quickly darted around the assemblage waiting for silence. Eventually, the hisses to hush and the poked ribs brought everyone to silence.

Nicholas felt the temptation to speak boil up within him, but decided not to. Without thinking, he placed his arm around Diana's waist, and she did not push it away. Instead, she gave Nicholas a small smile. He glanced at Lionel and saw the lordling's scowl. Nicholas felt a bubble of contentment like he had never before.

"Procolon is a great kingdom, perhaps the greatest in all the world," Randolph said and then cocked his head to the side and attempted a modest smile. "Absolutely the greatest. So, you there, lord Turbid, isn't it? I can't help but wonder.

How many feast days will there be? How many parades?"

"Tetris, not Turbid," Lionel's father growled. "But never mind about that. For being a master, I am surprised at the flaw in your logic. From what I observed, my brave son, his fiancé, and this, what, initiate, here were the ones who did whatever it was they did to stop Hector's explosion. Without their swift action, we would be hailing another master instead."

"What? What you say? A pampered son, a mere initiate, and a woman. They were but the instruments of my powerful magic. I am the one who conceived what had to be done. Surely, you jest."

"I will consult with the rest of the fiefholders of course," Tetris said. "But if there is to be any celebration, it will not be for you — master, ah, Rundown, is it?"

Randolph's eyes flared. With a dramatic whirl he gathered his deep blue robe about him and stalked away into the streets of the city.

The crowd grew silent, and then in twos and threes began drifting elsewhere. Lionel shouted some commands, and the queen and her entourage returned to the bailey. Vendora silently entered the keep and began climbing the stairs to the royal apartment. Evidently, what had happened was all too confusing, and the queen had nothing to say.

Nicholas felt Diana's arm slip away. She ran back to Lionel and kissed him on the cheek. It was over, Nicholas thought as he watched her depart. All over. Perhaps eventually some scribe will attempt to add what had happened to the sagas but… He shrugged. Wasn't the hero the one who wins the fair maiden? A happy ending and it was all over? Nicholas sighed and shook his head. There was no more to be said.

⓵⓷

Birds of a Feather

RANDOLPH WANDERED aimlessly without purpose through the streets of Ambrosia. Scoundrels, one and all, he still fumed, even after more than a month had gone by since the keep had been saved. It was simple. The magician's litany of logic repeated over and over again in his head.

There had been a formal agreement made with the queen. Hector tried to destroy the keep. *I* resolved to defend it. The tower did not fall, ergo, I won. *I* am the one to be feted. Ambrosians are no better than the simple barbarians to the far north. Somehow, I will make them pay; make them all pay.

He heard loud voices ahead and decided to investigate. They came from the market.

"What do you mean? My scrip is good. The queen guarantees it."

"Guarantees what?" a merchant growled back. "Every hour, the rate escalates. Now, the exchange for a single brandel of gold takes twenty vellums. I will no longer accept paper."

"Then you will get nothing," the customer said with frustration. His face filled with anger and when it became too much to bear, he grabbed the belt he wanted from the display table. "This is not right," he yelled. "I have traded with you fair and square."

"What! Let go of that," the merchant commanded. "Give

248

that back to me." He picked up a short club from the table and started pelting the customer on his head.

"Then, give me back my money." The shopper hunched under the sudden flurry of blows. "Twenty, you say," as the barrage continued. "If so, then all of these are mine as well." He swiped his arm across the table with his free arm scattering belts everywhere.

Like a flash of fire in dry brush, the surrounding crowd erupted. A dozen hands reached forward and seized the remaining belts. Then, the gowns to the left vanished almost as fast. In the blink of a demon's eye, the looting spread from stall to table. The entire market became a seething maelstrom.

Randolph stepped away from the chaos and tried to exit but discovered that he could not. A small squad of city guardsmen had appeared and slammed into the most violent offenders, trying to wrestle them to the ground.

A rock sailed overhead and then another. "Where are these missiles coming from?" Randolph wondered aloud.

"From the rubble of Vendora's castle wall," a voice behind him said.

Randolph stopped and looked about. He saw nothing.

Suddenly, a hand was placed over his mouth, and he was manhandled into an alleyway away from the growing chaos.

"Psst!"

"Hector!" Randolph exclaimed when he was able to squirm and see his assailant. "How did you get away?"

He breathed deeply. Both his arms began to shake.

The other magician shrugged. "There was total confusion. No one knew what to do."

"Your men. You must have had more than a dozen. What happened to them?"

"Vanished," Hector said. "Wandred and the others. All of them. If you do not pay, you do not get any work done for you."

"I was robbed," Randolph said. "Denied the accolades I was due." He swept his arm around the scene as more and more guardsmen arrived to help subdue the crowd. "And it is all your fault. Your petty schemes are the cause of everything. Get away from me. I want nothing to do with you."

"Never mind about all that has happened," Hector said. "What is important is that there is still gold to be had. The keep stands over the treasury the same as always." The magician paused and puffed out his chest. "And as always, I have a backup plan I am sure will work. It will be, as they say, one last heist."

"Another of your get rich quick schemes," Randolph said as the action continued to swirl around the pair. He shied aside as two more guardsmen began grabbing rioters and subduing them.

"I know where we can go," Hector said.

"Where? What do you mean?"

"Come with me to a little lair I have built — not far from our magician's palace on Honeysuckle Street. It is ironic, isn't it? The countryside scoured to find me, when all the time, I holed up right under Vendora's nose."

Randolph looked again at the riot coursing around him. "Why should I follow you?" he demanded. His face took on a crazed look — one that abandoned the hold of reason.

"You want to achieve your fame, do you not? If so, then work with me. There are enough details to be managed that you will not be bored. And as the sagas say, there is more than one way to stuff a goose."

"I will not follow your lead," Randolph shook his head. "The gold in Vendora's vault was never something I coveted."

"I know," Hector said. "And better than that, I understand. Come with me, and I will show you the way for your name to be on the lips of everyone on the globe — well, along with mine of course, but nevertheless, worldwide fame."

Randolph glanced again at the swirling action. He saw some of the more resistant around him be dragged through the dirt and mud. He breathed deeply and gradually calmed himself.

"Equal partners," Hector continued. "And when we appear together, I will even let you be introduced first."

Randolph watched the indignities being unleashed before him over and over again. One resister, a gentleman by the looks of his robe, had his clothing stripped away and was pushed into a caged wagon already overflowing with squirming bodies. He shuddered at the thought of what would be happening next — the interrogations and even possible tortures.

"Last," Randolph said. "The most important is presented last."

"Last it is," Hector laughed. "Now come. I have much to show you."

14

Urias Again

"YOU SEE, Randolph, our so-called magician's palace is not the only charade on Honeysuckle Street." Hector pointed at an abandoned warehouse with boarded up windows and no signs anywhere. Instead, its bare façade was almost covered, street to roof, with several piles of dirt and sand.

"Only a third of a league distant from where you, Antron, and I set up shop. I first met Urias there."

"A novice alchemist," Randolph snorted. "Of what use would he be to masters like ourselves?"

"Pleased to meet you, Master," Urias bowed slightly. "Ah, I guess I haven't had the time to thank you for the spare glassware I bought from your neophyte — what was his name — Nicklesworth — something like that? The alchemist I resold them to tidied me a profit. He said that he was brewing something that would be jaw-dropping."

"What are you talking about?" Randolph snapped. "Alchemists are not all powerful. They are no better than magicians, even though they brag many times as much. They fiddle with chemicals in the hopes of achieving some great power, but all they end up with are sweet smelling salves that reduce the itching of poison ivy." He pointed at the logos on his robe. "At least the things we sell work exactly as advertised."

The magician took a deep breath. "Which apothecary are

you associated with? Not this place, surely. What purpose does it serve having a façade so tall? Wouldn't you worry about leaks from the upper story to the one beneath?"

"No problem with that," Urias rushed to answer. "Come inside, and you will see."

"I remembered what Urias had said when he visited our palace," Hector interrupted. "Sought him out when I had more than a few brandels in my pocket from the original robbery. Able to finance the construction as well as contribute to the design."

"I still don't see —"

"Look, Randolph, climb down from your inflexible mountain of thought," Hector interrupted. "There are things that can be accomplished if one is willing to experiment."

"Not this tale again," Randolph huffed. "We never agreed on approach before, so I do not see why we should now." He glared and waved his arms. "Never, I say."

"I think that Urias's machine, after I modified his original concept, is going to work," Hector said.

"What machine?"

"Let's show him, Urias."

Hector opened the door, and the trio walked into the building. Randolph scowled as he stepped inside. It was completely dark.

"A moment, Master," Urias said. "I will get some candles."

Randolph heard some fumbling, and then a while later the two-story high room blazed with light. His jaw dropped when he saw what was illuminated — a tall, man-sized cylinder made of glass. It was not empty. Inside at top and bottom were horizontal bands of what looked like steel.

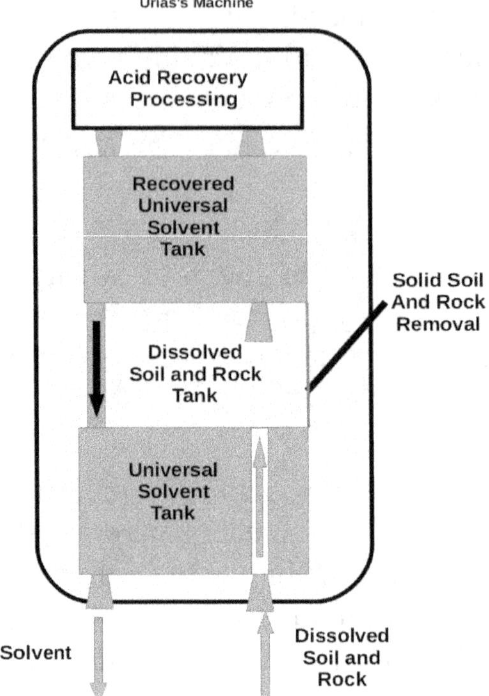

"Yes, impressive, isn't it?" Hector said. "Until the opportunity to be named Vendora's regent came along, I had been formulating an even better plan. What you see is the result."

"Impressive, yes. I guess I give you that, but to what purpose? Size alone means nothing."

"Remember all the trouble we had trying to get slabs that were perfectly flat — what was needed as the first step in making magic mirrors?"

"I remember. A single little mishap in one of the ritual steps and one got curved blanks rather than flat ones. A waste of time and materials."

"Exactly. But it occurred to me to embrace what was happening. Perform steps that accentuated the curve rather than fighting it. It took only a few trials to modify the ritual and produce a perfect cylinder that could not be broken — or even melted, no matter how hot it would get on the outside."

"Of what use is it?" Randolph shrugged as he pointed to the structure that had been revealed.

"It is like a flat-roofed tower — a rather sleek one, don't you agree? It cannot be broken because of the magic, and it can hold quite a large amount of …" Hector paused for effect. "A large amount of universal solvent."

"Universal solvent!" Randolph scoffed. "That is obviously impossible. There is no such thing. If there were something that could dissolve everything, then what would you hold it in?"

"Listen up for a moment, won't you," Hector snapped. "You have always been like this. No one else can get a word in slantwise."

Randolph sighed. "Alright. Tell me its purpose, then perhaps I will become more interested."

Hector smiled. "This machine," he said, "is how we are going to loot *all* of Vendora's treasure. And this time, no one will be the wiser. All gain and no risk at all."

His smile widened as he looked directly at Randolph. "And as a final bonus, when we are done, then, indeed, you will be world-renown."

"How?" Nicholas asked, suddenly interested. "Surely, it does not rest upon what an alchemist hawker says. It relies on a universal solvent, you say. Come now."

"Begging your pardon, Master," Urias said. "As is well known on the street, something called a universal solvent is, well, a *bit* of an exaggeration. A standard marketing technique, some alchemists say."

The novice gathered up his resolve. "But there is something of alchemy that *does* dissolve *most* everything. But not the magic glass. The solvent does not react to it. See the bottom of the cylinder here. The lowest band is a container made of the special alloy. It is filled with solvent as we speak, and yet none is leaking out."

"Alright, I am not sufficiently conversant in the subject," Randolph shrugged. "I grant you that such a powerful chemical known to alchemists possibly could exist. So what? Why would you want to tinker with something like that?"

"To build a tunnel." Hector said.

"Idiot," Randolph said. "Why? From where to where else?"

"From right here."

"Of course," Randolph scowled. "When no one is looking, you pour some the solvent on the ground and then — "

"I am trying to finish the thought before your closed mind interrupts again," Hector said.

"This is a story for which even a novice alchemist like this one here could see the flaw," Randolph continued. "The capacity of a jug of solvent cannot dissolve what it encounters forever. A given amount of it must have a finite capacity. What has been dissolved is suspended within it. Otherwise, a single drop could create a hole all the way to the center of our planet. It would take thousands of hogsheads of the stuff, maybe even millions, to go from where we are now to, say…, well, I don't know where."

"Yes, yes, exactly," Hector said. "Of that, Urias and I are well aware. Look more closely at the other parts of the machine we have created."

Randolph leaned forward, suddenly intrigued. Hector seemed to him to be so composed, so self-confident, Had the other master actually come up with something new? He looked upward and saw the glass cylinder was suspended by a block and tackle pulley system attached at the top and anchored in the rafters. The suspension ran from a nearby spool of thick rope that looped three times around and ended in the ring at the very bottom that was attached to the machine. Then downward, he observed that the device was not standing on the ground but gently swayed over a dark pit — one so dark that he could not see the bottom.

"You are saying this novice here has been able to manufacture enough of this solvent that you were able to dig this void? I can't really tell, but it looks like it is deeper than three times the height of a man."

"No, only a modest amount of solvent is being used," Hector shook his head. "Maybe a third of the cylinder's volume contains the chemical, but not more."

"So how did you excavate this — "

"On the base of the machine are two orifices," Urias cut in. "One for squirting out solvent and one for sucking up the saturated liquid that results. I tried it out while Hector was busy interacting with the queen. I was to be ready in case his more direct course did not work out."

Randolph scratched his chin. "So, the device dissolves the rock at the bottom of it and then does what — eject it out the top? After that, it can move downward in the hole created and repeat the process: squirt, suck, expel, sink. Clever. But eventually you run out of solvent, right?"

"No," Hector shook his head. "There is more to the design than that."

"What?"

"Despite his lack of credentials, Urias here is a clever lad. I did not know this until he told me, but by changing the amount of reactive hydrogen in the slurry of solvent and solute, what had been dissolved precipitates back out as inert sand and dirt. The solvent is not dense, and it rises to the top, totally recovered for additional use."

"Reactive hydrogen means?"

"Available in many forms. Urias and I are using oil of vitrol. It is readily available." Hector shrugged. "And then there are some more steps to recover the acid for reuse as well."

"This sounds like the tale of the cat and rat farm," Randolph snorted. "One feeds rats to the cats, kills them when they are big enough to eat and sells their pelts. Their carcasses are the food for the rats. The cycle repeats and there are no expenses, only pure profit."

"No, no," Hector laughed. "Of course, eventually in the process there are inexpensive chemicals that are consumed, and the pulverized rock has to be disposed of, but that is not the point."

"So, then, the point is what? Why do you want to dig a man-sized hole into the ground?"

"As you probably know, the surface soil in Ambrosia is not very deep — merely an accumulation from spring river overflow."

"Yes, I know all that."

"Underneath that topsoil is basalt — solid bedrock. Ambrosia is built over the remains of many ancient lava flows."

"And so?"

"And so, If you want to go deeper then, pick and shovel takes too long and costs a fortune. It is the reason why the alchemists tinkered until they came up with solvent. Without that, even a lord could not afford a basement."

"I repeat, and — "

"After we are at a sufficient depth, the machine will be turned on its side, the one the wheels are on. Then, we tunnel all the way across Ambrosia into the depths of Vendora's castle, directly into her vault. We can rob the entire treasury at our leisure and no one will be the wiser."

"There are some more details involved," Hector rushed on, "The tunnel will have to be enlarged manually at the proper depth so that the machine could be rotated, but Urias found some out-of-work thaumaturges to do that. Everything has been taken care of. Well, everything except for one."

"Which is?"

"From where we stand now, we have to dig down to a sufficient depth so that when the machine is tipped on its side to bore horizontally, we do so at the proper angle. And that calculation is tricky. Vendora's castle is uphill from here. Too shallow an angle when we bore horizontally and we rupture existing basements and are discovered. Too deep and we miss the treasury entirely."

"Easily enough solved," Randolph snorted. "A matter of simple geometry."

"Yes, yes, I understand that in principle," Hector said. "But, well … I am unable to do these geometry calculations accurately enough. That is where *you* come in."

Randolph did not immediately answer. He grabbed the other magician's arm. "They laughed at me, Hector," he growled. "I must make them pay."

"Let go of me," Hector commanded. He looked into Randolph's contorted face and called out to Urias. Quickly bring a jug of brandy. Master Randolph needs to calm down.

"Look, ah, partner. Can you not see it? The most pain you can inflict on those who might laugh is by absconding with their wealth. Join the effort. I promise you that your revenge will be oh so sweet."

Randolph did nothing for more than a dozen ticks of a clock. He sighed. He released his grip. "Yes, your theorem is sound, Hector. Count me in."

(15)

Knowledge Never Hurts

A FEW days later, Urias dumped an evening meal on the table in front of the two masters and moved out of sight as they ate. "How are you coming along, Master Randolph?" he asked as he started to leave.

Randolph smiled. Although his own task had been simple, it was beyond what Hector could do. A small victory compared to what he had desired, but a victory, nonetheless. And even better chances lie in the future.

"The calculations were easy, simple geometric transformations," he called back to the novice. "Only an hour's work to check and recheck that they were correct. And I added a few things to the engine that Hector has forgotten about as well."

"Forgotten? Hector wrinkled his brow. Like what?"

"Like the mirror I placed on the top of your machine. Well, it will be on the end when it is turned sideways."

"What do we need that for?" Hector asked.

"You said so yourself," Randolph answered. "The angle of the tunnel must be precise enough to have little error over half a league of distance. Merely pushing the device along as it does its job is not enough. We have to make sure that a beam of imp light from here always strikes the reflector. Makes sure that the machine stays on track."

"Ah, I see." Hector wiped his chin. "I am glad you have

bought into this. Probably no one could have done the calculations quicker or better than you."

Randolph ignored the compliment. "Tell me, Hector. No matter how clever your machine is at recycling resources, what do you do with all the excavated sand and dirt."

Hector shrugged. "The thaumaturges I have hired take care of that. What they do with it, I don't know."

"Thaumaturgy?" Randolph replied. "That craft is simple: 'Once together, always together' and 'Like produces like.' Nothing of any real power there."

"Nevertheless, the craft has its uses," Hector said. "With solvent, digging basements is not complicated work. But without thaumaturgy, nothing over three stories tall would ever be built in Ambrosia. Too many complications — how thick to make support beams and all the rest.

"But, more importantly right now, most of the practitioners of the craft are starving. With most commerce stopping because of the scrip panic, they will do almost anything." Hector shrugged. "It is happening everywhere. There is a good chance this year's harvest will not occur at all because no farm worker is accepting paper for his labors."

"These thaumaturges work for free?"

"Of course not. But they are fair with their numbers. They will add the time for the manual excavations to rotate the engine to what they will spend hauling away the dirt and sand for the shaft and tunnel."

"The *manual* excavations?"

"The ones that allow enough room to turn the machine on its side when it is at the proper depth you have calculated." Hector shrugged. "It turns out to be quite a large volume, and I don't want to raise any suspicions with large piles of dirt amassing outside in the street. Just enough each day so that it all can be hauled away in the night."

He paused for a moment. "You should talk to them a bit.

Interesting guys. Entertaining. They know a lot besides mechanics — weather prediction, what they call earth-study, ocean currents and more stuff besides."

Randolph's eyes got a far-away look for a moment. "I think I will do that. Yes, Hector, I think I just might do exactly that."

16

Awkwardness

A FEW days later, Nicholas stretched. He felt both tired and exhilarated at the same time. With no interruptions to impede him except for keeping Antron fed, he discovered he could study from morning to night, as long as he chose. It had taken him almost a fortnight, but gradually, he was gaining a fuller grasp of the craft of magic.

A persistent tapping sound penetrated his reverie. Someone was knocking at the apothecary's front door.

Nicholas hurried to open it and blinked. "Diana!" he gasped. "Why are you here? Shouldn't you be busy with preparations for your wed — "

Diana placed her fingers gently on his lips. "The protocols are endless," she said. "How many guests from each of the fiefdoms, which dress color best agrees with — "

"Why are you here?" Nicholas persisted.

Diana thrust an envelope into Nicholas's hand, one with a fancy seal filling the central third of the flap. "It is your invitation," she said. "As a bride, as they say, not of proper birth, I get to select only three of my own."

"I, I guess I am lucky," Nicholas stammered. "Who are the other two?"

"Nobody else," Diana said softly. "You are the only one I truly want to be there. It does not look like I will be seeing much of you after that." She shrugged. "You know, the formal balls, the teas..."

Nicholas tried to smile. "Thank you," he said as he opened it and read. "In three days at noon in the queen's ballroom. How many will be there?"

"I don't know." Diana shrugged again and looked towards the door. She scowled. "My guard will be getting anxious. A lady of the court cannot spend too much time unescorted — "

"Wait, stay a while," Nicholas interrupted. "This means I won't ever see you again, right?" His shoulders sagged. "So then, wait a few moments. I want to tell you about some of the things I have learned."

"All right," Diana paused and smiled back at Nicholas. "A few minutes more won't hurt. We have a lot of memories together that we can recall."

THE THAUMATURGES had quit for the day from hauling away almost all of the last of the new dirt from enlarging the pit. Finally, now the excavations needed for turning the machine could be started. When they were all gone, Urias locked the front door, thrust his key safely away and smiled. Hector and Randolph reconvened near the top of the machine.

"I admit I am excited." Hector said as he watched Randolph perform a final test of the imp light and mirror. "Soon, all we will have to do is lower my machine to the proper level, rotate it horizontal and start dissolving a tunnel in front of it."

Hector breathed a satisfying lung full of air. "And after this works, we can travel to every kingdom on our globe and take all their treasures as well."

Randolph did not immediately respond.

"Well?" Hector asked. "Don't you understand now?"

"No, we are *not* going to follow any plan like that,"

Randolph suddenly growled.

"Wait, what? What do you mean?"

"They ignored me, Hector. And then they started laughing. Whenever it is quiet, I can hear them. Don't you understand yet? That was *not* the plan. *I* was to be the one who was to pull the bat out of the hat and save the day. Instead, they ignored me, and when the keep was saved, they started to laugh."

"Look, Randolph, every kingdom throughout the globe will change their attitude after they learn what we have done here in Procolon. They all will start paying ransom so as not to have their treasuries repeatedly robbed as soon as they are replenished.

"Why, after a few exploits, we will not even have to use the machine at all! Just threaten to do so, and accept annual payments for, what is it called, *protection*, instead. Yes, protection. What the lowest level of those who dwell here in Ambrosia state what they are providing. but, of course on a much grander scale."

Hector stopped and studied Randolph carefully. He did not like the maniacal visage now on the other magician's face "You're not listening, are you?"

Randolph did not reply. His focus was elsewhere.

Hector shook his head and sighed. "Give it a rest. What is done is done." He put his hand on Randolph's shoulder. "*I* am not laughing at you. I, I respect you as a partner. I always have."

"*Respect*?" Randolph shouted. "Merely respect. I have been thinking and have decided that I deserve more than that."

"What then?"

"They are laughing at me, Hector. They must be. This has to stop."

"You don't know that. The world does not revolve around

what are the latest happenings with a single magician.”

Randolph’s eye started to twitch. “Yes, I do know, Hector. I can feel it. And it must stop.”

“For the last time, what is it that you want? What will make you stop this brooding that comes over you and to remain focused on the steps we have left to perform.”

“What will make me stop? I will tell you what. The — fear and trembling — of — every single person who walks our globe.”

Randolph scowled. His face distorted into a mad rage, both eyes bulging and his teeth bared. His left eye jittered like the panic of a captured moth. “And I will do it by destroying the *entire city of Ambrosia*. They are going to pay, Hector. They are going to pay.”

Hector put his hand on Randolph’s shoulder to calm him, but it had the opposite effect. Randolph flung Hector’s grip away.

“Randolph, you’re making no sense again,” Hector pleaded. “Calm down and drink a little more brandy.”

“No! Instead, I will explain. *I* am the one who will pilot this machine. *I* am the one who will direct where it goes.”

Hector frowned. “Vendora’s treasury, right?” He paused for a moment and then sighed. “If it calms you down, you can control the first run. There will be plenty enough for both of us after the tunnel is finished.”

Randolph shook his head. “Only one run, Hector, only *one*. And not to a petty queen’s little trove of metal.”

“You’re still making no sense. *To where* then?”

“Don’t you recognize the basic flaws in your design?” Randolph waved at the bin of dirt and sand still waiting to be hauled away the first thing the next morning. “Think of it. You push the machine a little bit forward. Drag it back out of the tunnel, turn it erect, raise it, and then empty the dirt. Repeat the process, step after tiny step. Terribly inefficient.

Have you bothered to calculate how long this repetition will take?”

“I do not deal with numbers well,” Hector said. “You know that.”

“So, I have made the necessary improvements,” Randolph replied. “Ones that anyone with a sense of design would have implemented at the first.”

“What?”

“Condense the pulverized rock, you idiot. But you did not think of that did you?”

“No, I did not. So what?”

“Yes, condense it as much as it possibly could be. If you had done that, you would have discovered that all the rock from one cycle could be squeezed into nothing more than the size of a small stone. Ejected from the side bathed in solvent and it would be embedded easily into the shaft wall. A simple part of the ritual running each cycle. One enacted over and over again by an *actuator*. Producing a pebble that can be ejected out the side of the machine and adhered to the wall.”

“Who cares about the size of each piece removed from the tunnel?” Hector said. “Waste dirt is still dirt.”

“No idiot. Don’t you see? If the output is only pebbles, extremely dense and heavy ones, admittedly, but because of their small volume, there is no need to return here and discharge contents every hour or so. Once the machine is set in motion it will continue to run. I have made the calculations and my plan will work.” Randolph laughed. “Perhaps a cat and rat farm after all.”

“We still have to guide the machine so it stays on target towards Vendora’s vault.”

“No, no, not at all,” Randolph almost shouted. “Not if the goal is to continue downward. Gravity furnishes whatever guidance needed.”

“Downward? To what purpose?”

"The lava pit under the Fumus Mountains. It extends underneath Ambrosia as well. The thaumaturges I have talked to have been quite informative about what would happen."

"Happen? What?"

"Well, they have not been totally clear. 'Hypothetically speaking' seems to be one of their favorite phrases. But if a shaft that is a direct pipeline to the lava pit would release the pent-up pressure. A volcano would erupt when a new opening is pierced."

Hector frowned in concentration for a long while. Then his eyes grew wide.

"The city would be destroyed" he finally gasped in comprehension.

"Yes. Almost everyone would die. And my name would be spoken of with reverence throughout the entire world."

"But you could perish along with all the rest." Hector said. "Snap out of the state you are in, Randolph. Stop this nonsense, now."

Randolph shook his head. He waved at the boring machine. "With my improvements, I can manage all of this by myself from a safe distance. They will stop laughing. All of them will pay. I will be well away, and all the laughs in Ambrosia will stop. There will be no one left to utter them."

"I have heard no such laughs on the streets," Hector protested. "You are making all of this up. You are, you are — mad."

Randolph shook his head again. He grinned at Hector. "And you are not going to stop me." He fumbled into one of the pockets of his robe, grabbed a hand full of small marbles, and threw them on the ground. When they hit, they all popped with tiny explosions and puffs of smoke.

Hector steadied himself as he felt the sting of acid from the smoke begin to attack his bare arms. Ignoring the sudden pain as best he could, he reached into his robe and extracted a small transparent packet that pulsed with magic. Inside was a coil of thin wire with wooden handles at each end. "A slicer," he mumbled through the smoke. "Able to cut through anything. Necks are easy. And I don't think, Randolph, that I need your mathematical proficiency anymore."

Randolph did not hesitate. He kicked Hector in his knee and smiled as the other master stumbled and fell. In the next breath, he flung himself down on top of him.

"Get off me, you oaf," Hector sputtered.

Randolph grabbed Hector's wrists and held the wire away from him. "Every living being will know my name."

"They will despise you as the worst villain ever." Hector strained against Randolph's surprisingly strong grip. "Don't you realize that?"

"I do not care. It is my *name* that will be on every tongue even if it is a curse, not a laugh."

Randolph strained and dragged one of his feet along the ground, sliding Hector's lower body off of him. The pair twisted onto their sides.

Then he released his grip on one of Hector's hands, reached again into his robe and extracted what looked like some sort of mechanical spider. He flung it onto Hector's face.

Hector screamed. He released the slicer and began clawing at his eyes. Without the handles gripped, the slicer fell harmlessly onto his chest. He fell to the ground as the spider bored through his eyes and up into his brain. After a moment, the mechanism, evidently sated, cracked open the top of an empty skull and scampered off in a puff of magical smoke.

"You are next, novice," Randolph shouted as he scrambled to his feet. "I command you to come to me. Come to me now. You are next."

Urias stared at Randolph and gasped. He was shocked by

the sudden wide-eyed abandon now in the master's eyes. The magician had lost his senses.

The novice inhaled one deep breath and decided. He bolted out of the warehouse. "The other magicians," he yelled as he ran away. "I must get the help of others in their craft to deal with what is going on."

17

Pupils Against A Master

URIAS RAN past the guard sleeping at the reins of the cart outside of the apothecary. He ripped open the doors and shouted. "Magicians, every one of you. I need you now."

Nicholas opened the door to the makeshift vault and looked out at the disturbance. Diana followed.

"I remember you," the initiate said. "The novice who bought — "

"Ancient history," Urias panted, shaking his head. "An emergency! Every master magician I can find is needed father up the street. NOW!"

"There is only one master here," Nicholas said. He frowned as he remembered how brash the intruder had been the time he visited before. "And he is probably too old to travel."

"You then!" Urias said. "The one named Randolph. He is intent on destroying all of Ambrosia."

"What! You have found where he slipped away to?"

"Yes, yes, but he has gone completely mad. He must be stopped."

Diana studied Urias's face. She grabbed Nicholas by the arm. "I believe what he is saying," she said.

Nicholas grunted in agreement. "Where?" he asked.

"In an abandoned warehouse farther up the street. We can use the cart outside. Bring everything magic that you can."

"There are only a few remaining mirror blanks and —" Nicholas began.

"Whatever, we have to stop Randolph before it is too late."

"What would be too late?"

"The rope threading the block and tackle. It is not all that long — only enough to lower Hector's and my machine to where it is to be turned on its side. Once it threads all the way through the pullies, we will be unable to recover the digging machine from the shaft, it will continue on its own —"

"You are making no sense."

"On our way, I will explain as we go."

THE TRIO arrived at Hector's lair and tumbled out of the cart. Nicholas grabbed the largest of Garavak's hemispheres, one that contained what he had brought. It was not much. One flask of unused fixer, two mirror blanks, and a pile of magic rings. How any of this would be of help, he did not know.

Once inside, Urias lit a few more wall sconces to increase the feeble light. He lit a torch burning from one and led Nicholas and Diana into the room nearest the front doors. Nicholas looked about. The room was huge. One could not even see how distant were the far walls.

Diana gasped. "Look!" she pointed.

On the floor sprawled a body with pieces of brain oozing from a cracked skull.

"Hector!" Urias exclaimed. "I recognize his tunic. We returned too late."

"There!" Nicholas ignored the announcement. "On the far workbench. Urias, bring the light closer. I think I recognize what it is."

"What?" Urias asked.

"You said on our journey back here that Randolph has mentioned something about an automaton," Nicholas replied. "They are the result of some basic magic that every neophyte learns. Once created and then started, they perform simple rituals over and over until they are stopped."

"It must be for controlling the machine's cycling process," Urias said.

"Cycling process?"

"Yes. I don't know what it sounds like yet, but it is caused by the pumping of the chemicals and motion of the machine."

Nicholas spotted a heavy hammer. With a swift blow, he shattered the little device on the workbench into splinters.

Randolph suddenly emerged from the shadows in the corner of the room and laughed wildly. He waved another automaton in the air as he pointed at the workbench. "What you just did will not stop me."

For a moment, none of the trio moved. Finally, Urias said "This place is not all that big. Let's split up and find him. We will have to destroy this second automaton as well."

"No, we must remain together," Diana said. "The horror sagas are full of tales that as soon as 'don't split up' is said, everyone wanders off separately and then are dispatched one by one."

"Then we stick together," Nicholas said. "Urias, you lead. You are the only one of us who knows every place to look."

But before any one of them took a single step, they heard the sound of a bar sliding into place on the other side of the door.

Urias ran to the entry and pushed, but the door did not bulge. "We're trapped!"

"Isn't there another exit?" Diana asked.

"No!" Urias answered. We're trapped in here! Trapped! And no one else knows." The novice began to shake. "I've always dreaded something like this happening."

For a moment, Nicholas did not speak. Then he asked, "Is there a keyhole saw in this place?"

"On the bench there, I think, but how is that — "

"Drill a small hole on the left, just above where the crossbar is hung."

"Why?"

"Just do it. Didn't you ask for help?"

Urias sighed and then nodded. He found a brace and bit, and started drilling.

"Why crossbar a door on the outside?" Diana asked.

Urias answered. "Probably to prevent tool pilfering by the workmen when this place was operating as a warehouse."

"I bet that there is a rattail file around here someplace," Nicholas said when Urias finished the hole. "It will take a while to enlarge the opening enough, but eventually I will be able to insert the keyhole saw and cut through the center of the entry bar, so that the two parts will fall to the floor." He shook his head. "Barricading a room filled with tools is not something that usually works to confine anybody."

SOMETIME LATER the trio paused searching the warehouse. "We've looked almost everywhere," Urias said. "All that is left is the room with the machine and pit."

"Then let's go there," Nicholas said.

The trio entered the room in the center of the warehouse. "What's that noise," Diana asked.

Urias looked to where the machine had been hanging suspended, but it was not there. "It's my machine," he shouted.

The three ran to the edge of the pit and peered down into the dimness. The light cast from a chandelier above the opening was faint. It took a few moments to be sure, but the trio realized from the sound coming upward that the device was doing something.

"Yes," Urias said. "A staccato downward march — dissolve, release, compress and eject. That is how the machine works since Randolph had improved it."

Diana pointed, "There!" As eyes adjusted, it was hard to be sure, but it looked like Randolph was sitting quietly on the top of the machine as it descended. The magician howled with laughter when he spotted the three peering down at him.

"It's hard to tell in the gloom," Urias shouted. "Already past the point where we wanted to enlarge the opening so the machine can be turned horizontal."

"Randolph, Stop! Stop your — your automaton," The novice stumbled over the word as he shouted down into the pit. He glanced at the large spool of coiled rope standing nearby. "We must pull you back up before the rope unthreads all the way out of the pulleys. Don't you realize? If we don't, there would be no way to retrieve my machine. You will perish, too."

Randolph laughed. "No, never. You cannot stop me now. You will pay for your snub, for your mistake. All of you will pay. All of you must be made accountable for what you have done— because it is my due. "

"I can't understand him," Diana said. "He's starting to sprout gibberish. He's completely mad."

"The machine is on its way to its first and only use." Randolph continued yelling. "Ambrosia will be destroyed. And when it is, I am the one who will be remembered. Remembered as the one who demolished it." The magician cackled as if he were already marked as a villain in the pages of the sagas.

Nicholas and Diana looked from one to the other. "I don't think any reasoning with him will work," the sorceress said.

"Somehow, we have to stop the descent ourselves,"

Nicholas agreed.

"My machine is quite heavy," Urias shook his head. "It takes three turns through the block and tackle to make it liftable by two men. Look at how fast Randolph is descending. By the time we have pulled it up one armlength, the machine will have fallen two."

"Sorcery then," Diana said. "I will try to enchant him. Cover your ears."

THE ONLY sounds coming from the pit were the echoes of Diana's words of enchantment, each one weaker than the one before. Urias's machine was getting farther and farther away.

"We need better light," Diana said as she leaned over the edge. "I can't see much down there at all. And with the echoes off the walls interfering, I don't think any of my charms are going to work."

"Then what?" Urias asked.

"Hang on," Nicholas said. He stared for a moment down the shaft the machine was creating." I just remembered something. I will get it out of the cart."

WHEN THE initiate returned, he lugged the Gavarak hemisphere with him. "Now, Diana, shine one of our lights down into the pit. Urias, hold me tight around my waist. We might have only a single shot at this."

Nicholas strained to keep his focus as Urias made sure of his grip around him. He slowly leaned over the edge of the pit. The top of the machine was barely visible in the gloom. Without thinking more, he dropped the heavy weight down into the shaft. "Something we learned from a king to the south," he said over his shoulder to Urias.

Within a heartbeat, there was a thump and startled cry and then silence. The trio looked downward and saw Randolph sprawled in a grotesque crumple on the machine's lid, blood oozing from his head.

"Is he still alive?" Urias called down.

Nicholas shook his head. "No, I think we have stopped him."

Urias sighed. He took a deep breath. "Now all we have to do is pull the machine back up and we are saved."

But the machine did not stop. The more they waited to be sure, the farther away it kept chugging along.

"It's the second automaton!" Nicholas realized. "Randolph, dead or alive, does not matter. Probably in one of the pockets of his robe."

"Don't those things have to be initialized or something first? Urias asked.

"Depends on the need," Nicholas said. "A master one can be set to broadcast its settings to others nearby. Looks like that is what Randolph has done here."

Without thinking more, the initiate leapt onto the suspension rope and started to lower himself towards the machine.

He was clumsy at first, but gradually was able to increase his speed. He began to anticipate when the device would take another step downward and grasp the suspension rope tightly when it did.

"Hurry," Urias cried out as Nicholas descended. "There is not much more rope on the spool that is connected to the machine. Hector only bought enough to get to the depth to turn horizontal."

NICHOLAS LOST all sense of time. He concentrated on

maintaining a firm grip on the rope as he shinnied down. Finally, he reached the top of the machine and collapsed onto Randolph's body. The master magician did not move. Nicholas checked for a pulse. Randolph was quite dead.

"Hurry," Urias shouted. "The last of the rope is leaving its spool. After it passes through the three loops on the pulleys, we will have no way to pull you back up."

"Then start pulling upward now," Nicholas shouted back as the machine fell farther into the hole it was creating.

"We tried that," Diana yelled. "But it takes two adult men to raise it, even with the block and tackle. I don't—I don't even weigh enough to help you."

Nicholas grunted. He began feeling each of Randolph's six pockets that presumedly were in the same places as those on his own robe.

Then, in the very last one, the initiate felt a bulge—another actuator! He fumbled it free, dashed it against the hard metal of the rock-borer, and sighed with relief.

But the machine did not stop moving. It descended another step.

"The rope end is in the first pulley loop!" Urias cried.

Nicholas could not believe it. Did Randolph have yet another backup? When he started one actuator, as a matter of course, were all that he possessed instructed the same way as well?

The initiate took as a large breath as he could and started to proceed more methodically as he patted down the magician's body again.

But he found nothing! All six of the pockets were flat and empty.

The machine lurched and descended another step.

Nicholas's pulse rate quickened. He breathed deeply to calm himself but it did not help. He racked his brain. There was yet another actuator, but where was it?

While he pondered, the machine descended another three steps.

"The trailing rope is in the second loop now," Urias cried. "Hurry!

Nicholas patted all parts of Randolph's robe again, this time as slowly and thoroughly as he could, but he felt no more bulges; only smooth skin underneath.

The machine lurched and settled lower, not once but twice.

"Hurry," Urias cried. "You have to find where the automaton is now."

All magician robes were the same, weren't they? Nicholas reasoned. He in fact was wearing the one that Randolph himself wore when he was an initiate.

"Do something!" Diana's words rained down on him.

Nicholas felt totally perplexed. His breath started coming in shorter bursts. This was worse than his failed exam. Worse than building the box around the magic object that would have destroyed Vendora's keep. He felt himself begin to freeze into complete inaction, but somehow willed himself to continue.

If not in a pocket, the initiate reasoned, perhaps hidden somewhere else on the robe. He began patting again, this time over each and every inch of the garment.

Wait! On the left, in the stitching in the armpit. It felt different there! He tore open a small compartment and breathed a sigh of relief. Yet another backup automaton! When Randolph initialized one, he must have broadcast the instructions to all that he had. With his bare hand, Nicholas smashed it against the machine's wall and started to exhale a sigh of relief.

But the machine lurched two more times as Nicholas hung immobile.

Nicholas started quivering head to toe. This was going to be the end — the end of everything for everyone. He spasmed and squeezed his arms around himself to stop the shaking.

As he did, he felt something. He became aware of the fabric of Randolph's initiate robe that he himself wore. It was crafted from a far better fabric than what he wore as a neophyte.

Nicholas's thoughts raced. Randolph's initiate robe. Perhaps it too could contain hiding places for automatons. He shed it and began patting it down just as he had for Randolph's maser robe.

Wait! On the left, in the stitching in the right armpit. It felt different there!

Yes, it bulged a bit. Something was present had been sewn in there. A small pouch that was about the right size and shape.

"The last loop!" Urias shouted.

Nicholas extracted the small little box he had felt, one that vibrated with the familiar feel of magic. Hanging on for dear life to the suspension rope with one hand, he switched off the automaton with the other. The machine lurched to a stop. The next sucking action did not happen. It stood on firm bedrock and did not move any more.

"Secure the rope tightly so it does not start to tumble down" he yelled up. "I will be back with you as soon as I am able."

NICHOLAS BREATHED deeply more than a dozen times. Gradually, he restored his calm.

The initiate looked upwards. How had he ventured so deeply so fast? He sighed, grabbed the rope and started the long process of shinning back up.

"WE DID it!" Urias exclaimed when Nicholas regained ground level. "We are saved from what Randolph was planning to do."

Nicholas studied the novice for a moment. "Not quite," he said.

"What do you mean?"

"I had plenty of time to think about things on my way back up," Nicholas said. He suddenly sprang forward and pinned Urias to the ground.

"IT'S DONE," Diana said as she motioned Nicholas to remove his hands from his ears. "Three hours of chanting to wipe everything from Urias's mind. The novice won't remember anything about this from start to finish. But why?"

"The basic idea of the machine was his from the very beginning," Nicholas said. "There would have been nothing to stop him from starting over again with someone else. Or even worse, bragging about what he had created. Can you even imagine what would happen if others found out and decided to build such machines as well?"

"So, we just let him go?"

"Not until after he helps with the shoveling. We will use the last pile of dirt that was yet to be removed. If we get it spread evenly enough, the machine will be covered and the pit will just look like a hole in the ground."

"Then what?"

"In the morning, I could get in contact with the thaumaturges and get them to bring back the dirt they have removed and then some more."

"It is a very large hole," Diana said. "Surely, it will create a lot of curiosity before it is totally filled."

Nicholas shook his head.

"I had plenty enough time to think while you were reciting the incantation that caused Urias to bury all of his thoughts about a boring machine. All we have to do is to tell the thaumaturges that we have reversed things in Hector's original agreement with them."

"Reversed?"

"Yes, they get paid when hauling away dirt, but it all cannot be a clear profit. They must have to pay for dumping it somewhere else."

"So?"

"So, you need to add a little bit to Urias's enchantment. Get him to offer the thaumaturges a cheaper dumping site than whatever they are using now. Urias will have a lot of shoveling to do himself in order to get the pit filled, but eventually it will be, and all will be well.

"But I am too exhausted to think about that any more now."

Nicholas took a deep breath and studied Diana for a long moment.

"What?" she asked.

"We make a good team, don't we?" He paused, then continued slowly. "But saving the world doesn't change anything that really matters does it?"

Diana was silent a long while before answering. At last, she spoke softly. "No, it doesn't. But please believe me, Nicholas, I have thought about things a lot."

"And you concluded what?"

"The single most important thing, the one thing that

everyone has *complete* control over, regardless of their wealth or their circumstances in life, is — ”

“Is what?” Nicholas could not keep quiet.

“Their *honor*,” Diana said. “I agreed that I would marry Lionel, and that is what I shall do. He is waiting for me back at Vendora’s castle as we speak.”

Nicholas blinked at the words. “For anyone else, I would understand. Perhaps even admired the speaker for such a choice being made. But you, Diana, you and me — "

Diana put a finger to Nicholas’s lips. “I know. I understand,” she said. “It is heartbreaking for me as well.” She kissed Nicholas gently on the cheek and then sighed. “I look forward to seeing you at the wedding.”

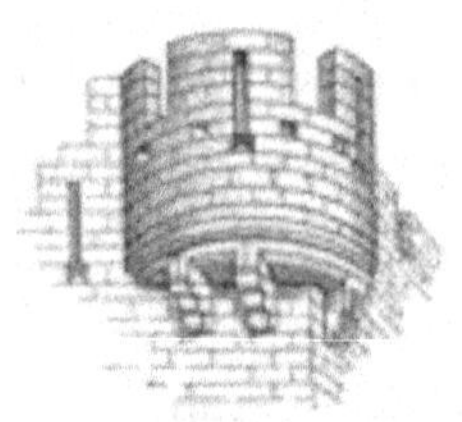

18
Final Decisions

DAYS HAD passed. Lionel stood in front of the queen on the raised platform at the north side of the ballroom. He looked out over the peerage who were assembled there. Every fiefholder in Procolon was present. Most were accompanied by wives who would not miss the event for anything. Everyone awaited the appearance of the bride.

Lionel's thoughts wandered. He had to admit that the past few months had a certain exhilaration to them. Captain of the city guard, then in charge of the workings of the entire castle. The leader who repulsed an attack from the south. Hector's attempt to destroy the keep averted. His idea of exchanging ten vellums of scrip for eleven brandels at the treasury had gotten around. The rioting stopped. Vendora was pleased. He smiled, admitting that, through it all, he liked being in charge.

To his surprise, the concept of regency had become an allure for him. It could never happen of course, but if it did, it would finally fulfill what he had always been looking for — *purpose*, a true reason for being, not merely finding something to do that filled up the hours of the day.

A quartet of musicians along the side wall changed their background music into a slow march. The bridesmaids started to enter. Lionel wondered how they had been chosen. Diana had not known her way through the minefield of who was to be selected and who not.

Diana, Diana. His thoughts settled on her. He breathed deeply, trying to fill himself with the intoxicating, addicting feeling of love. He *did* love her, did he not? Of course, he did. There was no doubt. Well, only a tiny one.

Lionel shook his head. The nagging small thought did not go completely away. Diana had told him and Nicholas about it. That she had cast a charm on them that entirely washed away all that had been induced before by her sorcery. So, his feelings now were true and deep — weren't they? His brow wrinkled. Could he ever be sure?

As was the custom, the bridesmaids, one by one, slowly marched past Lionel for the traditional final inspection. They dipped with a small curtsy as they did — the indication that they accepted he was no longer available to be pursued.

Lionel recognized the last. It was Rachel, the terrified youngster he had met at her first ball! He blinked. It could not have been that long ago. But what a transformation had occurred. She had blossomed. No longer a girl, but — but a woman!

She smiled with a saucy confidence as she passed. "You had your chance," she whispered. "And just so you know, it is not a doll that keeps me company now when I sleep."

Lionel felt a thickening in his loins. "Ah, thank you for being part of the ceremony," he managed to say at the very end. He scowled. What was he thinking? He should not be having any more such thoughts. Where was Diana? Shouldn't she be appearing by now?

DIANA FLUFFED up her dress and tried to reach around and straighten her train. *Wasn't it what she had always dreamed about?* she thought. Lionel was an honest and decent man. In the little time she had been at court, she could see the degree of respect he was being given. Eventually he would even inherit a fief. She would be not only a lady but the *lady of a lord*. Be bathed in luxury. And if Vendora suddenly were to pass, her wildest fantasies might be more than fulfilled.

But if so, why did her chest feel so tight about what she was doing now? Because of what was happening to him, a voice inside of herself said. Lionel was no longer an errant lordling looking for himself. That he had found. Now he had responsibilities, duties to fill. His future was bright — so long as he followed all the rules and he had a wife to help him obey them.

Diana sighed. The pressure upon Lionel to succeed would push everything else aside. She would be a lord's lady, yes. Within reason, indulge in her slightest whims. But she also would become merely another object, another piece of property to be possessed.

Lionel was so unlike Nicholas, another waif like herself. She had not really known how deeply she felt about the initiate until he had rushed into the keep with his cart of magic mirror blanks. On impulse, she had followed, knowing in her heart he was about to do something that had to be done, no matter what the cost. How they worked so smoothly together to stop an errant magician who had wandered astray. And not once but twice, they had saved the day.

She looked at Lionel as she drew closer to him. It would all be so perfect — if only the most important question would go away. Did Lionel really love her? Or instead, was she merely another piece of fine jewelry that befitted a lord? There was no more time left. What should she decide?

NICHOLAS SLIPPED into the back row of watchers. No one gave him more than a single look. Why would they? He was merely an initiate. But, if nothing else, he wanted to see

Diana again, even if it were for the very last time.

The music changed and became more forceful, filling the air with inevitability. Diana drew closer to where the queen and wedding party stood waiting for her, and his heart seemed to skip not one beat, but two. She was beautiful. Well, she always had been, but, somehow, now in the sumptuous gown —

He smiled ruefully. Wasn't this the place in the sagas where an outsider rushes in and yells 'Stop the wedding'?

A few heartbeats passed. But that did not happen. Diana joined Lionel in front of Vendora.

Is this really what I want to do?, Diana asked herself. She remembered her first tea with the ladies of the court and all the like rituals that followed. And what Nicholas and she had done together at the abandoned apothecary. What kind of life did she truly desire?

The queen donned reading glasses, something she did not normally do in public.

"By the power invested in me as the supreme ruler of Procolon," she began.

"I want to make a statement," Diana interrupted.

Vendora frowned at Diana. "Didn't the matrons school you on all the aspects of the ceremony?" she whispered.

"Yes, my liege," Diana dipped slightly. "But the instruction included the part where the bride can make a statement of conditions if she so desires."

Vendora looked shocked. She summoned one of her courtiers to her side. A hurried discussion ensued.

"Yes, you are correct," the queen sighed, "but this is most irregular. What is it you wish to say?"

Diana filled her lungs. She looked at Lionel. "I accept the man standing beside me as my husband," she said. "But not as my lord and master."

A flurry of hushed conversations coursed through the audience. A bailiff off to the side banged a small drum for order.

"But that is the tradition," Vendora said.

"I understand, my queen," Diana replied. "But I have thought on this for many hours." She looked at Lionel. "I honor this man as my — my friend. We have been on several adventures together. I will serve by his side as required by all the functions of state. But, not in his bed. I am my own person. I will not bear any of his heirs. *I* will decide to whom I give my heart."

For a moment, Lionel looked stunned. Everyone, that is every last lord in the kingdom, was there. He could hear the gears starting to churn in their heads. He looked at the line of attendants standing obediently at the side. Rachel was the closest. She would have to do.

Lionel grabbed her from the line and positioned her beside himself. "By your leave, my queen. Let us continue."

LATER, NICHOLAS and Diana walked hand in hand towards the market to sell some more magic rings.

"You know," he said, "an initiate without a magician's palace will not garner much money."

"I know," Diana replied. "Doesn't bother me. We will think of something."

Author's Afterword

Did you enjoy *One Last Heist*?

Do you know some others who might like it, too?

Why not contact them right now?

Do it while *One Last Heist* is fresh in your mind. It will take only a few minutes.

Just send an email to *two or more* of your friends, telling them what you liked about my book.

[Warning! Tongue-in-cheek logic follows]

Why two or more? Well,you could be part of something to brag about!

If all of your friends also buy *One Last Heist,*then they will get to read this request too! Then they each recruit two or so more friends…

Boom! Things exponentially explode! Eventually, every single person on the planet ends up reading this book! You will be able to tell your grandchildren that, yes, you were part of making this explosion happen.

[Warning! Tongue is now safely retrieved from cheek]

Seriously, word-of-mouth is the most powerful form of promotion that there is. If you like what I have written and want me to write more, you can help me a lot by spreading the word!

To score a small appreciation gift for your effort, point your browser at:

https://www.alodar.com/blog/im

You will be transferred to where you can download three connected novelettes set in the same world as *One Last Heist*

You will not be added to any email list for having done so. It is presented to you on the honor system. Of course, if you do not send the emails to your friends and yet get free copies of the *Island Magic* novelettes anyway, I will not be responsible for your shame that will result.

But, if you did help me out, thank you very much!

Leave a review

You can also help by posting a review of this book on a blog or bookseller site. You can find a link to the sites of booksellers who carry my books here:

https://www.alodar.com/blog/books-2/one-last-heist"

Please sign up to my newsletter anyway

I promise not to spam you. You will get an email only every three or four weeks or so. In it, I will have things like:

- Notifications of new book availability

- My recommendations for books by other authors that you might enjoy reading

- Some of my favorite games and past-times

- Zany things that have happened in my life

To newsletter subscribe, point your browser at:

http://www.alodar.com/blog/subscribe-to-newsletter

Thanks again for jumping through these hoops.

What's next

I hope you enjoyed *One Last Heist*.

It is the seventh book in the series titled Magic by the Numbers.

Unlike many other series, however, these books can be read in any order.

None end in a cliffhanger trying to compel you to run right out and purchase the next.

A happy hero and heroine do not break up and then in the next book discover that they were meant for each other after all.

Instead, each book has a distinct *theme*. Each deals with different *settings* and *situations* in which rigorous magic is involved.

The only purpose of the series number is to help you keep straight which you have already read.

The following pages give you a brief idea of what each book is about.

What secret lay in the depths of the volcano?

How could anyone survive there in the blistering heat?

Would the struggling journeyman last long enough to discover what was there?

Could he learn something that would help him in his quest for the love of the beautiful queen?

Based on the magic folklore of our own world, the quest of Alodar, the journeyman, takes him from one form of magic to the next, each with its own unique rules and constraints. Each step requiring him to press on. Each one brings everyone in the world closer and closer to everlasting enslavement.

Order Master of the Five Magics here:

https://alodar.com/blog/mfm

How could Astron ever stand up to any of the other demons?

Why couldn't he have been born with more than mere stubs for wings?

What secrets lay in realms even more exotic than his own?

Why had the prince chosen him as the one to travel there for the answer to the ancient riddle?

The cover of the book depicts an event that takes place in the palace of Elezar, a demon prince. Most of the realm of demons is a featureless void. It is hard to transport solid matter there from other places, and it is extremely valuable. The utmost ecstasy for a lightning djinn is to blast something of beauty into a scatter of individual atoms.

Order Riddle of the Seven Realms here:

https://alodar.com/blog/rsr

Is time immutable? There is no way to go back and change things without creating paradoxes?

Or perhaps a demon like the succubus, Lilith, is really in charge?

Could Figaro Newton, the struggling physics grad student go back in time and save Marie Antoinette?

Order Magic Times Three here:

http://www.alodar.com/blog/mtt

A fantastic aspect of our universe is existence of black holes.

Why do the bad guys want to travel to one?

Even if we wanted to stop them, wouldn't it take several generations in order to do so?

Is there something about the realm of demons that would help?

Order Double Magic here:

http://www.alodar.com/blog/dm

Could Briana, the fourth daughter of the Archimage, emerge from the shadow of her famous father?

Will she go off on her own and try something rash in order to make a name for herself?

Is alien first contact anything like it is cracked up to be?

Especially when the real threat has been hiding undetected on the earth for thousands of years?

Order The Archimage's Fourth Daughter here:

http://www.alodar.com/blog/afd

Could Jason, the wordsmith, somehow overcome his writers block?

Will Delia, the escaped slave girl, remain free?

Are there really only five types of magic?

Nope!

Okay then, are there really only six?

Nope again!

Order Secret of the Sixth Magic here:

http://www.alodar.com/blog/ssm

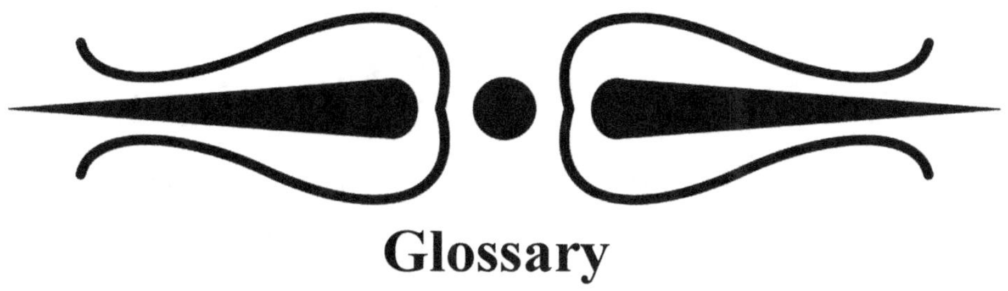

Glossary

Alchemy

On earth, the root of the word comes from the Greek for transmutation. In the Middle Ages, alchemy focused on changing baser metals into gold, finding an elixir of life and a universal solvent. Some alchemical practices ultimately became the basis for modern chemistry.

In *Master of the Five Magics* and its sequels, alchemical procedures were described by formulas of arcane symbols kept in grimoires. Formula success was governed by probability; the more potent the result the less likely it was to succeed.

On earth, the most similar craft is that of a chemist.

Wikipedia: http://en.wikipedia.org/wiki/Alchemy

Barding a horse

Since ancient times, armor had been a part of warfare. But not only for the warriors. If horses were involved, then they were armored as well. The horse's armor was called barding.

Wikipedia: https://en.wikipedia.org/wiki/Barding

Charm

On earth, a synonym for spells in general. In *Master of the Five Magics* and its sequels, a sorcerer's spell in particular.

Wikipedia: http://en.wikipedia.org/wiki/Charm

Crystals

In three-dimensional space, there are only five regular solids with three-dimensional symmetry.

One might think that if there are only 5 regular ones, there should be roughly the same number of different crystal types also.

But this is not true! Crystal types refer to structures that are *repetitive* — but they are not necessarily *regular*.

Crystal types can be divided into a hierarchy of classifications beginning with *lattice systems* such as cubic and hexagonal.

When all the possible arrangements have been considered, it turns out there are 230! ways for a basic pattern to repeat itself and hence form crystals.

Wikipedia: https://en.wikipedia.org/wiki/Crystal_system

Dark Energy

In physical cosmology and astronomy, dark energy is an unknown form of energy that affects the universe on the largest scales. The first observational evidence for its existence came from measurements of supernovas, which showed that the universe does not expand at a constant rate; rather, the universe's expansion is *accelerating*.

What is causing this?

Our current theory about our universe states that it started with a big explosion. Roughly some 13 billion years it spang out of nothingness. This conclusion came about because observations of distant galaxies in the early twentieth century showed that, by far, most of them were moving away from us.

Was this because we as a species have body odor? Well, probably not. Just as a police siren lowers in frequency when the police car is moving away, the frequency of the light from most of these far away galaxies were shifted towards the red from what they would be if they were remaining stationary or were approaching us.

It also turned out from distance measurements that galaxies the farthest away were the ones traveling the fastest - - because they had been travelling the fastest to begin with. This phenomenon would be what one would expect to happen from an explosion - some pieces traveling fast and some slower.

Extrapolating back in time, the conclusion was that there was a single point of nothingness thirteen billion ago from which everything sprang. Additional observations that the very low energy background radiation surrounding us now was very *uniform*, pretty much the same no matter which way one looked. This helped confirm the big bang theory. (And rather than think of matter expanding in space, the equations that are used to describe this are now thought of as describing the expansion of space itself, not expansion in space that is already existing)

As the number of powerful telescopes improved, the makeup and nature of individual galaxies were measured with increasing detail. Problems began to emerge. Galaxies are made up of stars, planets and dust -- clumps of matter held together by the universal attraction between all of the pieces for one another. Only because the stars and gas in a galaxy was whirling around its center is this inward attraction resisted -- the reason that galaxies have survived for as long as they have.

By measuring the amount of light produced by the stars in a galaxy, one can estimate how massive they are -- how large is the central gravitational force of the central stars holding the galaxy together against the outward centrifugal force.

Alas, it turned out not to be large enough. The total mass of all the stars in a galaxy are insufficient to hold the structure together. Over the billions of years of its lifetime, something else must be preventing the galaxies from dissipating into isolated stars surrounded by emptiness. Even when there is a black hole at the galactic center, there still is not enough mass.

The solution finally accepted was that, although stars make up the bulk of the matter in a galaxy, it must not be the *most* of it. Instead, in each galaxy was something else that was dark and did not show up in our telescope images. With their usual flair for style, scientists agreed to call this matter that was dark and could not be seen -- dark matter.

(With similar panache, when two more quarks were proposed to complete a sextet of (what is now anyway) the most fundamental of particles, it was suggested by some that they be called "truth" and "beauty". What wonderful, poetic names!

The suggestion was not adopted. Instead, the top and bottom-most of quarks are known today as "top" and "bottom".)

Still with me? Okay, the universe has been expanding ever since the big bang, thirteen billion years ago. There is something called dark matter that is holding galaxies together while this is going on. But even over cosmic distances, the rate of expansion should be slowing down. Galaxies are still composed of matter, light and dark, and all matter attracts other matter. But instead of slowing down, the rate of expansion is increasing!

Yes, in the flight of all the galaxies from one another, as time goes on, they are being driven apart faster and faster. Something else is happening here.

So then, what is it? Well, it cannot be dark matter. That name is already taken. But it is dark. Our telescopes do not see any evidence of it. It is something else that we cannot see.

And what is the most famous equation in all of physics — Einstein's $E = mc^2$, of course. There is an *equivalence* between mass (i.e., matter) and energy. And so, the answer is obvious.

We don't know what this new kid on the block is, but his

name is *dark energy*. The present thinking is that our universe is made up of three components as shown here.

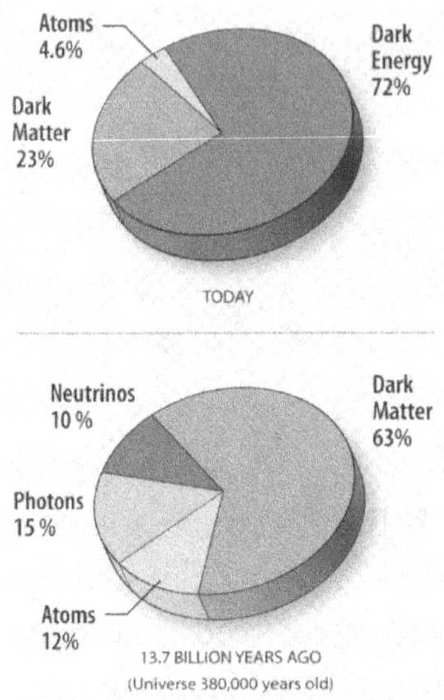

Some physicists still have the guts to be a little poetic. Another name for dark energy is *quintessence*. The term quintessence goes all the way back to the ancient Greeks. Contrary to some popular lore that the Greeks thought of everything being formed from the four basic elements: earth, air, fire, and water, there were in fact five elements, with quintessence being the fifth — the aether that surrounds everything.

As originally proposed, quintessence was what is called a scalar field — something that is just everywhere pushing everything apart. And it turns out that Einstein in his original formulation of general relativity had in it what he called the "Cosmological constant". He later repudiated it, saying that it was the biggest blunder he ever had made. So, one take on quintessence is that it is simply Einstein's constant reborn and therefore we could use the original term and forget about the aether.

Presently then, there are three components of the universe: ordinary matter, dark matter, and dark energy. As you can see, everything we are familiar with is a small minority.

Wikipedia: https://en.wikipedia.org/wiki/Dark_energy

Types of demons

As those of you who have read my fantasy novels might be able to guess, I delight in creating new types of demons with very specialized characteristics. They divide into three basic categories: imps, sprites, and djinns.

As the *Magic by the Numbers* series developed, the types of smaller demons proliferated. Roughly speaking, the most powerful are djinns. Smaller ones are sprites and imps.

Category Name	**Description**
imps	
drinkdribbler	pokes holes at the tops of drink glasses
dynamite	microscopic imps requiring high energy to transfer to our realm
hairjumbler	snarls hair when you are sleeping
glowimp	used for lighting
hoseherder	switch socks from one clothes-dryer to another
nosetweaker	gives your nose a workout
waterwisp	a computer part

sprites

gargoyle	likes to hang out over a church roof
pigmy afreet	a computer part
pufferscamp	an inflatable gas bag
rock gremlin	enjoys fouling up electronics
rockbubbler	able to move through solid rock
whilrling dervish	likes to spin as rapidly as he can
will-o-the-wisp	able to manipulate water
watersprite	alternate name for a will-o-the-wisp
ice sprite	able to manipulate ice, sleet, and hail
fire devil	able to manipulate fire
winged fire devil	able to manipulate fire and can fly
maxwell	able to manipulate individual molecules
siren	enchants with its voice
banshee	instills panic and dread with its voice
glowsprite	a large glowimp with delusion of self-importance
ticklesprite	able to tickle with the slightest touch

djinns

lightning	fights with lightning bolts
splendorous	largest and most powerful
splendiforous	same as splendorous
succubus	seductive female
incubus	seductive male

> shield demon able to block lightning djinn strikes
> quake demon able to shake the ground

Festination

This effect is real, not something I made up. The effect is frightening. You feel like you can't stop walking. Worse, that you cannot stop walking faster and faster with each step.

Festination is linked to Parkinson's disease and other neurological problems. Not a good thing to have if you are a performer of magic rituals.

Wikitionary: https://en.wiktionary.org/wiki/festination

Gresham's Law

"Bad money drives out good"

Sir Thomas Gresham was an English financier who urged Queen Elizabeth I to reestablish a firm foundation for the English economy.

The basic concept is that if there is more than one base for a currency, then the one which is sounder will demand a premium when exchanged for the one less so.

Wikipedia:
https://en.wikipedia.org/wiki/Gresham%27s_law

Magic

The use of means outside of those normally available to affect change. On earth, the terms magic, sorcery, thaumaturgy, and wizardry are roughly synonymous.

In *Master of the Five Magics* and its sequels, each have distinct meanings. Magic is performed by the exercise of rituals, the steps of which are derived from extensions of rituals deduced previously.

The goal of these exercises is the production of magical objects, things that are perfect in what they do, such as mirrors, daggers, swords, and shields. Once created, with few exceptions, they last forever.

The power of magic is limited by the time and expense involved in performing magic rituals. Some take several generations and the involvement of many participants. Because of the effort involved, magical objects are quite expensive.

On earth, the most similar craft is that of a mathematician.

Wikipedia: http://en.wikipedia.org/wiki/Magic

Metamagician

The word "meta" comes from the Greek meaning "beyond" or "after". In English it is used to denote a concept that is behind another.

A metamagician, therefore, is a magic practitioner whose craft underlies the seven magic laws in my books. Indeed, as *Secret of the Sixth Magic* reveals, there is a lot going on in the foundation from which these laws emerge.

So, how are which laws chosen to be in effect? Which ones in the larger set can be selected?

This is where what are called *metalaws* come in. Metalaws are laws about laws. These laws *about the laws* of magic is the central theme of *Secret of the Sixth Magic*.

I had wanted *Metalaws* to be the title of my second book, but my editor, Lester del Rey, insisted that it would not be understood as a sequel by readers.

He proposed instead, *Secret of the Sixth Magic*.

"Sixth Magic?" I protested. "There is no sixth magic mentioned in the book at all."

Del Rey approximately countered with, "Here's what you do. Part way through the book, you have your protagonist say something like, 'Hmm, maybe there is a sixth undiscovered magic operating here … No, on second thought, that's can't be right. Something else is going on.' The term 'sixth magic' is mentioned, so the title is 'justified'. All is well."

Oil of Vitriol

An old name for sulfuric acid

Wikipedia: https://en.wikipedia.org/wiki/Sulfuric_acid

Parallelepiped

The general term is a three-dimensional figure formed by six parallelograms.

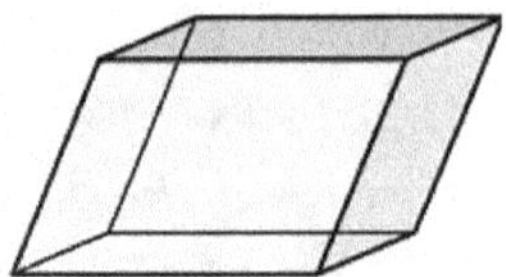

Wikipedia: https://en.wikipedia.org/wiki/Parallelepiped

Nicholas used the term in a more restrictive way. Each of the six parallelograms was in fact a rectangle. This more restrictive figure is called a cuboid.

Plover

In the 1970s when computers were first becoming more available, Nick Mofort at MIT wrote what is regarded as the first interactive fiction. By today's standards it is quite primitive. The display is an alphanumeric cathode ray terminal and the user has a limited vocabulary of actions that he could take -- things like go north, drop sword, and so on. The goal was to garner points by picking up treasures. scattered at undisclosed places in a cave of twisty little passages.

All I can say is that, at the time, it was quite addictive. You can find out more about *Twisty Little Passages* at:

https://en.wikipedia.org/wiki/Colossal_Cave_Adventure

This glossary entry is not so much about the game as it is about what I call the *Impact of Accomplishment*.

When I was in charge of what called a laboratory at TRW, at lunch time we played the game on a Digital Equipment

Corporation PDP 11-45 mini- computer.

We divided into teams, each of which huddled around a VT-100 terminal. The goal was to be the first to find all of the treasures and return them to the point where credit points were awarded.

I don't recall how long it took, but after several weeks every team was tied. All of the treasures had been found by everyone except for the elusive emerald in the Plover room.

You could pick it up, but if you did, you could not exit the room. The opening was too small with the huge gem in your hand.

Don Brabston, a fellow engineer, and I comprised one of the teams and after a long time with no progress we were quite frustrated. We had tried everything: drop everything that you were carrying, drink the oil…

One day after at least a full week had gone by with no one advancing, a cheer of triumph came from one of the other teams. "Oh, by gosh!" I said to Don, "Somehow, they have figured it out."

The winning team was congratulated, but no other competitor wanted to have the answer for this final riddle handed to them on a plate. We all had to continue trying.

But I was completely stumped. I could not think of anything else possibly to try. The lunch hour ended and we all went back to work.

When the workday was over, Don found me and said, "I

have something to show you." We went into the computer room, and, son-of-a-gun, Don was able to retrieve the emerald.

"How were you able to do this?" I asked.

"Well", Don said. "Once I *knew for sure* that a solution existed, the answer came to me in a flash."

The point of the story is that, somehow, when one knows that there is an answer to a riddle and that others have solved it, getting the answer becomes easier.

Reflections

In our own world, when we think of reflections, mirrors come to mind. We do not have ones that can look elsewhere in the world or into the future. (Or if you do know of some, then please let me know where I can buy one!)

But we do have some pretty amazing mirrors here on earth, nonetheless. They are prized because of their high degree of reflectivity. Almost all of what goes into one is reflected back. And reflectivity is more complicated that it seems.

Click here to find out more.

Robe

Practitioners of each of the five magics are distinguished by the capes and robes they wear.

Thaumaturges wear brown covered with what is on earth the mathematical symbol of similarity.

Alchemists wear white covered with triangles with a single vertex bottom-most symbolizing the delicate balance between success and failure when performing a formula.

Magicians wear blue with the palest for a neophyte and the darkest for the master and covered by circular rings symbolizing the perfect mathematical object.

Sorcerers wear gray covered with the logo of the staring eye symbolizing the ability to see far in time and place and into another's inner being.

Wizards wear black covered with wisps of flame symbolizing the portal by which the realm of demons and the realm of men are connected.

Royal Water

A mixture of hydrochloric and nitric acids that produces a fuming liquid. It was so named by alchemists because it could dissolve gold and platinum.

Wikipedia: https://en.wikipedia.org/wiki/Aqua_regia

The alchemists of Nicholas's world are market savvy and market it as a universal solvent, although it is not true.

Shapes

Some of the earliest efforts of geometry were ones of definition and description. Of particular interest were naming objects that had some simple recurrent properties. Part of the game was discovering which had a lot of them.

For example, things composed of three straight lines connected to one another were dubbed triangles— because of the three angles created where each pair of lines met. If these three angles all turned out to be the same magnitude, then what we had was an equilateral triangle. Besides having three angles with the same number of circular degrees, the three sides were the same length as well.

At some point, the term *regular* began to be used to define an object where all of its attributes were the same. So, after square (an object with four equal sides with all angles the same number of circular degrees) we had regular pentagons, … regular octagons, … regular dodecahedrons, and so on, an infinite progression of n-gons as large as we wanted to think about.

A natural extension to this line of thought is to ask what can be done with more than a single example of an n-gon.

BTW, the famous mathematician, Fredrick Gauss, was so enamored of his discovery of how to draw a heptadecagon (a regular 17-gon) on paper using only a straightedge and a compass that he had one inscribed on his gravestone. See Gauss' Regular 17-Gon Construction" for how to do this.

This pursuit of naming things extended into three dimensions as well. A most notable example is the cube. It is built of six squares of equal area and all the angles where three edges meet are ninety degrees. But unlike the infinite chain of named objects we can conceive of in two dimensions, there are only five regular shapes in three dimensions that are also regular — not an infinite number, but only five!

Besides the cube, the additional four regular solids are the tetrahedron, octahedron, dodecahedron, and icosahedron. Their discovery has been attributed to Plato and hence are called the Platonic solids.

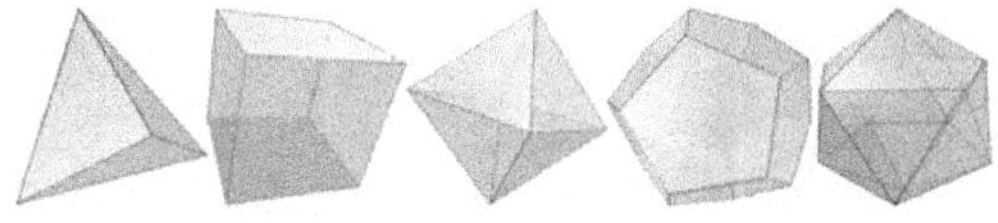

Wikipedia https://en.wikipedia.org/wiki/Platonic_solid

The aspects of these solid that are regular are:

- All of their faces are identical in shape and size (congruent)

- All of the faces are regular polygons (all edges and angles identical)

- The same number of faces at each vertex

So, in three dimensions, we cannot get something more symmetric than one of these five.

Or can we? See the glossary entry on Tiling.

Simple Machines

Wikipedia defines what are called *simple* machines. These are devices known from ancient times. There are six of them:

Lever

Wheel(and axle)

Inclined plane

Wedge

Screw and Pulley

A simple pulley is a wheel with a grove around the edge into which a rope can be placed. By suspending it and tying one free end of the rope to a heavy object and pulling on it, the object can be lifted off of the ground.

Such a maneuver changes the vertical position of the object but does not provide any mechanical advantage. If the object weighs, say, 100 pounds, it would require 100 pounds of downward tugging on the other end of the rope in order to lift it.

The advantage comes if the rope is looped several types rather than just once in what is called a *block and tackle*. The simplest one uses three pulleys with two independently mounted at the top of the mechanism and one more freely hanging at the bottom.

The rope is threaded over one of the pullies at the top and then down and around the one at the bottom. After that back up and around the second one at the top.

If this is done, a *mechanical advantage* results. Unlike the simple pulley, a 100-pound weight can be lifted with only 50 pounded of tugging.

The reason for this is that there is not just a single rope pulling on the weight but effectively two of them — each sharing half of the load.

With more and more pulleys added at the top and bottom, the easier the lifting becomes.

Is there a catch for this? After all, in our universe, one cannot get something for nothing. And in the case above, one must pull the rope downward by two feet for every foot the weight is hauled higher.

For Diana and Nicholas, the weight is reduced by a factor of three and each downward motion of the boring machine by one foot would uncoil three feet of rope.

Sorcery

The use of means outside of normal availability to affect change. On earth, the terms magic, sorcery, thaumaturgy, and wizardry are roughly synonymous.

In *Master of the Five Magics* and its sequels, each, along with alchemy, have distinct meanings. Sorcery is performed by the recitation of charms, the steps of which are revealed from self-enchantment.

The power of a sorcerer is limited by the fact that each casting takes some of his life force, and eventually he succumbs when he has no more to give.

On earth, the most similar craft is that of a psychologist.

Wikipedia: http://en.wikipedia.org/wiki/Sorcery

Spell

On earth the terms cantrip, charm, enchantment, glamour, incantation, and spell are synonymous — the performance of an act of magic.

In *Master of the Five Magics* and its sequels, except for the word spell itself, each of the others have particular meanings. The word spell is a generic umbrella for any of them.

Thaumaturgy — incantation

Alchemist — formula performance

Magician — ritual exercise

Sorcerer — charm recitation

Wizard — invocation

Subordinate

The first four crafts have named subordinates in *Master of the Five Magics* and its sequels.

Thaumaturgy — Journeyman, Apprentice

Alchemist — Novice

Magician — Neophyte, Initiate, Acolyte

Sorcerer — Tyro

Symmetry

A word that we all use but probably have a hard time defining what it means. The answer depends upon what exactly we are talking about, of course, but basically is about changing something and, after we have done so, things look the same.

In geometry, the concept applies to objects such as circles, squares, cubes, pyramids and even objects in higher dimensions. For example, we say that a circle has rotational symmetry. Take one and spin it around, or change where we are observing it from, and it still looks like it did before. A square also has symmetry but not as much. It looks the same only if it is spun a multiple of ninety degrees.

Why is this important? Well, basically, it is part of our struggle to precisely define things so that we can communicate with others about them. But the benefit goes deeper than that. Once we have a list of symmetries that something has, there are deductions that can result.

For a grossly over-simplifying example, we experimentally observe that when we move things around in a freshman physics lab, the laws that are in play, to a first approximation, do not depend on where we conduct them — on one side of the room or another. From this simple fact, it can be deduced the fundamental law that momentum is conserved!

Likewise, doing the experiment on Friday instead of Monday also has no effect. From this, it can be deduced that energy is conserved, too. Or going the other way — if energy is conserved, then doing our experiment on Tuesday or Wednesday will produce the same result.

Wikipedia: https://en.wikipedia.org/wiki/Symmetry

Thaumaturgy

The use of means outside of normal availability to affect change. On earth, the terms magic, sorcery, thaumaturgy, and wizardry are roughly synonymous.

In *Master of the Five Magics* and its sequels, each, along with alchemy, have distinct meanings. Thaumaturgy is performed by the reciting incantations that bind together objects at a distance that once had physically been together and with a source of energy that can perform work.

The power of thaumaturgy is limited by the fact that all incantations must conserve energy or, as sometimes stated, the first law of thermodynamics.

On earth, the term derives from the Greek for miracle and the most similar craft is that of a physicist.

Wikipedia: http://en.wikipedia.org/wiki/Thaumaturgy

Three-dimensional tiling

A tiling or tessellation of the plane is covering it with one or more geometric shapes, called tiles so that there are no overlaps and no gaps. This might sound trivial, but instead it is a complex mathematical subject called Tesselation.

Wikipedia: https://en.wikipedia.org/wiki/Tessellation

A regular tiling is one that has a repetitive pattern.

An additional (arbitrary) proviso is that the tiles must be selected from a small number of shapes. The two most obvious examples are to use squares or hexagons. Evidently, hexagons are the tilings of choice for many civic building bathroom builders.

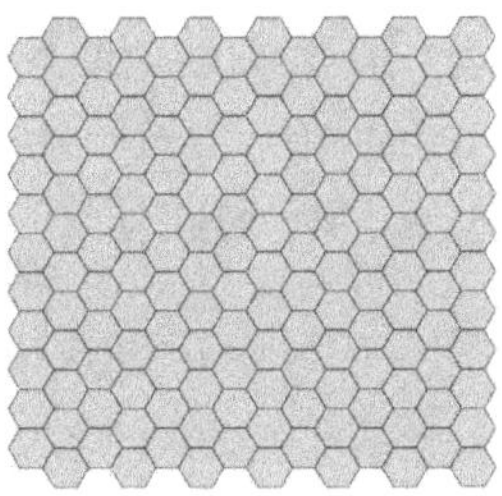

If more than one type of tile is allowed, more exotic tilings can be posssible.

The study of tiling extends beyond that of a periodic repeating pattern. The effort here is directed at finding the smallest number of distinct types of shapes that tile the plane but in a way that is non-periodic…no piece of the tiling ever reoccurs.

In 1974, the mathematician Roger Penrose developed a set of only *two* tiles that not only cover the plane, they do so in a pattern that has no periodic repetition. (It turns out to have a five-fold rotational symmetry, however.)

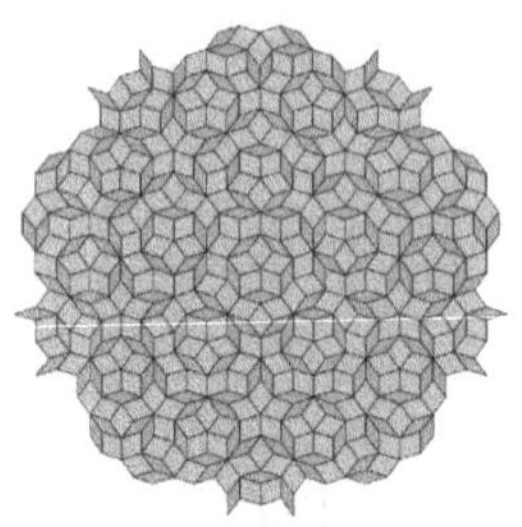

Wikipedia:
href="https://en.wikipedia.org/wiki/Roger_Penrose">

In 2022, the math hobbyist David Smith did even better. He discovered a 13-sided tile which he appropriately named "einstein" that tiles the plane aperiodically all by itself.

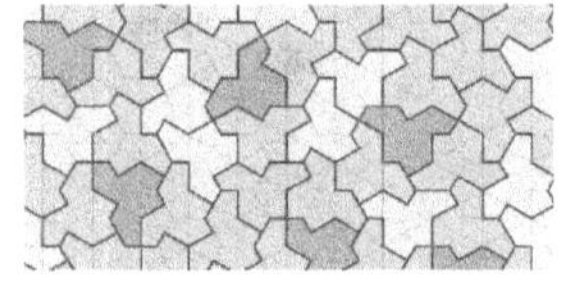

Wikipedia:
href="https://en.wikipedia.org/wiki/Einstein_problem">

It is fun to look at the pretty pictures generated by tilings, but the important aspect for the story here is tiling in not *two*, but *three*, dimensions.

Yes, there is the simple answer of just stacking up cubes on top of one another. But suppose you wanted to use more complex building blocks — ones in the context of the story here that would cause an even more coupling with dark energy. Ones that would cause an even more powerful explosion?

Well, it turns out that three-space can be tiled using two of the Platonic solids — tetraherons and octahedrons.

Wikipedia: https://en.wikipedia.org/wiki/Tetrahedral-octahedral_honeycomb

Universal Solvent

A liquid that can dissolve everything.

Also known as Alkahest. Allegedly even more powerful than mere aqua regia. But probably just aqua regia, or royal water as it also called, along with some fancy sales talking.

Wikipedia: https://en.wikipedia.org/wiki/Alkahest

Wizardry

The use of means outside of normal availability to affect change. On earth, the terms magic, sorcery, thaumaturgy, and wizardry are roughly synonymous.

In *Master of the Five Magics* and its sequels, each have

distinct meanings. Wizardry is performed by the invocation of demons from another realm from that of the earth.

The potency of a wizard is limited by the power of the demons that he can dominate.

On earth, there is no such craft as such, although one could argue that the practices of witches and warlocks are similar.

Wikipedia: http://en.wikipedia.org/wiki/Witchcraft